CO-APX-071

SPIRIT OF THE TOWERS

THE OMNI TOWERS SERIES BOOK 6

JAMIE A. WATERS

Spirit of the Towers © 2018 by Jamie A. Waters

Cover Art by Deranged Doctor Designs
Editor: Beyond DEF Lit

ISBN: 978-1-949524-00-0 (Paperback Edition)
ISBN: 978-1-949524-01-7 (eBook Edition)

Library of Congress Control Number: 2018909905
First Edition *December 2018

THE OMNI TOWERS SERIES

Spirit of the Towers

CHAPTER ONE

VALENTINA CREPT OUT OF BED, timing her movements to coincide with Sergei's deep and regular breathing. From all appearances, he was fast asleep and had been for some time, yet she waited, watching the rhythmic motion of his chest for any variations. He could be sneaky when it suited him, and she didn't trust he was truly asleep.

She picked up Sergei's shirt and pulled it over her head before glancing down at him again. The sight of him in the dim lighting took her breath away. Although, in all fairness, Sergei was just as alluring in the stark light of day too. His blond hair was brushed away from his face, revealing his chiseled jawline and lips that were more than kissable.

Watching him in this unguarded moment gave her a pang of regret, and she wished she could curl up beside him again. Having him within touching distance again didn't seem real after being so long without him, and it made it even harder knowing that if she slipped back into bed, his arms would immediately encircle her. She could fall asleep within minutes, basking in his comforting warmth. But she couldn't risk any delays. Not tonight.

Taking the opportunity to escape, she slipped out into the hallway and closed the door silently behind her. Nikolai's room was across the hall, and even though light shone from underneath the door, she didn't want to disturb him. Hopefully, if Sergei were feigning sleep, he'd believe she was in there talking with Nikolai. It was a common enough occurrence that it might work. At least, she hoped.

She moved silently down the hall and stopped outside Yuri's room. Not bothering to knock, she slipped inside the darkened room and closed the door behind her.

"Tired of Sergei already, Valya? You're always welcome to share my bed." Yuri muttered sleepily.

Valentina grinned and reached over to activate the lights. With a wide yawn, Yuri stretched, causing the blankets to shift and making it apparent he was sleeping nude again. Lovely.

Averting her eyes, she grabbed his discarded clothing from the floor. She tossed them on the bed strategically over certain body parts she didn't want to look at longer than necessary. "I got a message from one of my contacts on the surface. I think he may have a lead about the missing weapons. I need you to come with me."

Ignoring his clothing, Yuri put his hands behind his head and leaned back. "It won't work. Sergei won't let you leave without him."

Her eyes narrowed. "I'm *not* asking him to go with me. He can't leave the towers without endangering himself. If Viktor was being honest with me, Sergei is a marked man. Not only that, Dmitri requested the meet."

Yuri made a noncommittal noise and scratched his chest. "Oh, I'm not disagreeing with your assessment. Sergei will likely kill Dmitri. I'm simply saying your plan to sneak out will not work."

Valentina ignored him and walked over to the bag she'd

hidden in his room earlier. If they hurried, they could be back before morning. She paused, tilting her head to listen for any sounds coming from the hallway. So far, it was still quiet, but that could change at any moment. Yanking open the bag, she strapped on her weapons and grabbed a pair of UV pants and shimmied into them.

"You know, I think I prefer when women take *off* their clothing in my room," Yuri mused thoughtfully, watching her from his position in bed. "This just doesn't have the same appeal. The weapons and black panties are a nice touch though. Are those new?"

Valentina scowled at him, withdrew a knife from her arm sheath, and flung it in his direction. It embedded into the headboard with a *thump*. Yuri glanced up at it and grinned, but he still didn't move.

She finished fastening her belt and put her hands on her hips. "I'll throw another knife if you're not dressed in five minutes, and this time, I may decide not to miss." She paused, considering for a moment, and added, "On second thought, maybe I should just ask Brant to join me. He doesn't give me nearly as many headaches or comment on my *panties*."

Yuri snorted. "You have as much chance of taking Brant as you do in avoiding Sergei. Open the door, Valya."

Valentina paused, her gaze darting toward the closed door. Dammit. She'd hoped to have at least escaped the towers before Sergei learned what she was doing.

At her hesitation, Yuri called out, "You might as well come in. She doesn't want to believe you're standing out there listening to every word."

"Traitor!" she yelled at Yuri as the door swung open. Valentina darted to the far side of the room, narrowly avoiding Sergei trying to grab her. Leaping onto the bed, she ignored Yuri's grunt as she scrambled over him.

Yuri grabbed her ankle and hauled her back, but she

kicked out, making contact briefly before rolling off the side of the bed and onto the floor. A second later, she was tackled and pinned facedown by a body she knew well.

"I win," Sergei whispered next to her ear.

Valentina blew her hair out of her face and laughed. "You cheated. Yuri helped you."

"Since when do we have rules, Valechka?" He chuckled and nuzzled her neck. "It was worth agreeing to take over two days of training Nikolai's new recruits."

She wriggled against Sergei's ironclad hold, plotting how she'd make Yuri pay. "Really, Yuri? You sold me out for two days of training?"

"I'm a cheap date," Yuri agreed.

"Just wait," she threatened. "I'll get you back for this."

Sergei slid her shirt off her shoulder and kissed her bare skin. She couldn't help the delicious shiver that went through her at his touch.

"Definitely worth it," he murmured and trailed several kisses along her shoulder and up toward her neck. "I'm trying to decide what I want to do with you now that I won."

She squirmed underneath him. "I have to go, Sergei. I can't play right now."

"Is that so?" He pressed a kiss right below her ear and slid his hand under her shirt, caressing her skin. His skin was hot compared to hers, and it only fueled her desire for him. "And where are you sneaking off to in the middle of the night?"

"I have a meeting with a contact," she managed, trying not to pant from his slow seduction. Her resistance was slowly starting to dissipate, and she was beginning to wonder if it were possible to push back the meeting a few hours.

"As entertaining as this is," Yuri began and yawned again, "you should probably let her get up. It's about the missing weapon shipments."

Sergei made a noncommittal noise but shifted off of her.

She rolled over, staring up into his gray eyes, mildly disappointed. With a knowing smile, he leaned over and kissed her. She rested her hand against his chest, the warmth of his skin surrounding her, and for a moment, she got lost in the kiss and him. He tightened his hand on her hip and shifted his leg to slide between hers as he deepened the kiss.

Yuri cleared his throat.

Valentina pulled away from Sergei with a disappointed sigh. Getting to her feet, she reached over, yanked her knife out of Yuri's headboard, and pointed the tip of it in his direction. "You should have held out for three days of training. Trust me, he would have agreed to it."

Yuri chuckled. "I'll keep that in mind for next time."

She sheathed her knife and winked at him. Turning back to Sergei, she tilted her head to regard him as he stood. Her heart always beat just a little faster at the sight of him. Since she was currently wearing his stolen shirt, he was only half dressed. The sight was enough to make her want to run her hands over his muscular chest again. She couldn't afford to be sidetracked though, at least not more than she already was. "How did you know what I was planning?"

Sergei chuckled and wrapped his arms around her. "While I immensely enjoyed your efforts to distract me earlier with sex, you were more... determined than usual. You also normally fall asleep the moment your head hits the pillow, and nothing short of an invasion will wake you. When that didn't happen, it only confirmed my suspicions." He paused and added, "I also caught some of your plans through our bond. I had no intention of letting you go to the surface alone."

She huffed. "That's why I came to drag Yuri out of bed. You can't go with me, Sergei."

He pulled her closer and nuzzled her neck. "Watch me."

Pushing against his chest, she said, "No. Until we clear

your name or find out who's responsible for the missing weapon shipments, you're a liability on the surface. Yuri can come with me while you stay with Nikolai. We'll be back before morning."

"No."

Valentina blew out a breath. Sergei could be stubborn and annoying when it suited him. He slid his hands under her shirt again, and she stepped away from him, lightly swatting away his roaming hands. If Sergei had his way, he'd seduce her back into bed. It wouldn't take much effort either. She needed to get out of there.

Turning back to Yuri, she said, "Get dressed. We need to go now."

Yuri arched an eyebrow and glanced at Sergei over her shoulder before grinning and shaking his head. "You might as well agree to take him, Valya. He'll just follow you anyway, and at least this way, you can keep an eye on him."

She clenched her fists and turned to glare at them. When the two of them teamed up, it was like trying to break down a wall with her bare hands. Part of her preferred it when they were at odds with each other. "Both of you are impossible, especially together. And don't think I'm unaware you just bribed him again, Sergei."

Without waiting for a response, she stormed past Sergei and back into the hallway to find a voice of reason. Opening the door to Nikolai's room, she found him working at his desk. He looked like he'd been sitting there for hours. It made her heart hurt a little to know how much effort he was pouring into keeping everything together for their people. They'd only been in the towers for a few days, but his duties didn't permit any sort of downtime.

It only reinforced her decision to meet with Dmitri to find out what he knew. She'd met with him last time in a more remote location away from his camp. Valentina didn't like meeting in places where someone might recognize her as being connected to Nikolai, but Dmitri's schedule restricted his movements. If she could help resolve the mystery of the weapon thefts or find a clue to clear Sergei's name, it would take some pressure off him *and* Nikolai.

Traveling to Dmitri's camp was a risk, but a necessary one, especially if he had information about the missing weapons.

"Take both of them with you, Valya," Nikolai said casually before turning back to his tablet. "You need backup, and if there's any trouble, the three of you will be in a better position to handle it. I would go with you, but it'll just raise more questions."

She blinked at him. "You can't be serious."

Nikolai shrugged. "Maybe Yuri can also keep Sergei from killing Dmitri, although I wouldn't mind terribly if he did. I'm not fond of him either." He paused for a moment and added, "I think Yuri probably could have gotten four days of training duties out of Sergei. I'm surprised he settled for only two. You might want to go back to bribing Yuri with food. He was much more amenable to taking your side when you smuggled him extra helpings."

"I'm really starting to hate this bond," she muttered, irritated they all knew what she was doing before she had a chance to do it.

Sergei wrapped his arms around her again, drawing her against his heated skin. "If our situations were reversed, would you let me go without you?"

She squeezed her eyes shut and sighed. "No."

"Then don't ask of me what you're not willing to do yourself," Sergei murmured in her ear. "And I would have agreed to any number of days with Yuri's annoying recruits for even one night with you."

She leaned back, unable to resist him. "Stop being charming. It makes it difficult to be annoyed with you."

He chuckled and pressed a kiss against her hair. "Come. Let's go meet your contact. When we're finished, I'll take you back to bed and try distracting *you* this time."

Despite herself, she couldn't help but smile. He was just too appealing for his own good. "Fine, but you need to keep your distance. I don't want people to know we're working together again. They'll be more inclined to talk about you if they believe we're still at odds."

He made a noncommittal noise. "Will you tell me about this Dmitri?"

When she hesitated, he turned her around and narrowed his eyes. "Who is he, Valentina? Why do Yuri and Nikolai think I'll want to kill him?"

She shrugged. "He's been a contact for a couple of years. He's not important. Only his intel is."

Yuri chuckled from the doorway. "It's not going to work, Valya. You're broadcasting your discomfort loud and clear. You might as well tell him. Besides, I could use a little more entertainment since you dragged me out of bed."

Valentina inwardly cursed, clamping down tightly on their shared connection. Alec and Ariana had been trying to instruct them how to control it since their bond changed, but certain things still filtered through. To make matters even worse, she was at the heart of the bond and who connected all of them together. While they only had to suppress one connection, she had to manage all three, which proved to be rather challenging.

Sometimes there wasn't a tactful way to handle an unpleasant discussion, especially where Sergei was involved. She pulled away from him and headed into the other room to collect the rest of her gear. "You were gone, Sergei. Did you really think I waited around pining over you?"

She felt more than heard the explosion of heat erupt behind her. Without bothering to turn around, she ducked back into Yuri's bedroom. Hopefully, Yuri and Nikolai could calm him down because she'd really rather not spend the next several years grooming another contact to replace Dmitri.

––––––––

VALENTINA STOPPED her speeder a short distance from the camp. Glancing at her display, she confirmed they were within the confines of the UV guard encompassing the area. She wasn't willing to advertise their presence more than necessary by engaging the one affixed to her vehicle. She climbed off just as Sergei and Yuri pulled up alongside her.

This camp was technically under Ivan's control, another one of their leaders, and a common stopping point for people traveling back and forth between the tower construction and river excavation sites. According to her contact, Ivan rarely visited this camp, so she should be able to move freely within it without arousing suspicion or being recognized. It was only when one of the camp's leaders was in residence or during an active operation in hostile territory that they increased security.

Sergei was still in charge of their people's involvement in both endeavors, so hopefully no one would question his presence, and, with any luck, he'd agree to keep a low profile. However, there were no guarantees with Sergei.

Glancing over at him, she noted the obvious rigidity in his shoulders through his UV gear. He was still angry about Dmitri, but there wasn't much she could do about it. Valentina suspected he was angrier at himself more than anything. Sergei had left her for three years, and even though she'd never been serious about anyone other than him, they'd both lived separate lives during that time. In all fairness, she'd probably have a similar reaction to learning about any of his lovers. For their sake, she hoped they were fast runners, though she might be inclined to run them over with a speeder... a few times.

With a sigh, she gestured for Yuri to try to run interference. It likely wouldn't work for long, but she needed to take this meeting. She finished adjusting the listening device she'd hidden in her arm sheath so Yuri could monitor her. She'd specifically asked him to keep Sergei away from the comms. Knowing Sergei, he'd come charging in the moment Dmitri opened his mouth.

"Valechka," Sergei spoke over her headset.

Valentina turned toward him, waiting expectantly.

"Be careful."

She tilted her head, considering him for a long time. Even now, he still managed to catch her off guard. He was one of the few who had that ability.

Sergei returned her gaze, and even though she needed to get to her appointment, some things were more important. With determination in her steps, Valentina walked back over to him and pulled off her helmet. The moment he removed his, she gripped his jacket and yanked him toward her. Pressing her lips against his, she told him without words how much he meant to her.

"I'm always careful, Seryozha," she reminded him when she pulled away. "But I will be especially careful now that I know you're waiting for me."

Sergei hooked his hand around her neck and pulled her closer again. Placing another kiss against her mouth, he murmured, "And I won't make any promises about not killing Dmitri, but I'll try to wait until after you get your information."

He released her again, and she bit back a grin, shaking her head in exasperation.

Leaving her helmet on the seat of her speeder, she headed into the ruins of an old city. The Coalition had constructed the camp by using the abandoned buildings as support structures, reinforcing some areas and constructing temporary housing for the workers. Various areas throughout the camp were sectioned off, indicating where excavations or demolitions were currently in progress. This camp's function was primarily to retrieve building materials and resources to be used in the construction of the new tower.

Valentina walked deeper into the makeshift town, surreptitiously scanning the area. Several people passed by her, but no one seemed to give her a second glance. She ducked under a fallen overhang into a small plaza, which was the designated meeting spot. Some lighting had been installed along the pathway, illuminating the area where several people were gathered. Even under the cover of darkness, the Coalition continued to work, taking shifts around the clock to meet their deadlines and ensure their continued survival.

"Valentina," Dmitri called out, his eyes warming at the sight of her. He dropped down from an elevated ledge where he'd been sitting and walked over to her, his gait confident and holding a hint of the swagger she'd always admired. Wrapping his arms around her, he pulled her against him in a tight embrace. She hugged him back and brushed a kiss against his cheek.

Dmitri leaned down and whispered in her ear, "I've missed you, beautiful."

"You're still as much a flirt as ever," she teased.

He rested his forehead against hers, still holding her in his arms. "You ran out on me too quickly last time. Is everything all right?"

"Just a small situation that required my assistance."

Dmitri searched her expression for a long moment. "Hmm. I'm assuming the situation has something to do with the rumors floating around?"

She pulled away, glancing around at the people nearby.

Biting her lip and lowering her gaze a fraction, she peered up at him through her eyelashes. "Is there somewhere private we can be alone?"

He took her hand in his. "There's a place not far from here."

Valentina followed him around the outskirts of the camp and into a nearby abandoned building. She took the opportunity to look around, noting the building had been well used over the past few months, most likely by lovers wanting a few hours of privacy.

She turned back to Dmitri to find him watching her with brown eyes that were far too perceptive. He was usually quick to smile or joke, teasing her out of her more serious moods. It was part of the reason she'd been drawn to him from the beginning. But now his expression was filled with concern, shadowing his usual mirth.

"I heard Sofia and Pavel hurt you," he said, taking a step toward her. "Rumors say you were taken to the towers for medical treatment. Is that true?"

She nodded. "Yes, but I'm fine."

He frowned, his eyes roaming over her before meeting her gaze again. Lifting his hand, he cupped her cheek. "Would you tell me if you weren't?"

"Dmitri," she began, placing her hand against his chest to stop him, "I didn't come here for this."

He put his hand over hers, holding her to him, and pretended to be affronted. "Shh. Give me a few moments to dream before you destroy all my hopes again."

Valentina couldn't help but smile. They'd had fun together a few times, but it had never been anything more than that. He'd made some suggestions about being open to something more, but she'd shut that down immediately. "Are you going to tell me why you asked me to meet you in the middle of the night?"

"You already said you didn't come here for that," he reminded her with a grin.

A laugh bubbled out of her. "If you don't start talking, I'll walk out of here and ruin your reputation. Whatever woman you're currently trying to lure into bed won't believe your claims about your prowess as a lover."

"You're a cruel woman," he lamented with a sigh. "Very well. They've got me on a rather insane schedule right now, but there's been some commotion lately and a lot of rumors. I heard Sergei made his displeasure known after you were hurt. Some of the people in Sofia's camp claim they heard Pavel's screams for over an hour."

Valentina nodded. "I heard the same."

"Ah," he murmured. "But did you also hear an attempt was made on Sergei's life?"

She froze. "What did you hear?"

"He was meeting with some representatives from the towers. Orders came down from the top that Sergei's life is forfeit. There are rumors he's been organizing a rebellion."

Valentina frowned. No such order had been issued, but if people believed it and possessed a vendetta against him, they might decide to target Sergei without fear of any ramifications. Someone was carefully planting seeds and hoping their machinations bore fruit. "Do you know who was responsible for the attempt on his life?"

Dmitri paused, studying her for a long time. "I was expecting more of a reaction from you, Valentina. You barely even blinked when I mentioned a possible rebellion, but you're fixated on Sergei? You've been keeping your own secrets, haven't you?"

Her body stiffened. "What do you know, Dmitri?"

He lifted his hand, brushing his fingers against her cheek. Valentina pulled back from him, suddenly wary. Dmitri didn't usually touch her again once she'd made it clear she wasn't interested.

"The last time you pulled away from me was also when I mentioned his name," he said with a frown. "Are you thinking about getting back together with him?"

Her eyes narrowed. "If you don't start talking, we're going to have a problem."

"Dammit, Valentina," he swore, running a hand over his closely cropped dark hair. "You need to stay away from him. People are already tying you two together again, especially after what he did to Pavel and Sofia. For fuck's sake, he tortured Pavel. Sergei made it clear that night that if anyone else put their hands on you, they'd meet the same end. Some of the men who cleaned up the bodies are still having nightmares."

"What's your point?"

Dmitri's jaw clenched, and he took another step toward her, backing her up against the wall. In a low voice, he warned, "Distance yourself from him, Valentina. He's being set up to take the fall for this rebellion. One way or another, he's going to be removed from the towers. If you're standing too close when it happens, you'll be dragged under too." He paused, his eyes roaming over her face again. He lifted his hand and brushed his thumb across her cheek. "I don't want to see anything happen to you."

She swallowed, putting her hand on his chest again. "Who's behind this, Dmitri? What do you know about the rebellion?"

Footsteps sounded from outside, and Dmitri's eyes widened before yanking Valentina against him. His mouth slammed against hers while his hands landed on her backside, a little more enthusiastically than necessary.

Inwardly swearing, she wound her arms around his neck, softening her body against his to make it appear they were engaged in a passionate embrace. Someone chuckled, and Dmitri broke their kiss to glare at the newcomer. She didn't recognize him, but that didn't mean much.

"What the fuck are you doing here, Marek? If you haven't noticed, I'm a little busy. I'm supposed to be off schedule for the rest of the night."

Marek grinned, eyeing her with appreciation. "Change of plans. You're needed back on duty."

Dmitri tensed, and Valentina's internal alarms started going off. Something wasn't right, and Dmitri knew it too. After their last meeting, he'd gone back on duty and hadn't had a chance to get a message to her until tonight. It wasn't normal for them to recall him so soon. If there was a problem with one of the excavation sites, Sergei should have heard something.

Dmitri shook his head. "I've been on for four days straight. Get someone else to cover for me."

Marek shrugged. "Sorry. I was told to bring you back immediately and not to take no for an answer."

Valentina pretended to pout and ran her hands up Dmitri's chest. Winding her hands around his neck again, she leaned against him and purred, "I came all this way to see you, Dima. I'm not sure when I'll get another chance to sneak away. I was really hoping to get some alone time with you."

Dmitri glanced down at her and muttered a curse before turning back to Marek. "Give me fifteen minutes, and I'll cover your shift tomorrow."

Marek hesitated, studying her again, and then nodded. "Hurry. I'll wait outside."

As soon as he was gone, Valentina frowned and whispered, "You can't stay here."

Dmitri turned back to her and arched an eyebrow. "Don't tell me you're worried about me." He grinned and added, "If you want to reconsider my earlier offer, we have fifteen minutes before I have to go back on duty. We can do a lot in that time. Maybe not as much as I'd like, but I'm willing to give it a shot."

"I'm serious, Dmitri," she hissed. "You know someone's suspicious or they wouldn't have called you back. You can't walk out of here and pretend nothing's changed."

"I don't have much of a choice," he said in a low voice, glancing toward the door. "If I leave with you, I might as well admit I'm guilty of something. You know better than anyone how people love to talk. If I stay, I can probably convince them out of whatever they're thinking."

"And if they think you're smuggling sensitive information to Nikolai, they'll execute you," she reminded him. "Did they act suspicious before I arrived?"

When he hesitated, she understood the problem immediately. This part was always difficult, especially when you'd been playing a role for a long time. Friendships and relationships were easily forged, but they made it harder to walk away. Dmitri was very likeable, and it was one of the reasons he'd been perfect for her purposes. People naturally gravitated toward him, and like he said: they loved to talk.

"I'm sorry, Dmitri. Someone must have recognized me and sent Marek to retrieve you. You managed to buy us a few minutes of time, but we can't spend it arguing. If you come with me now, I can offer you a place in the towers or in one of Nikolai's camps off-continent. It's your choice. Please don't take a chance with your life. It's not worth it."

Dmitri squeezed his eyes shut and sighed. "You're right. You told me to watch for anything out of the ordinary, and this isn't typical." He opened his eyes again. "I have a speeder and some UV gear stashed not far from here. It's in one of the outbuildings."

She nodded and pulled out her commlink. "Good. Give me the coordinates."

He rattled them off, turning to watch the door while she sent the information to Sergei and Yuri with instructions to meet her there. Even though Yuri was monitoring, she didn't intend to announce that to Dmitri. People frequently opened up more when they thought conversations were private.

She slipped her commlink back into her pocket and glanced around the room. This building was in better shape compared to some others in the area, but there were limited options as far as escaping. "What's the best way out?"

"I scouted this area before I brought you here. We can climb up to the second floor and cross through to the next building." Dmitri took her hand again and led her to another room where the ceiling was partially collapsed. Some supply crates had been pushed to the side of the wall, creating a rather unsteady staircase.

Valentina carefully climbed to the top and used her arms to pull herself up through the hole in the ceiling. If the crates had been wobbly under her weight, they were even worse for Dmitri. He'd almost reached the top when one of the crates shifted, and he fell to the floor with a crash. She started to move forward to help him, but footsteps came rushing into the room. She scrambled back and waited, making sure to keep out of sight.

"What the fuck is going on in here?" Marek demanded.

"Would you believe it was a sex game gone wrong?" came Dmitri's pained reply.

Valentina scanned the second floor. Aside from a window that looked out over an adjacent building's roof, there was another small hole in the floor on the opposite side of the room. It would be a tight fit, but she didn't have much choice. She crept forward, trying to keep her movements silent as she avoided various pieces of debris.

"Not a chance. Where's your girlfriend? Caz said you were up to something."

From this new position, she was situated behind Marek and out of his line of sight. He was currently holding an electrolaser gun on Dmitri, who was still lying prone on the floor. It was unfortunate he'd chosen to bring out the weapons and escalate the situation. Not only was it an obvious sign Marek was an excitable amateur and therefore unpredictable, but it also limited her options in handling the situation. Above all else, she couldn't risk Dmitri being captured and interrogated.

Dmitri's eyes widened at the sight of her through the ceiling. Marek's shoulder's tensed and he started to turn, but Dmitri groaned and clutched his balls. "The bitch took off. She not only left me high and dry but had the nerve to kick me first."

Valentina gripped the edge of the ceiling and lowered herself down, dropping to the ground as soon as Dmitri started moaning again. Withdrawing the knife strapped to her back, she silently moved forward. With one quick thrust, she shoved the knife between Marek's ribs, puncturing his lung so he couldn't call out. She yanked it back out as he dropped to his knees, unable to take a breath. Moving forward, she roughly grabbed his hair and shoved the blade upward again at the base of his neck, severing his brain stem. She twisted the knife, and his body twitched, falling to the ground with a *thump*.

"Fuck," Dmitri muttered, shock and horror filling his expression. "I just thought you'd hit him over the head or something. Did you have to kill him?"

"Get up," she ordered, yanking out her blade and ignoring his question. Valentina couldn't afford to doubt herself or her actions. The time for that would come later when they were out of danger. She picked up Marek's abandoned weapon and began searching his body until she located his commlink. She pocketed both items and lifted her head to find that Dmitri still hadn't moved.

"Don't make me say it again, Dmitri. You either come with me and keep your mouth shut about who you've been working for, or I can end your life right now. You have ten seconds to decide."

Dmitri blinked at her. She narrowed her eyes at him, knowing he was just now coming to the realization Nikolai was the one truly at risk if he opened his mouth. She might like Dmitri, but her first loyalty was always going to be to Nikolai. She'd kill Dmitri in a second if it kept him from talking and implicating Nikolai in their subterfuge. Even though she'd been the one who had enlisted Dmitri's help to gain insight into what their other leaders were doing, Nikolai was the one who'd be held responsible.

Dmitri scrambled to his feet, his expression both wary and fascinated. "You're very good at making people forget who you really are. Now I can't decide which version of you I like better. This one is pretty hot."

"It figures. I seem to attract a specific type," she muttered, gripping his arm and pulling him toward the main room. Valentina stopped him before they got to the door. Reaching down, she quickly unhooked his belt and unfastened the top button of his pants. When he arched an eyebrow at her, she said, "Fasten it when we walk out."

He nodded and grinned. She pulled out her ponytail and shook out her hair. The chestnut color with its reddish undertones was distinctive, but she hoped having her hair down would alter her appearance enough to make someone pause for a few seconds and question whether it was her. At the very least, it would lend some believability to the appearance they were lovers who'd just finished engaging in a tryst.

Taking Dmitri's arm again, she leaned into him and kept her

hand close to her weapon as they headed outside. No one was within the immediate vicinity, but that didn't mean no one was watching. They only had a handful of minutes until someone came looking for Dmitri and discovered Marek's body.

They walked quickly around the back of the building, ducking between partially collapsed structures and climbing over rubble. It was too risky to pull out a light, so they navigated as quickly as possible with the limited moonlight. Valentina's commlink buzzed in her pocket, and she knew it was either Sergei or Yuri checking in to see if she needed assistance. She pressed a button, letting them know she was on her way, and slid it back into her pocket.

This next part was going to be far more challenging. She'd managed to keep Dmitri alive so far, but she wasn't sure she'd be able to protect him from Sergei. Having them meet each other face to face had never been part of the plan.

CHAPTER TWO

VALENTINA AND DMITRI walked into the abandoned building where he'd hidden his speeder. Sergei and Yuri were already there and waiting for them, and neither of them looked particularly pleased with the unexpected company.

Dmitri muttered a colorful oath under his breath. "This should be fun."

Sergei straightened as they approached. His gaze swept over her, and she knew he was making sure she was unharmed. But then his eyes narrowed on Dmitri, and they were anything but friendly.

Yuri arched an eyebrow. "Really, Valya? Introducing Dmitri to Sergei? If you wanted him dead, you didn't have to bring me along. You could have let me sleep."

"Nice to see you too, Yuri," Dmitri said and gave Sergei a curt nod.

"I recognize you from somewhere," Sergei said, his voice almost eerily calm, but the energy surrounding him sparked to life.

Valentina studied him carefully, prepared to intervene if things escalated. Sergei had been working with Hayden to gain better control of his energy when it came to her, but this was the first time they'd had a chance to experiment. It wasn't an ideal location or test, but facing a former lover was better than having Sergei witness her being injured.

Dmitri nodded. "We met briefly a few years ago at the summit meeting when you were offered your own command."

Sergei cocked his head. "That's right. You led the special reconnaissance team for the OmniLab facility. You were there to report your findings." He glanced at Valentina briefly before focusing again on Dmitri. "This particular assignment seems a bit... out of character for someone with your skill set."

"Let's just say I was looking to diversify. I met Valentina shortly after that meeting, and her proposal was... intriguing," Dmitri replied and placed his hand on Valentina's back.

She tensed as Sergei's eyes narrowed on Dmitri again. The energy in the building began crackling with electricity, and she mentally willed him to pull it back. Sergei had always excelled at retaining control in difficult situations, but it was different when she was in the room.

Yuri chuckled. "Our Valya frequently has that effect on people. Granted, she doesn't usually fuck her informants, but it appears to be a very motivating tactic. Dmitri's been quite *satisfied* with his position... or maybe it's her position under him."

"Dammit, Yuri," she hissed as Sergei started to take a step toward Dmitri, murder in his eyes. It was bad enough Dmitri had put his hands on her, but Yuri had to push Sergei just a little more, knowing his control was still tenuous.

"Better we find out now, Valya," Yuri said with a shrug.

Valentina moved in front of Sergei and pressed her hands against his chest to stop his advance. Sergei encircled her wrists with his hands, his touch gentle but firm as he moved her to the side—or rather, tried to move her. Understanding his intent, she leaped onto him, forcing Sergei to grab hold of her so she wouldn't fall. No matter how angry he was, Valentina knew his first inclination was to protect her from harm, and she was counting on that now.

He gripped her tightly, and she wrapped her arms and legs around him. As long as his hands were occupied with her, he wasn't going to be killing anyone. She leaned her head against his shoulder and said quietly, "Dmitri has information we need, Seryozha. You know what you mean to me."

Sergei held her against him, and she allowed her cool water energy to envelop him as she slid down his body. He lifted his hands to cup her face and lowered his head, claiming her mouth. Instead of a gentle kiss, it was full of possession and need. She met him head-on, demanding with her lips and tongue the same thing he wanted from her.

She poured every emotion she felt into that kiss, reminding him he was her chosen mate and the only one she wanted. Without exception, he'd always held her heart, and no matter what happened in the past or future, nothing would ever change that. He pulled back gently and looked down into her eyes, the small flame around his iris flaring brightly with the knowledge of everything she'd communicated.

He released her and turned back to Dmitri. "You know about Pavel?"

When he nodded, Sergei continued, "Good. If you ever put your hands on Valentina again, what I did to Pavel will seem like a merciful death."

Dmitri's jaw clenched, but he wisely didn't argue the point. Valentina blew out a breath. They didn't have time for this. "Yuri, can you run a check on someone named Caz working in this camp?"

Yuri nodded, and she turned back to Dmitri. "Did Marek report directly to Caz?"

Dmitri continued to eye Sergei and didn't answer right away. She had the impression they were both sizing up the competition. This was absurd. They needed to focus on learning about the man she'd just killed, who he reported to, and whether he posed a threat to Nikolai. Engaging in this testosterone-laden version of chest thumping while the two of them glared at each other was counterproductive.

Before she could snap at them to knock it off, Dmitri crossed his arms over his chest and said, "Not directly. Marek was fairly new to the camp, but he followed whatever orders Caz threw at him. Caz was always angling for a way to get pushed up faster through the ranks."

While Yuri worked on his tablet, Valentina handed Marek's commlink to Sergei. "Can you search this device? I'm especially interested in any messages about me or Dmitri."

Sergei frowned. "What happened?"

"I think I may have been recognized," she explained as Yuri entered some additional information into his tablet. "I had to eliminate Marek, but I couldn't risk leaving Dmitri there if they connected him to me or Nikolai."

Yuri handed Dmitri the tablet. "Which one is Caz?"

Dmitri scrolled through the tablet, and Valentina leaned over his arm to look at the screen. Images of several people going by that name or some variation were displayed. Dmitri pointed to one of them. "That's him."

She took the tablet from him, pulled up Caz's information, and studied the picture of the man. Nothing was remotely familiar about him. If she'd ever met him, she didn't have any recollection of it. She looked up to find Sergei frowning at the tablet. "You know him?"

"No, but I recognize him. He was in Sofia's camp that day when Ariana was taken and held captive. I have no idea what he was doing there if he works here in Ivan's camp."

Valentina frowned. Many of the camps in the

surrounding area fell under Sergei's command as part of their initial planned acquisition of OmniLab. Sofia's camp had been one of them. But once the Coalition had formed an alliance with OmniLab and they agreed to help construct a new tower, everyone had quickly realized their preliminary numbers weren't going to be sufficient for such an endeavor.

Several of the Coalition's leaders had volunteered their people to work under Sergei's direction while still retaining ultimate control of their camps. This agreement allowed Sergei the flexibility to further the Coalition's efforts in completing the construction as he saw fit. It also had the added benefit of keeping their leaders abreast of the current situation by having their people report directly to them regarding the progress. It all came down to accountability.

Unfortunately for her, having so many of their people in proximity to one another also increased the likelihood of accidentally crossing paths with someone. The more well-known Nikolai became, the more people began to recognize her. Most of the upper tiers of their government knew her by sight, but that knowledge was now starting to trickle down the ranks. It didn't help that she'd stormed into Sofia's camp and had thrown Nikolai's name around to rescue Ariana either. She usually tried to keep a low profile but hadn't had many options in that case, especially with their alliance at stake.

Dmitri frowned. "Caz sometimes runs deliveries between camps. Not often, but now and then when he's trying to collect favors."

Valentina blew out a breath. "Dammit. If he was in Sofia's camp that day, he definitely knows who I am. He could have been hoping to use that information to his advantage."

Yuri walked over and took the tablet from her. He entered a few commands to display a map of the camp and thrust it toward Dmitri. "Show me the location of Caz's bunk and his current assignment."

Dmitri circled the areas. "If he's waiting for me to show up, Caz will probably be in one of the tents right outside his assigned area."

Yuri studied the map, most likely memorizing the layout of the camp. He handed the tablet back to Valentina. "Let me know if Sergei gets anything else off the commlink. I'll be back shortly."

Valentina nodded, watching as he headed out. Yuri rarely had much interaction with the other camps, so his presence would mostly go unnoticed while he handled Caz.

Turning back to Sergei who was still studying Marek's commlink, she considered their options. If she were going to have a chance to get more information out of Dmitri, the time was now. Sergei lifted his head and frowned at her, obviously displeased with her silent request, but he gave her a curt nod to indicate he wouldn't interfere.

Valentina turned back to Dmitri. "Will you tell me what you know about this rebellion?"

Dmitri darted a quick look at Sergei before responding. "I don't know much. There are just some rumors floating around that Sergei is orchestrating it."

She tilted her head to study Dmitri. He was wary, especially about discussing anything in front of an audience. Based on their conversation earlier, she suspected his feelings for her ran deeper than he'd initially led her to believe. It hadn't helped that she'd made her reconciliation with Sergei clear by kissing him. Dmitri wasn't going to divulge any information easily, but she didn't want to resort to harsh measures. Yet.

Taking a step closer to him, she placed her hand on his arm. He tensed, glancing at Sergei before focusing on her again. She bit her lip and lowered her head, peering up at him through her lashes. "Dmitri, we've known each other for a long time. I wouldn't have asked you to work with me if I didn't trust your judgment. If there's a threat to our people, please tell me."

"You know I would tell you if I knew anything definite."

Valentina sighed and squeezed her eyes shut. "Sergei, can you give us a moment alone?"

There was a long pause. Finally, Sergei said, "Very well. I'll be outside."

She listened to his retreating footsteps but knew he'd remain within earshot. She didn't particularly mind. If she were in his position, she'd do the same.

"What the hell, Valentina?" Dmitri demanded. "How long have you two been back together?"

"We've been talking for a few days," she admitted quietly. "You know the attempt on his life you heard about?" When Dmitri nodded, she said, "Sergei thought they were aiming at me. He pushed me out of the way and almost died as a result. They were barely able to get him to the towers in time to save him."

Dmitri let out a breath and ran a hand over his head. "Dammit. I don't want to be grateful to him of all people." He frowned and glanced in the direction Sergei had gone. "Does Nikolai know about you two?"

"Does it matter?"

He sighed. "I suppose not. I just know Nikolai's possessive of you. He wasn't happy when we became close, and I know he had a falling out with Sergei years ago. I don't want to see you get involved in something dangerous."

Valentina moved closer to Dmitri and looked up into his eyes. He really was a good man. In some ways, he'd reminded her of Sergei and it was those similarities that had drawn her to him. When it came down to it, though, there was no comparison.

"I wanted you to know about Sergei so you would understand my motivation. I need to find out who's framing him, Dmitri," she whispered, letting a trace of her fear and vulnerability edge into her voice. "He saved my life. I have a responsibility to do the same for him."

His gaze softened as he reached up to touch her cheek, stopping before he made contact. He lowered his hand and sighed. "I don't know much. I overheard a conversation several days ago between two people running deliveries to the towers and outlying camps. They were talking about a shipment of weapons and having to divert it from going to the towers because their contact wasn't responding. I knew you were looking for information on a missing shipment, so I stuck around to listen. I thought it was odd that weapons were going there instead of being sent to one of the other camps."

She frowned. "Did they say who their contact was in the towers?"

"No. I had the impression they were both worried about not being able to reach him. The woman had some concerns about arming the Omnis and having them turn on us. The man with her said it wouldn't come to that. Sergei was going to be held responsible for it and removed from command. The weapons would be confiscated and returned to our people."

"Did you hear any names?"

Dmitri shook his head. "My supervisor saw me, and I couldn't sneak away to follow them without arousing suspicion."

"Thank you, Dmitri," she said and leaned over to kiss his cheek.

"Valentina," he began and glanced toward the door, "I know you feel a sense of loyalty toward him for saving you, but can someone like him truly make you happy?"

She smiled. There was no doubt in her mind. "Yes."

———

SERGEI LEANED against the wall outside and listened to Valentina and Dmitri. When he heard her soft voice saying he could make her happy, something within him loosened at her words. It had only been a few days since he'd managed to convince her to give him another chance. He knew she was still a bit wary, but every day, she was letting him back in a little more. Even playing with her and Yuri earlier had been reminiscent of their time together before he'd left.

Her voice caught his attention again, and he heard a trace of wariness in her tone. "What happened?"

Sensing her distress and urgency through their bond, he straightened and headed back into the building to find her speaking with someone on her commlink. Valentina started pacing the length of the room. "Yuri's cleaning up a situation. As soon as he finishes, we'll head back. Do we have copies of the security feeds?"

She paused to listen, stopping a short distance away from him, and lifted her gaze to meet his. "Sergei might have a way to bypass it."

He took a step toward her as she bit her lower lip. "Yes, he's with me." She held out the commlink to him. "It's Nikolai."

Sergei accepted the device and held it to his ear. "What's happened?"

"I wanted you both with Valentina to keep her safe. Are you aware she was almost caught? That's why she had to eliminate Marek," Nikolai replied, his tone laced with irritation.

Sergei's jaw clenched, and he glared at her. She simply blinked at him with her big blue eyes. He'd suspected as much based on Dmitri's presence, but Yuri had been the one monitoring her comms and hadn't shared the details of what happened. He'd given Valentina some space to do what was necessary, recognizing his own barely suppressed energy when it came to her, but now he was starting to question that wisdom. Yuri must have either told Nikolai what transpired, or he'd been listening in on Valentina's comms from the towers.

Looking at her now, with her chestnut hair loose and framing the delicate features of her face, she was the quintessential vision of innocence. He resisted the urge to snort. She was very, very good... and in a great deal of trouble once he got her alone again.

"I'm aware now."

"Don't let her out of your sight again," Nikolai ordered. "I've had a bad feeling since the three of you left, but I knew she wouldn't return until she spoke with Dmitri. To make matters worse, we now have a situation here in the towers. Lars said some of our people were arrested at Hayden's club. They got into an altercation with some tower residents. You're going to need to get back here as soon as possible to help untangle this mess."

Sergei frowned. Hayden was the fire channeler who had been training him. His club had been designed to integrate the people living in the towers with some of the Coalition and ruin rats. Sergei had only visited the establishment once, but he knew it was becoming increasingly popular with some of his people. "How bad is it?"

"At least one dead and several others injured. We're still gathering information. Security managed to contain the situation, but a tower resident was in possession of one of our weapons. OmniLab is currently searching their quarters for any other weapons."

Sergei resisted the urge to curse. If their stolen weapons were already circulating through the towers, the situation had become dire. Alec and the rest of the tower leadership couldn't afford to allow this to continue. Once again, it looked like their alliance was in jeopardy.

When the original terms of their agreement were negotiated, OmniLab had demanded that no one affiliated with the Coalition be permitted to bring weapons into the existing towers. Sergei hadn't objected, especially since the tower residents weren't permitted to carry lethal weapons. He'd managed to get around that rule by entering through the Inner Sanctum as Lars's guest, but everyone else was searched and all weapons confiscated.

"Did they mention any names or how they acquired them?"

"No," Nikolai replied with a sigh. "They're not talking yet, and these Omnis tend to take a more passive approach than I'd like. At my request, they've agreed to hold our people who were involved in the altercation in their security offices, waiting for us to handle their interrogation. At this time, there's no way to know if any of them provided the weapon in question. They were searched, but nothing was found. I've also asked Hayden to pull the security feeds for the past two weeks so we can determine who else may be a suspect."

Sergei pinched the bridge of his nose. It was going to be a long night. "I'll speak with them once I return."

"I assumed as much, but that brings us to another problem. Once Hayden supplies us with the security feeds, we won't be able to run the images through our system for identification without alerting the rest of our leadership about the problem. If they investigate, you'll be blamed for this too."

Sergei remained silent. He didn't particularly care if he were blamed or not. As long as Valentina knew he was innocent, that was all that mattered. In his experience, the truth usually had a way of coming out. His bigger concern was their alliance and what it would mean for their people if it fell apart.

After a brief moment, Nikolai sighed and added, "Someone's gunning for you, Sergei. I think Valentina's right, and we can't sit on this any longer. Until we get a handle on this situation, Alec is talking about imposing restrictions to prevent our people from accessing their towers. If that happens, the Coalition will be united in taking action against you and having you removed from command. We'll need to act decisively to prevent this alliance from crumbling and you being made into a convenient scapegoat. You may not care what they think of you, but Valentina does and this is hurting her."

Sergei walked a distance away, making sure he was out of Dmitri's earshot. In a quiet voice, he said, "See if you can get Alec to hold off temporarily. I can set up a relay here to mask the signal, and you can run a search through the database. It'll appear as though it originated from here. I just need to get access to their computer system."

"Do it," Nikolai ordered. "Once you have it set up, let me know so I can start running the analysis. I'll speak with Alec and explain the situation. If he agrees to give us a bit more time, we'll likely only have a day or two to get to the bottom of this. Either way, this is going to affect future negotiations with them. We can't afford to ask their people for more favors without losing standing. Someone needs to be held responsible."

"We'll take care of it," Sergei promised and signed off the call. He walked back over to Valentina and handed her the commlink. Setting up a relay wouldn't be all that difficult, but Dmitri's presence was an unwelcome complication. They needed to avoid letting him know what was going on. Depending on how strongly Dmitri felt about Valentina, he might be inclined to use the information for his own means.

Sergei glanced over at the dark-haired man, remembering

the familiarity Dmitri had shown when touching her. It was his own fault for walking away from her for three years, but it was still tempting to "accidentally" snap the man's neck. Dmitri crossed his arms over his chest and glared at Sergei with equal dislike.

Sergei narrowed his eyes, but Valentina put her hand on his arm. With an amused smile, she shook her head. For whatever reason, she wanted Dmitri alive. Sergei sighed and said, "I need to see the camp layout map again."

She handed the tablet to him, and Sergei pulled up the image. He should be able to access their network from any terminal, but it would be better if he could use someone else's credentials. Eyeing Dmitri again, he considered the possibility of using his credentials for about half a minute before Valentina narrowed her eyes at him. Too bad. It would have been a tidy solution.

According to the information he'd learned from reviewing Marek's commlink, Caz should have the necessary access he needed. Caz most likely wouldn't have a need to use his credentials again once Yuri was finished with him. Sergei pulled out his commlink and sent a quick message to Yuri telling him what he needed. He glanced over at Valentina, uneasy at the thought of leaving her alone. Nikolai wouldn't have issued a warning without reason.

She frowned and took a step closer to him, searching his expression. "What's wrong?"

"I'm going to need your help," he said and walked over to Yuri's speeder. He opened the side compartment and pulled out a hat for her. Without questioning him, she immediately pulled her hair back into a bun and placed the hat on her head. He reached up and tucked a few loose strands of her hair out of sight.

"You can't be serious," Dmitri said, walking over to them. "If someone recognized her, a hat isn't going to cut it. Whatever you need her for, it's not worth it. Valentina should wait here where it's safe. If you need help, I'll go."

Valentina paused, a slight trace of temper in her eyes before softening her expression and turning back to Dmitri. Sergei bit back a smile. If there was one thing she hated, it was someone being overprotective when they hadn't earned that right. She might give Sergei, Nikolai, and Yuri some leeway, but only up to a point.

"I appreciate your concern," she said gently, "but you've worked in this camp for months, and the chances of you being recognized are much higher. They've already sent Marek out to retrieve you, and I'm sure an alert with your name will be issued as soon as they discover his body. If you'd like to wait here for us, we won't be gone long. Otherwise, I can give you the coordinates and you can head directly to Nikolai's camp. I'll send instructions along to provide you with accommodations until you decide where you'd like to be relocated."

Dmitri's jaw clenched. "I'll wait here."

She inclined her head and gestured for Sergei to lead the way. He grinned and headed out of the ruined building.

———

VALENTINA FOLLOWED Sergei through a maze of abandoned buildings. They were trying to stay on the outskirts of camp, but what they were attempting was still risky. Not only was it difficult to navigate in the darkness, but they wouldn't have a good explanation for why they were skulking around in the middle of the night.

Sergei slowed his steps and said quietly, "I need to meet up with Yuri to get Caz's credentials to set up the relay. I could override the system, but it may alert security there's a problem. We need to buy Nikolai as much time as possible to run the search."

She carefully climbed over some fallen masonry. "You didn't really need my help, did you?"

"Nikolai's worried about you," he admitted, glancing around a corner before leading her through a narrow alley. "I couldn't say anything in front of your... *friend*, but Nikolai wants either Yuri or me to stay with you. I don't know if his concerns are related to the new training we've been doing, but I'm not willing to take the chance."

Valentina frowned. One of Nikolai's talents was precognition. On occasions in the past, and during times of extreme stress, he could see a few minutes ahead in time. It had saved their lives more than once, but his ability was erratic. Ever since their bond changed a few days ago, Nikolai was getting other flashes or insights, but it had become harder for him to make sense of them.

"You need to keep a low profile, Sergei—more so than any of us. This camp is under Ivan's jurisdiction, and you don't have any business here. Someone will recognize you."

"I know," he agreed. "I'll try to keep out of sight unless there's no alternative. I'll have Yuri bring the credentials to us, but I need to find a network access point to use them. You might need to provide a distraction."

Valentina opened her mouth to respond, but Sergei held up his hand to halt her progress. She froze. Based on the sound of the footsteps and hushed voices, at least two people were approaching from an adjacent alleyway. She motioned to Sergei, and he nodded, backing up quickly and darting into a partially collapsed doorway with her. He put his arms around her, holding her tightly against him as they waited for the group to pass.

The cadence of the voices led her to believe it wasn't just a routine patrol. They were on edge about something, but she couldn't make out the individual words. If she had to guess, she'd say someone had probably discovered Marek's body or Yuri had already eliminated Caz. Either way, the approaching group was in a heightened state of awareness.

Sergei stroked her side with his thumb, and she lifted her head. He nodded, indicating he understood the same thing. They'd take action if necessary, but they both hoped the people would pass without noticing them. Sergei carefully withdrew his commlink, angling it so they could both read the message on the screen. Yuri had managed to acquire the necessary credentials and was on his way back.

Valentina took the commlink from Sergei, her position affording her more mobility. She sent their coordinates, along with a warning about the patrols. When she finished, Sergei slipped the device back into his pocket just as the sound of the patrol's footsteps began moving in the opposite direction. This time, their luck had held.

She moved away from Sergei, and he motioned for her to follow him into a nearby building. They couldn't go far until Yuri joined them, but they were too exposed waiting in the alley. Sergei ducked down to avoid the low, overhanging beam and began investigating the building to catalogue all the exit points. Valentina took up position near a broken window, keeping watch for anyone who might approach.

Sergei came back and hunched down beside her. "If there's a problem, there's a window in the next room we can use as an exit."

She nodded, still watching the alley, and settled in to wait. So far, other than the small group they'd seen, everything was quiet. This time of night was her favorite to do this type of work. The moon cast an eerie light over the ruins and provided ample shadows where they could hide. Even the air was different, cooler somehow with a hint of moisture that was usually absent in the sunlight.

With Sergei beside her, a strange sort of contentment filled her. It reminded her of all the past times when they'd gone on surveillance missions together. She never thought they'd be doing this together again. Even now, it was a little surreal.

Sergei was quiet for a long time before he spoke again. "What did you see in him, Valechka?"

Valentina frowned, surprised by the question. "Do you really want to have this conversation now?"

"Might as well."

She glanced over at him. His body was tense, and the whole thing with Dmitri appeared to really be bothering him. With a sigh, she turned back to watch for any sign of Yuri or more patrols. "He made me laugh. Sometimes, he would say or do something that reminded me of you. No one else other than Yuri or Nikolai has ever played around or teased me like that. It was nice."

Sergei fell silent again for several more minutes. "Do you care for him?"

Valentina lifted her shoulder in a half-hearted shrug. "Yes, or I wouldn't have been with him. I missed you, and I didn't think there was a chance I'd ever have you back in my life. Being with him made the pain a little easier to manage, but he was never any sort of substitute. I love you, Seryozha. It's always been you for me."

"I'm sorry I hurt you, little dove," he whispered.

She turned toward him again, the pain in his eyes as vivid as hers had been. She placed her hand over his. "I'm sorry for your hurt too."

He frowned, and she knew he was thinking about the fire he'd caused in the facility after she'd been injured. Too many had died, and he'd carried the weight of his guilt for years. Determined to distract him from the painful memories, she said, "I'd ask about your other lovers, but I'm not sure I want to know how many you had."

Sergei winced. "Perhaps we should find out what's taking Yuri so long."

She huffed and turned back to watching the alley. "It figures. If any of them are still around, you might want to suggest they leave the continent before I find out about them."

"No one has ever come close to comparing to you, Valechka," he said quietly. "But maybe I'll make that suggestion... just in case."

Yuri slinked around the corner. Valentina stood and stepped out of the building, motioning for him to join them. He ducked inside and handed Sergei a small keycard. "They found Marek's body. It will take them a bit longer to locate Caz. I found a nearby terminal you can access, but we're going to need to hurry. I overhead them issuing a campwide alert, and the patrols are getting heavier. We need to get rid of Valentina's lover before they realize he hasn't checked in."

"We're not killing Dmitri," Valentina reminded them. "But I agree. Whatever we're going to do needs to be done quickly."

Sergei nodded and pocketed the keycard. "How many people are guarding the terminal?"

"At least two," Yuri replied, wiping the sweat from his brow. "It's not as heavily manned as some others, but I didn't have time to fully scope out the building."

Valentina frowned. "If they're already in a heightened state of alert, a simple distraction may not be enough. What's their positioning?"

Yuri crouched down, grabbing a few nearby pebbles to create a rudimentary map. "If we're here," he began, pointing to one area, "then the building they're located in is over here." He gestured to another pebble. "The two people I saw are stationed inside near the front, but we may be able to lure them out. If so, Sergei can sneak through the side entrance." He traced the path with his finger. "If there's anyone else there, Sergei will have to deal with them."

"I'd rather not kill them, if we can avoid it," Valentina said, trying to think of a way to distract them. A thought struck her, and she smiled.

Sergei lifted his head and frowned. "I'm not sure I like that look in your eyes, Valechka."

"Oh, you're definitely going to hate this," she agreed.

CHAPTER THREE

"You can't be serious," Sergei argued. "You and Yuri are going to pretend to be lovers?"

She grinned and swatted him playfully. "Keep a lower profile next time and *you* can play the part with me. Besides, it's just long enough to distract the guards. We'll cause a commotion or a lovers' spat, and they'll have to investigate."

"We're going to have to make this believable," Yuri suggested, waggling his eyebrows. "Maybe a little groping, some tongue..."

Sergei glared at him. "Just remember... You have to sleep some time."

"Come on," Valentina said, tugging on Yuri's sleeve before Sergei seriously thought about strangling him. Yuri put his arm around her shoulder as they headed out into the alley. This time, they weren't hiding. There was still a risk someone might identify them, but hopefully, she and Yuri could limit their exposure. If everything went well, the whole operation should take less than fifteen minutes. If not, well, they'd always excelled at improvisation.

"Maybe I should put my hand in your back pocket

instead," Yuri commented as they walked down the street toward the building where the terminal was located.

"Only if you don't need that hand," she replied sweetly. "Sergei might not wait until you're asleep to carve you up if you start groping my ass."

"Hmm. Sounds like foreplay to me."

A laugh bubbled out of her. "You're impossible."

Someone called out, "Valentina? Is that you?"

She froze, inwardly cursing and praying she was wrong about the identity of the person speaking to her. Turning around, she pasted on a brilliant smile even as her heart thudded in her chest. This definitely wasn't good.

"Uncle Grigory, it's wonderful to see you again."

An older man with salt-and-pepper hair approached her and held out his arms. She went to him immediately, and he wrapped her in a tight hug. Leaning back, he looked her up and down. The affection in his eyes was obvious. "My God, it's been a few years, but I would have recognized you anywhere. You're almost an exact replica of your mother, right down to her laugh. You may be even more beautiful than she was at your age."

Valentina smiled and lowered her gaze. "And you're much as I remember you—still full of hot air."

He let out a big booming laugh and draped his arm over her shoulder. "And your companion is Yuri, correct? It's been a while, but we've met before."

Yuri gave him a polite nod. "It's good to see you again." He frowned at her and added, "I wasn't aware Grigory was your uncle, Valya."

"Oh, no," Grigory said, waving off the comment, "we're not related by blood. Her parents were in my unit when we were younger. I knew them well. I've tried to keep tabs on Valentina over the years, but she's very good at staying below the radar. Well, except for tonight apparently."

Valentina smiled, but she still felt a familiar pang of sadness when she thought about her parents. They were killed when she was a child, but she'd been fortunate enough to be raised by her wonderful and loving grandmother.

"What are you doing here, Uncle? I thought you were overseeing one of the construction crew camps."

He nodded. "Yes, but I needed to meet up with Ivan about a shipment that's been delayed. Sometimes a personal approach is necessary to get things done. Your Nikolai understands that well. It's one of the things I respect about him."

She frowned. Ivan wasn't supposed to have been in the camp, and his presence made what they were attempting even riskier. Dammit. Security was going to be tighter than usual. "I've heard about other shipments being delayed, but I didn't realize Ivan was having problems too. If you don't mind me asking, what was in the shipment?"

"Mostly general supplies... some food, hydrating packs, and medical items. Why? Do you know something? Ivan assured me it would only be a minor delay."

"Maybe that's all it is," she agreed, considering the possibilities. Grigory had been allied with Ivan for a long time, but maybe they could use this situation as an opportunity for Nikolai to make inroads with them. "If Ivan runs into a problem, will you let me know? Nikolai may be able to offer you both some assistance if your camp is running low on necessary items. I know he'd be willing to help such a dear friend of my family."

Grigory arched a brow. "And what would Nikolai expect in return for such an offer?"

Valentina gave him a small smile. "We're a people of one circle. We'll square accounts later."

"And now I see your father in you," he murmured with a grin. "Very well. I'll give Ivan a few more days, but if we can't locate the shipment, I may need to take you up on your offer."

She nodded, unsurprised by his answer. "If you send me the list of supplies you need, I'll see what we have in our storage and make sure we hold them in reserve for you."

Yuri cleared his throat. She glanced over at him, and he gave her a meaningful look. She nodded. They still needed to distract the people inside the building so Sergei could set up the relay. "Uncle, forgive me, but we were just about to head out. Nikolai is expecting us. I had no idea you were going to be here or we would have stopped by to pay our respects. Perhaps we can get together soon?"

"Your aunt would love to see you again," he agreed. Lowering his voice, he said, "I would suggest you stay away from Ivan's camp from now on, Valya. A body just turned up, and your presence is somewhat suspicious. You're lucky it was me who came along."

She blinked at him. "How terrible. We certainly don't want to get caught up in any trouble here. Nikolai wanted me to extend an invitation to Ivan to join him for dinner one night, but his camp troubles need to come first."

Grigory studied her for a long time. He grinned and shook his head. "You're even better at playing the game than your mother was." He paused and added, "Ivan's locking down the camp right now. Lena's going to be here any minute, and it's too big of a security risk for you to remain. Your window to get out is closing."

Valentina tilted her head, curious about the purpose in two of their more established leaders meeting together in the middle of the night. If Ivan and Lena were working together, that might have all sorts of political ramifications. "Lena's meeting with Ivan?"

Grigory nodded. "A personal meeting of sorts. Now, shall I escort you out of here?"

Valentina frowned. She hadn't been aware they were sleeping together, but that might be something to explore later. Unfortunately, Grigory was determined to shoo her and Yuri out of the camp. She hadn't wanted to involve him, but her options were limited.

Making it a point to avoid glancing toward the building where Sergei was probably already in position, she said, "You have my word we'll leave in ten minutes, but there's something I need to do first."

Grigory arched an eyebrow. "And what's that?"

"Valya," Yuri began, obviously worried about involving someone else.

She put her hand on Grigory's arm. "Uncle, I have nothing but the utmost respect for you. But I would be remiss in sharing my plans with you. You have my word I don't have any ill intent toward Ivan or his camp. We are simply gathering information on a matter that affects all our people. Once I'm free to do so, I will gladly share the outcome of this investigation."

Grigory considered her for a long moment. Finally, he inclined his head. "Very well. I'll leave you to it. But Valya, you should consider getting out of this line of work. Your parents were taken from us too soon, and I don't want to see the same thing happen to you. Get married. Have babies. Life is far too short for it to be all about duty."

Yuri made a strangled noise and quickly covered it with a cough when she glared at him. Turning back to Grigory, she pasted on a pleasant smile. "Thank you, Uncle. I'll keep your words in mind."

Grigory chuckled and kissed her forehead. "You are definitely just like your mother, except she would have taken a knife to me for suggesting the same thing. I'll look forward to seeing you again soon."

She watched him walk back down the alleyway, waiting until he was out of sight. That was a little too close.

"Babies, huh?"

"Shut up," she muttered, grabbing Yuri's arm and dragging him toward the building. Of all the people Grigory had to say that in front of, it had to be Yuri. Although, Sergei wouldn't have been much better. Oh, who was she kidding? There wasn't a good option. Valentina blew out a breath, determined to focus on their objective. "Let's do this before Sergei gets impatient or we get interrupted again."

Yuri chuckled. "I'm just trying to imagine you married with a baby on your hip. Although, he did say babies... as in more than one. So two? One for each hip?"

They were close enough to the building for their plan to work. A little deviation was warranted. Whirling around, she shoved Yuri a little harder than necessary. Raising her voice, she shouted, "For the last time, I'm not getting married and having babies, so drop it!" Without another word, she ran toward the building.

One of the men caught her around the waist as she entered. She covered her face with her hands, pretending to burst into tears.

"You're not supposed to be here."

"You don't understand," she wailed, still covering her face. Dammit. She hated trying to cry intentionally. Maybe she should have pretended to get angry at Yuri for feeling her up instead.

"What are we supposed to do with her?" one of the men spoke to someone else, his voice slightly panicked.

"I don't know. Get her out of here though. We're supposed to be on lockdown."

"I'm sorry, miss," the first man spoke again. "You're going to need to leave."

He started to drag her to the door, but she buried her face

against his shirt and sniffled. "I'm sorry. I just... I need a minute. He's so unreasonable. He keeps talking about marriage and babies!"

The man holding her hesitated. She clutched him a bit tighter and lifted her head. Blinking back tears, she put a slight hitch into her voice as she said, "Would one of you talk to him for me and get him to back off? He might listen to you. I just... I can't talk to him about this right now."

The man standing behind them said, "For fuck's sake, Anton, just take her back to the boyfriend and deal with this. We've got work to do."

Well, that wouldn't work. She needed both of them engaged in this little charade. Leaning against Anton, Valentina buried her head against his chest, pretending to cry even harder. "I don't understand how he can be talking about babies when I know he's been sleeping with that whore on the construction crew!"

Anton floundered. "You're going to need to talk to him and get him to back off. She won't get off me."

"Fine," the other one snapped, and she heard his boots stomping toward the door.

Excellent. One down. And Yuri would get to deal with someone who was convinced *he* had babies on the brain. Ha!

As soon as he was gone, Valentina lifted her head and sniffed. She caught a glimpse of Sergei sneaking into the room behind Anton. "Will you go with me when I go out there? If he starts making promises, I'm not sure I can handle it. I just don't know what to believe anymore."

Anton sighed. "Fine. You're going to need to learn how to handle your man on your own. Babies, indeed. Who the hell wants to deal with them anyway?"

She nodded. "I know. I really appreciate your help though."

———

"REALLY, VALYA?" Yuri muttered as they headed back to where the speeders were parked. "I was somewhat looking forward to groping you in front of Sergei. Instead, those two recruits spent over ten minutes telling me I was an idiot. Apparently, *I'm* the one obsessing about babies."

She snorted, climbing over a pile of rubble in the darkness. "You inspired the idea with your baby talk. Besides, you sold me out to Sergei earlier. Maybe you'll rethink that next time."

He chuckled. "Maybe I'll—" Yuri froze, grabbing her arm and hauling her back. He ducked down, and she immediately did the same. Peering over the rubble, Valentina saw a group of people walking in their direction. One of them was carrying a handheld light, and it illuminated enough of their faces for her to recognize Lena's entourage. Dammit. They'd be doing a full sweep of the area, if they hadn't already started.

Valentina pulled out her commlink and quickly sent a message to Sergei. They were going to have to find another way around. Unfortunately, they were now sandwiched between Ivan and Lena's people. This was going to be a problem; the darkness wouldn't mask their identities if they got too close.

Yuri leaned over and whispered, "We're going to have to backtrack and find a place to wait until they're gone."

She nodded, not seeing an alternative, and slid her commlink back into her pocket. They started to go back in the direction they'd come from, but footsteps were rapidly approaching. Yuri grabbed her arm, and they ducked behind a crumbling wall. They were still somewhat exposed, but it would hopefully provide them with some temporary cover in the darkness.

The footsteps stopped almost directly in front of them. Yuri pulled out his knife and waited. Valentina put her hand on his arm, a silent gesture to hold off. If necessary, she'd come up with something. They couldn't risk dispatching anyone this close to Ivan or Lena's inner circle.

A woman said, "After you finish, get a copy of Ivan's shipping schedules for the next two weeks. I suspect he's asked me here to help supplement his missing supplies."

"Of course, Lena," a man replied.

"I need a breakdown of everything we have left in our holding location. If we need to move anything out, I want a heavy escort with it when it's transported. Also, find out what's going on in the towers. Now that the construction crews are back at work, they should be expecting another delivery soon. I want to know what and when." There was a lengthy pause before Lena said, "Ivan, it's wonderful to see you again."

"Lena," Ivan replied. "It's my pleasure. I trust your trip went well?"

"It was as expected..."

The voices trailed off as they began moving away.

Valentina frowned. The conversation was troubling. Lena didn't care much for Nikolai or his politics, but Ivan had always been neutral. If Lena was offering to bail Ivan out of trouble, she might demand he agree to certain concessions. Depending on what they were, it might not bode well for Nikolai's future endeavors.

Lena's mention of a holding location was also somewhat curious. Nikolai used various storehouses around the world to store excess supplies while keeping smaller supply caches with them. His network of camps wasn't as vast as Lena's though. Valentina hadn't heard about Lena missing any shipments, but the woman was secretive. It was possible she was trying to prevent additional thefts by using holding areas to stockpile supplies and then distribute them in a controlled manner, but there was no way to guess. Valentina didn't know enough about the inner workings of Lena's camps.

Valentina had contacts within some of them but not anyone close to the older woman. The personal connection between Lena and Ivan was worrisome as well. If the two of them were in bed together, a merger between them could shift the entire power structure within the Coalition. As two of the longest-held leadership positions, their combined holdings dwarfed most of their other leaders.

What they needed was more information. Grigory might be willing to share some insight about Ivan, especially in exchange for supplies. But she had the suspicion Grigory would be reticent about saying anything negative about him.

Ivan had known Valentina's parents too, but she'd never shared the same type of familial relationship she had with Grigory. Dammit. She needed more information.

Yuri tapped her wrist to get her attention and gestured toward the alley. She nodded and followed him, careful to keep her movements silent. It would take a lot longer to get back to Dmitri and the speeders, but it was better than the alternative. They'd already had too many close calls for one evening. Finding out more about Ivan and Lena was going to have to wait until later.

CHAPTER FOUR

VALENTINA AND YURI climbed up the hill toward where they'd left Dmitri and stashed the speeders. Sergei emerged from the shadows. "Are you all right, Valechka? What happened?"

"We almost ran into Lena and Ivan on the way back, so we had to go a different direction," she admitted, stepping over some debris. "Apparently, the two of them have been sleeping together and decided to use this camp as a meeting place. That's why security is tighter than we expected."

"At least I'm not the only one having their evening interrupted because of clandestine meetings," Yuri muttered.

"I offered to bring Brant with me instead," Valentina reminded him.

When Yuri grumbled something derogatory under his breath about Dmitri and Brant, Valentina decided to ignore him. "Ivan's having problems with shipments going missing too. We also overheard Lena asking one of her people to get Ivan's shipping manifest. I don't know if she's investigating Ivan or considering bailing him out."

Yuri frowned. "I'm not sure how much they're working

together. Otherwise, Lena would have gotten the shipping information directly from Ivan. For all we know, she could suspect Ivan's involvement and is looking for proof, or her people could be behind the thefts and looking for a new shipment to target."

"You're right, but I think we can narrow down a few things based on what we've learned so far," she admitted, taking Sergei's hand as he helped her over a ruined wall. "We have three possible suspects: Ivan, Lena, and Peter."

"Other than Nikolai, Oleg is the only other leader in the area," Sergei said, ducking under a low-hanging beam.

She nodded. "But we've ruled out Oleg as a suspect. I have a contact amongst his advisors, and Oleg isn't responsible for the thefts. He's just curious about OmniLab and interested in the new tower. So it's just the other three we need to consider."

"I wouldn't put it past Peter," Yuri muttered.

Valentina glanced over at him. Yuri's perspective had shifted dramatically a few days ago after she'd met with Viktor, Peter's second-in-command. Through Viktor, Peter had extended Valentina an offer to join his camp. Yuri hadn't taken it well. Granted, she had her own issues with Viktor given he'd stabbed Sergei and nearly killed him.

"I'm not fond of him, either, but we need more facts," she reminded him gently. "When I met with Viktor in the towers, he insinuated one of our leaders was responsible for the attempt on Sergei's life. Our stolen weapons were used during that ambush, so it's safe to assume there's a connection between the thefts and the person who targeted Sergei. We need to start ruling people out, and I intend to start with Ivan. From there, we can investigate Lena and Peter."

Sergei stopped while they were still far enough away so Dmitri couldn't overhear their conversation. He studied her for a moment and said, "You've thought of something, haven't you?"

"A loose plan, but yes," she agreed. "One of Grigory's shipments went missing. He was here speaking with Ivan about it. I offered to have Nikolai replenish his missing supplies, and in exchange, I'll ask him for information about Ivan."

Sergei's entire body stiffened. "You ran into Grigory here?" He glared at Yuri. "You didn't think to intervene? Grigory's always been a wildcard. He's supposedly allied with Ivan, but he does as he damn well pleases most of the time."

"You mean, *Uncle Grigory*?" Yuri said, crossing his arms over his chest. She glanced over at him and frowned. Apparently, he was still a little annoyed she hadn't shared that information with him.

Valentina sighed and placed her hand on his arm. "My history with him wasn't important, Yuri. I'm sorry I didn't tell you, but I haven't seen him in years. His interests rarely intersect with Nikolai's ventures. I'd never intentionally keep something like that from you."

Yuri's shoulders relaxed, and he nodded. "Does Nikolai know about your connection?"

"Yes, but he suggested I not use our friendship unless it was necessary. I agreed, and until now, there's never been a need."

"That sounds about right. Nikolai's always been a righteous bastard," Sergei muttered.

Yuri smirked and gestured toward the building where Dmitri was waiting. "Speaking of bastards, do you think he's still alive? Or should I take Valentina for another trip around Ivan's camp so you can take care of him?"

Sergei grinned.

"Very funny," Valentina retorted, but she was secretly glad Yuri had gotten over his snit. He was so strange sometimes—

leave it to the threat of murder and mayhem to brighten his mood. "Were you able to set up the relay, Seryozha?"

Sergei nodded. "Nikolai is running the club surveillance images through the database now. We should have at least a partial list by the time we return."

Sergei placed his hand against her back and led her into the building. The sun would be coming up soon, and they needed to be gone before then. The effects from her earlier adrenaline rush were starting to fade, and this was the time when mistakes were easily made. They couldn't afford more.

Dmitri was pacing when they entered but stopped short at the sight of them. "Are you all right, Valentina?"

"Mmhmm," she agreed, heading over to Yuri's speeder to retrieve a few hydrating packs. She tossed one to Yuri and Sergei before opening hers. Over the years, she'd come to realize she needed to drink more often, a direct correlation to her water channeling abilities. She drank it and then disposed of the empty container. It helped clear her head a bit, but they'd all need to get some rest soon.

Picking up another hydrating pack, she walked over to Dmitri and offered it to him. "Thirsty?"

While he opened it and took a drink, she said, "I need to meet Nikolai, but Yuri can take you back to our camp until we alter your records to mask your identity. It'll only take us a day or two at the most to change them. In the meantime, if there's a particular place you have in mind where you'd like to be transferred, we can begin making the arrangements."

Dmitri finished his drink and crumpled the hydrating pack. "I'd prefer being stationed in Nikolai's camp. I understand he's been expanding quite a bit. He's going to need more team leaders soon."

Valentina nodded, not terribly surprised by the request. "Very well. I can't promise you the position, only the opportunity to apply. Nikolai handpicks his team leads since he works so closely with them. But if you wish to join his camp, I'll make sure you have a place there. If you change your mind later, let me know and we can transfer you."

Yuri chuckled and slapped his hand on Dmitri's shoulder. "If you think staying near Valya will increase the likelihood of getting back into her bed, you're going to have a lot of lonely nights in your future."

Dmitri kept his gaze on her. "I'm willing to take that chance."

Sergei straightened and picked up her helmet off his speeder before handing it to her. "When we changed locations to meet you here, we had to leave your speeder behind, Valechka. We'll need to collect it later. In the meantime, it looks like I'll be the one," he gave a meaningful glance at Dmitri, "giving you a ride tonight."

Dmitri's jaw clenched, and he glared at Sergei.

Yuri guffawed loudly.

Valentina blew out a breath. It was definitely time to get out of there. She pulled on her helmet and followed Sergei over to his bike. Climbing on behind him, she wrapped her arms around his waist as he started to pull out of the ruined building. Thankful Dmitri couldn't hear her over the headset, she let her hands slip under his jacket. "Very cute, Seryozha. But if you want to give me a ride, maybe you should hurry back to the towers."

Sergei chuckled. "We don't have to wait. I could always pull over and find a spot somewhere."

Yuri pulled out behind them and said over the headset, "Oh, that reminds me... Sergei, Valya's uncle thinks it's time for her to get married and start having babies."

Sergei swerved and braked hard. "Babies?"

"Dammit, Yuri," Valentina muttered, tightening her arms around Sergei. "You're such a pain in the ass."

Yuri laughed. "I love you too, Valya."

"Wait," Sergei interrupted. "What's this about babies?"

She sighed. "Just drive, Seryozha. Preferably before I throw a knife at Yuri."

————

THE SUN WAS JUST BEGINNING to peek over the horizon by the time they made it back to the towers. Valentina placed her helmet on a nearby rack and stretched her tired muscles.

Sergei finished securing their speeder and said, "They're holding our people in the security offices. I'm not sure if Nikolai's there or back in Lars's quarters."

She nodded and pulled out her commlink to send Nikolai a quick message letting him know they were back in the towers. "I'll go with you to the security offices. If Brant's there, he can fill me in on what's happened. I'll find Nikolai afterward and we can compare notes. Yuri should be back by then too. It won't take him long to get Dmitri checked into our camp."

Sergei walked over to her, wrapped his arm around her waist, and pulled her tightly against him. Lowering his head, he pressed his lips against hers in a passionate embrace that sent her senses reeling. She curled her fingers into his jacket, giving herself over to his kiss, and softened against him. No one else had ever affected her so much or filled her with such need. It was as though every worry or irritation drifted away as soon as he touched her.

He eased away, and she blinked up at him, getting lost in the depth of emotion in his eyes. He cupped her face and ran his thumb over her cheek. "As soon as I'm finished, I intend to take you back to bed, little dove. I believe I made a promise earlier about distracting you."

She couldn't help but smile. "I have a lot on my mind. Do you really think you're up to such a challenge?"

He arched a brow. "Shall I take you back to my room and show you now?"

Valentina threw her head back and laughed. "If I say yes, neither one of us will leave for the rest of the day."

Sergei smiled and gave her another quick kiss. "You're right, and the thought isn't exactly discouraging. I suppose we need to take care of business first, but you make it very difficult to think of anything else. Although, I'm very interested in hearing what exactly Grigory said to you about getting married."

Her eyes narrowed. She had no intention of discussing anything of the sort with him. With a grin, he took her hand and led her toward the elevator. The security office wasn't too far from the garage area where they'd parked. They entered the stark, utilitarian office and were immediately greeted by an armed guard.

"Ah, welcome, Ambassador. Brant Mason's been expecting you," the guard said as he pressed a button on a console. "He'll be out in a moment, if you'd like to have a seat."

Sergei declined and leaned against the counter, angling his body so he could observe both exits. Valentina ignored the guard's curious gaze on her and wandered over to a screen on the wall, where various helpful tips about respecting your neighbors were displayed. It cycled through to some other strange advertisements about products that appeared largely unnecessary and even frivolous. Some luxuries were understandable, but these Omnis carried it to excess.

Overall, she wasn't impressed with the guard or area. There were cameras at key locations, but other than the security personnel carrying weapons, it didn't appear very secure at first glance. It probably wouldn't be terribly difficult to break out of the facility.

Valentina turned around when she heard approaching

footsteps. Brant walked down the hall toward her. He looked tired but smiled warmly at her.

"Valentina, I didn't think you'd be joining us."

She smiled. "I hope you don't mind if I observe the interviews."

"Not at all." He glanced over at Sergei and inclined his head in greeting. "Thanks for coming here directly. We've detained eight of your people. They're currently in holding cells, but now that you're here, we'll begin moving them into one of our interrogation rooms."

Sergei nodded, and they followed Brant down the narrow hallway. He led them into a small room set up with various consoles and chairs. A special mirrored glass had been installed to view the adjacent interrogation room.

Brant gestured to the chairs. "Nikolai and Lars are on their way down. Nikolai wants to view the proceedings, and this room is secure. Your people won't know he's watching."

Valentina frowned. She'd prefer if Nikolai stayed away, but he'd never agree. Part of her was surprised he'd refrained from coming down and interrogating their people himself. She walked over to the consoles, studying the displays. It appeared that even though the Omnis excelled with their energy abilities, they still relied on technology for some purposes. The consoles were designed to monitor room and body temperature, facial expressions, and even body language. She wondered how difficult it would be fool them.

Sergei leaned over to study the displays. "Do these devices record?"

"Yes. They record audio and video."

"Turn them off," Sergei ordered and pulled off his jacket.

Brant frowned. "Whatever you're thinking about doing—"

Sergei narrowed his eyes on Brant. "You have your way of

dealing with your people and we have ours. Turn off the recording. Now."

Brant's jaw clenched, and he looked as though he were about to argue.

Valentina stepped forward and said gently, "Brant, we don't have a problem if you wish to observe. But some information could prove to be... sensitive." She lowered her head to soften her expression even more. "We've shared many of our secrets with you already, but Alec expressed concerns about the trustworthiness of other people within the towers. I'm sure you understand why we're worried about having anything recorded. We may trust *you*, but we don't want any sensitive information falling into the wrong hands."

"Of course." Brant walked over to the console and entered a few commands. Valentina paid careful attention to the codes he entered to disable the surveillance. She never knew when such a thing could come in handy.

Sergei winked at her, indicating that had been his intention. She bit her lower lip and shook her head. He was such a troublemaker.

Brant turned around and gestured to one of the seats. "Would you like to observe in here? I can arrange to have some tea brought to you."

She beamed a smile at him. "That would be lovely."

Sergei frowned at her, but she simply smiled sweetly at him.

"I'll be back shortly. They'll bring the first of your people in a moment."

As soon as Brant left the room, Sergei prowled toward her. "Even though he knows we're bonded, he still looks at you as though the sun rises and sets with you."

She trailed her fingers down his chest. "Don't tell me you're jealous, Seryozha."

He yanked her close and kissed her as though he couldn't

survive another moment without her. She whimpered, and he fisted his hand in her hair. He deepened the kiss, tasting and teasing her with his lips and tongue. When he pulled away, she nearly swayed from the abrupt sense of loss.

"I'm not jealous of him, but part of me is tempted to have my way with you right here and damn the audience."

Valentina blinked up at him. "Do you expect me to argue after that kiss?"

He grinned. "I should have taken you back to my room first."

"Interrogate them quickly," she gripped his shirt and pulled him back toward her, nipping at his bottom lip, "and I'll take you back to mine and have my way with you instead. Maybe we'll see which of us can disarm the other first. If you win, I'll grant you another favor."

"Fuck," he muttered, scanning her up and down, and she knew he was mentally cataloging each of her weapons.

She laughed in delight. "We'll have to continue this later. Your first suspect just arrived."

Sergei frowned and turned toward the window. She moved beside him to get a better look. An OmniLab security officer had brought in a young man in his early twenties who appeared more curious than concerned. He had a small bandage on his wrist, which led her to believe he'd been up close with the altercation.

"Do you recognize him?"

"Yes," Sergei admitted. "We have several hundred people working on the construction of the new tower. I've only gotten to know a small percentage of them, but I know this one. He worked in one of the camps I oversaw before the attack on the towers. Given his age and temperament, it's unlikely he's working for anyone else. I doubt he'll have much knowledge to share with us. He's never struck me as particularly observant."

"As soon as Nikolai gets here, I'll get the background information on each of the detainees." Valentina pulled out her commlink to let Nikolai know what was happening. "How would you like to handle the interviews?"

"I should be able to get the story from this one within fifteen minutes. That will give you enough time to find out what Brant knows. You can decide if your presence is necessary after that."

When she nodded, Sergei headed toward the door and walked into the next room. She leaned against the wall, watching as the first flicker of worry crossed the young man's face at the sight of Sergei. Good. He was realizing the severity of the situation. Sergei would probably have the story in closer to ten minutes.

The door opened a moment later, and Brant entered the room with a large cup. She smiled at him and accepted the offering, noting he was now wearing a special translating device. It made sense if he planned to listen in on the conversations.

Taking a sip, she realized he'd added a bit of sweetener. Touched he'd paid attention to her preferences, she said, "Thank you, Brant. It's perfect."

"It's rather nice knowing you trust me enough to accept a beverage without wondering if it's safe."

She laughed and offered him the cup. "I can still share, if you'd like." When he waved her off with a grin, Valentina gestured to the suspect in the other room. "Do you have the names of our people who are being detained? Sergei happened to know this one, but I want to review the background information of the others when Nikolai arrives."

Brant nodded, walked over to the console, and entered a few commands. A list populated the screen. He pointed to the first name and said, "We'll bring them into the interrogation room in this order, unless you tell us otherwise."

She put the cup down and used her commlink to send each name to Sergei. When she finished, she slid the device back into her pocket and watched through the glass. Brant had the volume setting on low, but she didn't bother to increase it. The young man now appeared downright scared with whatever Sergei was saying to him. She didn't need to hear to know the young man was probably about to spill whatever information he knew. Sergei was obviously motivated to find out the truth in record time.

Turning back to Brant, she asked, "Will you tell me what happened at this club?"

With a weary expression, Brant sighed and sat in a chair facing the window. "We've been gathering information and processing the scene all night. It appears the altercation originated between some of our residents and your people. A few of them got into a verbal sparring match that evolved into some shoving. It was minor until Aiden got dragged into the argument."

"Who's Aiden?"

"He's an Inner Circle member who was standing nearby. I don't know what was said, but one of our residents threatened Aiden with a gun."

Valentina frowned. "Was he injured?"

"Aiden managed to disarm him with his wind talent, but the display of his abilities was enough to incite some of the people to attack him and others to run in fear. Aiden's in the medical wing being treated for severe injuries, but he'll survive. Ariana's with him now, healing the worst of his injuries. Not everyone involved were that lucky though."

She lowered herself into a chair beside him. This was worse than she'd realized. It was doubtful even Nikolai had known how bad the situation was when she'd spoken with him, or he would have asked them to return immediately.

OmniLab couldn't allow this to stand. "How many were hurt?"

"Two of our people were killed. The second died from his injuries a short time ago. We have almost two dozen seriously injured, some from the fighting and others from the stampede of people who were trying to get out of the way. A few of your people were also taken to the medical ward and then brought to a holding cell for questioning."

Valentina gazed through the window at Sergei. He must be hearing a similar story because his entire demeanor had changed. The young man with him was speaking rapidly and using expressive gestures. She glanced over at Brant. "You don't know how your people acquired one of our weapons?"

"No," Brant admitted. "The man in possession of the gun was one of those who died. We didn't have a chance to question him, and a search of his quarters didn't reveal any other weapons. He could have gotten it at the club earlier last night or even days ago. We're interviewing his friends and family now. We're hoping Sergei's interviews may be able to shed some light into the situation."

She sighed. "I appreciate you telling me all this, Brant. I know you're not under any obligation to answer my questions. We're going to do everything possible on our end to get to the bottom of this."

"I know. Alec does too. Nikolai's already been very cooperative. I'm afraid the problems are stemming from both our people, though, so it's far more complicated than we expected."

Valentina was quiet for a moment, considering the possibilities. Unfortunately, she didn't have as much knowledge of the procedures in the towers compared to their camps on the surface. "I've noticed most of your people don't carry weapons, but it wouldn't be difficult to find some if you were determined. What methods do you use to prevent weapons from getting into their hands?"

Brant frowned. "Weapon access is mostly limited to security officers and specially trained personnel. They're monitored closely, and very few have access to lethal weapons. You're right, and anyone can create a weapon with a little ingenuity, but I don't think many of our residents would consider attempting such a thing. We've had some problems in the past, but not significant ones—at least, not for the past fifteen years or so. Our punishment for such a crime became rather severe, and it deterred a lot of people from considering it."

"What happened fifteen years ago?"

He sighed and leaned back in the chair. "It was before I began working as a Shadow, so most of this is what I heard from other people or read about in our security archives. We had a regime change, and there was a lot of unrest. People were unhappy with the way things were being handled, how much authority was in the hands of the Inner Circle, and especially of their abilities. Some of our residents began rioting."

She bit her lip. It sounded similar to what was happening within the Coalition ever since they'd formed the alliance with OmniLab. Many people were afraid of anything they didn't understand. Granted, their situation wasn't quite as bad yet. But some people weren't pleased about the thought of joining together and what it meant for the future of the Coalition. Pride, superstition, and fear could be a deadly mix.

"How bad was it?"

Brant's jaw clenched. He stared through the window, but she didn't think he was really seeing the room beyond it. "Edwin Tal'Vayr took control of the High Council. He banished people from the towers, had some imprisoned, and tortured others for information about anyone who was instigating the unrest. People became fearful, but it worked. The riots stopped, yet the resentment remained. It was just buried."

"That must have been difficult for you," she said softly. "Ariana told me you and Alec are half-brothers. Edwin was your father, wasn't he?"

He met her gaze and nodded. "Yes. It's now common knowledge. Edwin was effective, but his methods were brutal."

Valentina placed her hand over his and squeezed it gently. "You're a good man, Brant. Sometimes, we learn more from our parents' mistakes than by the examples they set."

Brant gave her a small smile. "Then I learned a great deal from mine." He paused and added, "Back then, some of our residents acquired weapons on their own. Some manufactured devices using schematics they managed to download from our archives. But this is the first time we've had this new type of challenge. Even when we dealt with the surface dwellers in the past, we were able to minimize possible threats by assigning traders to act as our representatives on the surface. I don't think any of us were prepared for this sort of fallout when we formed an alliance with your people."

She gazed at Sergei through the window again. The interview had concluded, and OmniLab security was removing the young man from the room. They should be bringing in the next detainee momentarily. Brant had given her a great deal to think about, but she didn't want to push him too much. A balance of perceived cooperation needed to be maintained.

Turning back to Brant, she said, "Nikolai said he'd acquired the club surveillance footage from Hayden for the past two weeks. We've already started running the images through our databases and compiling a list of names. We'll investigate and interview each one of them until we figure out who's distributing these weapons to your residents."

Brant nodded. "Alec mentioned that's why you were delayed. He's already getting pressure from the High Council, especially since someone from the Inner Circle was so severely injured. Alec's meeting with them right now to do some damage control. Some of them are demanding we close our towers to your people until we get to the bottom of this."

Valentina squeezed her eyes shut, wondering how much that would set them back in their progress. The Coalition's leaders were already concerned about OmniLab's continued cooperation. If OmniLab closed their towers to their people, it might be enough to tip the arguments in favor of permanently severing their alliance. If that happened, the Coalition may decide to take the towers by force. They had too much invested to walk away now.

The door opened, and Valentina looked up to see Nikolai and Lars enter. Her heart clenched at the exhaustion etched on Nikolai's face. The dark circles under his eyes hadn't been as noticeable a few short hours ago. She immediately went to him and hugged him tightly.

He wrapped his arms around her, and she instinctively knew he'd needed her but hadn't wanted to call her back to him before she finished on the surface. Nikolai always tried to do too much on his own and was reluctant to make any demands of her. The four of them were still getting accustomed to using their abilities in front of others, but no one in this room would have an issue with it. It wouldn't matter if they did; Valentina had no intention of letting anyone she loved suffer a moment longer than necessary.

Reaching out through their metaphysical connection, she embraced him with her water energy and let it flow over him. Nikolai sighed, the tension in his body beginning to dissipate. He pressed a kiss against her hair and murmured, "Thank you, Valya. I'm glad you're back safely."

She released him. "Brant just finished telling me what

happened. I'm sorry it took us longer to get back than we expected."

Nikolai handed her his tablet and glanced toward the window where Sergei was sitting. "I appreciate you setting up the relay. I just finished running the images from the security footage through our database, and I have a list of names. Unfortunately, it will take time to analyze them all. I hadn't realized how popular this club was with our people. Alec also provided me with the names of everyone who was detained tonight. I checked through the information, and they all work on the construction crew. Only one of them wasn't part of Sergei's original team."

Valentina studied the tablet with the information on each detainee's history. There was nothing remarkable about any of them, but that wasn't a guarantee of innocence. It was easy enough to change information to mask someone's true purpose. She'd done the same often enough for her contacts. Sometimes, small discrepancies could be discovered, especially when conducting an interview. It was easy for people to forget the details of a carefully crafted lie.

"I've seen him before," Lars said, gesturing to the new man being brought into the room. "His name is Jaro, if I remember correctly. He was one of the people who escorted me to the underground river site when I dueled Alec."

Valentina turned to regard the dark-haired man seated in the interrogation room with Sergei. The detainee's body language was self-assured and confident, indicating his innocence. But when he sat down, she noticed he kept glancing at the door, a sign that he was uneasy. If she had to guess, she'd say he knew something but had reservations about sharing that information. Valentina pulled off her jacket, allowing her weapons to be easily seen. In her experience, the threat of violence was sometimes more effective than the actuality.

Tossing her jacket over a nearby chair, she tucked the

tablet under her arm. "I think I need to go sit in on this interview."

Nikolai nodded. "I agree."

She opened the door and walked to the interrogation room. The man seated at the table glanced up at her when she entered. From all appearances and his unconcerned demeanor, he didn't recognize her.

Sergei leaned back in his chair, a slight smile on his lips. "Ah, Valentina. I'm pleased you could make it. Would you like to sit?"

She leaned against the adjacent wall so she could watch both men. "No, I'll just observe for now."

"Of course," Sergei replied and gestured to the man sitting across the table. "Jaro, this is Valentina. She's here as Chairman Nikolai's representative. I'm sure you understand how serious we're taking this situation."

Jaro's body tensed. She nodded at him in greeting but didn't say anything else. Her presence would be enough to make their intended point.

Sergei started asking general questions about the club and how often Jaro visited the establishment. Apparently, he'd been a frequent patron over the past couple weeks, which put him as a prime candidate for information gathering. Jaro admitted to knowing several people who frequented the club, and Sergei went over the list of names.

Valentina glanced at the mirrored window where she knew Nikolai was watching. He was most likely recording the names so they could compare them with the list they'd obtained. If there were a discrepancy, it would only direct suspicion to those people who weren't being named.

She turned back to study Jaro again. Sergei was walking him through the events of the evening. Later, he'd circle back around and start breaking down Jaro's story.

Sergei excelled at interrogation, but he and Valentina had

different methods for extracting information. They knew one another's strengths and weaknesses, and together, they'd always made a very effective team. If she were honest, though, he'd always been better suited to this head-on style of interrogation.

She preferred a subtler approach and usually in an informal setting. In some cases, being a woman was an advantage. People had an easier time confiding in someone they considered less threatening. She didn't have a problem using her sex to accomplish her goals; it was just one more tool in her arsenal.

Valentina listened absently but focused more on the man's body language, assessing his comfort and discomfort levels. One of the first things she'd learned was that it was easy to lie with your face, but as you moved down the body... your body language became more honest. Right now, she was focused on Jaro's feet and how one of them was noiselessly tapping the floor. He was uncomfortable, but it wasn't the same sort of worry the last detainee had exhibited. Her initial assumption was most likely correct. Jaro knew something but wasn't sure if it was in his best interest to share it.

Sergei leaned back in his chair, and a subtle wave of heat began filling the room. "Did you see where he got the weapon?"

The foot jiggle ceased abruptly. Both feet were now pointed directly at the door, a clear indicator he wanted to escape. Badly. "No."

Her gaze immediately flew to Sergei. He arched a brow at her in response, and she blinked at him in surprise. She'd planned on waiting a bit longer to intervene, but what he was doing was risky. Brant had stopped the recording devices in here, but she didn't know if anyone could pick up on his energy from another room.

Valentina approached the table and sat in the chair across

from Jaro, blocking his direct line of sight to the door. Sergei leaned back and smirked at her. She paused, studying him for a moment, and then narrowed her eyes. Sergei was up to something.

Jaro's gaze shifted to her, and she smoothed out her expression and focused again on the detainee. Forcing her body to relax, she decided to embrace a more nonthreatening mien. She needed Jaro to be cooperative but also understand she was still here as Nikolai's representative. She'd deal with Sergei's shenanigans later and in a much more private setting. "I reviewed your service record before I came in here, Jaro. It was somewhat surprising."

Jaro's face remained carefully blank. "Why is that?"

"Well," Valentina began and leaned forward. Resting her wrists on the table, she slowly spread out her fingers. It was a subtle move, but on a subconscious level, Jaro would be aware it would take a little longer for her to draw a weapon. It was her way of indicating she didn't consider him a threat and this was a friendly interview. Besides, Sergei deserved a little payback for whatever scheme he was concocting—a reminder there were other ways to get information.

"You've worked with Sergei for several years now. Before that, your evaluations were very positive. You joined his team with some of the highest recommendations. But you've stayed in the background since taking over this new position."

Valentina swept her gaze over Jaro, pretending to assess him. She tilted her head and frowned. "I can't help but wonder... Is it Sergei's failure to see your potential? Or yours in not showing it?"

Jaro stiffened and darted a quick glance at Sergei. "I simply haven't had a chance to prove myself yet."

Valentina nodded in understanding. *Ha. Take that, Seryozha. Less than two minutes.* "Of course. We all need to take the opportunities as they're handed to us. Fortunately, one has just made itself known." She smiled and stood. "If you'll excuse me, gentlemen, I believe you have some things to discuss. I'll be sure to let Nikolai know how cooperative you've been."

Without saying another word, she walked out of the room.

CHAPTER FIVE

V ALENTINA WALKED BACKED into the observation room. Nikolai put his arm around her waist and kissed her temple. "Nicely done. Sergei's using his truth barrier abilities, isn't he? That's why you intervened so soon?"

"Yes. He's very subtle. It's unlikely anyone would have noticed, but it's still risky, especially here."

Lars frowned. "He's probably just eager to wrap up these interviews. I'm sure he's tired. You guys have been out all night."

Valentina made a noncommittal noise, but she knew the real reason. "That must be it. I'm sure he's just... eager to go to bed."

Nikolai arched an eyebrow, and she blinked up at him innocently. He chuckled and shook his head. "I should have known. You challenged him, didn't you?"

She looked through the window at Sergei and bit back a smile. From all appearances, he'd managed to elicit Jaro's cooperation. "I may have... offered some encouragement."

Lars cleared his throat. "Ah, I'm sure. If he's in a hurry to wrap this up, perhaps I should act as a stand-in and pretend to hold the truth barrier. Some of your people may recognize me, and it will limit his exposure. Even if someone can't feel it, they'll know something is wrong when they try to lie."

"That's not a bad idea," Nikolai agreed, tracing his thumb absently in a pattern on her side. "You were a common enough fixture in our camps that your presence will not be surprising. When Sergei is finished with this interview, your assistance would be appreciated."

Someone knocked on the door, and Brant opened it. A security officer was standing outside with Yuri. The officer gestured to him and said, "You asked me to bring him here when he arrived."

Brant stepped aside so Yuri could enter. Nikolai nodded at him in greeting and quickly updated Yuri on everything that had transpired. Yuri's expression clouded, the energy in the air swirling with his barely restrained anger. "How far has Sergei gotten with questioning our people?"

Valentina glanced at the window. "This is his second interview."

Yuri crossed his arms over his chest and turned to Brant. "Have you begun searching the towers for more weapons?"

Brant nodded. "Yes, but it's an enormous endeavor and may take weeks to complete with our current manpower. That doesn't even include our residents' private quarters. We won't check those without cause."

Yuri frowned. "That's unfortunate. We can't even offer our people to assist in the search since we don't know yet where the problem originated. Until we have more leads on our end, our ability to help will be limited."

"Maybe not," Valentina began and approached Yuri. She put her hand on his arm and felt his body immediately begin to relax. Ariana had been explaining some things during their training, and it was strange to see it in practice. Valentina had found that touching people, especially her bondmates, seemed to calm some of the negative emotions they were experiencing. Nikolai had often told her she helped him focus his thoughts, but she'd never realized she also had a similar effect on Yuri until recently. Ariana suspected it was tied to her abilities somehow.

Yuri studied her curiously. "What are you thinking?"

Valentina glanced toward the window again. Sergei was escorting Jaro into the hallway where a security officer was waiting. "This last detainee knows something. Sergei's been trying to convince him to work with us."

A moment later, Sergei entered the room. His eyes immediately went to her, and he arched an eyebrow. "I do believe you cheated that time, Valechka. Interfering with my interrogation before I finished establishing a baseline?"

She grinned. "Aren't you always telling me we don't have rules? Besides, the end goal is still the same. You wouldn't have intentionally provoked me if you didn't want to hurry things along." Scanning him up and down, she debated which of his weapons she'd take first. Or maybe she'd let him keep one. It might make things more fun. His expression heated at her perusal, and she bit her lip. He was far too distracting. "What agreement did you come to with Jaro?"

Sergei closed the distance between them and put his arms around her. "You were right. He's ambitious and eager for an opportunity. Based on what he shared with me, I don't believe the weapon was acquired last night. Jaro has attended this club often, and he's noticed some strange meetings between our people and the Omnis. Apparently, Pavel frequented this club too."

Nikolai nodded. "Yes. We caught your former second-in-command on the surveillance video. I wanted to discuss the possibility of whether or not he might have had any involvement."

Valentina frowned, remembering when she'd stolen

Sergei's notes from his tablet. She'd been bored to distraction reading through some of them.

Placing her hand against Sergei's chest, she looked up at him. "You told me Pavel handled the inventory for the tower construction. Could he have been helping to smuggle the weapons in here?"

"It's definitely possible, and that's my suspicion as well," Sergei agreed and idly began running his hand down her back. A small band of his heated fire energy swirled around her, and she leaned against him as he continued the leisurely movement. "I'll check Pavel's notes again for any obvious errors, but we'll need to perform a complete audit on the inventory we've set aside for the construction. Even if we don't know the exact number of weapons that are missing, we may be able to make an estimation by shipping weight discrepancies. I don't think they're being stored in the construction tower, but I intend to find out."

Yuri nodded. "That's something we can do from our end. Nikolai would be well within his rights to demand such a review, especially since he's now taking such an interest in the construction progress. We can bring in some of our people to help conduct the audit and have them stand under a truth barrier first to make sure they don't have any involvement."

"That takes care of one problem," Nikolai agreed. "Valya, did Dmitri have anything useful to say about the missing shipments?"

Valentina bit her lip as she tried to put together everything in her mind. She didn't want to say anything in front of Brant about someone trying to set Sergei up to take the fall, so she'd have to tell Nikolai privately later. Sharing knowledge like that could backfire on them too easily.

"Actually, yes," Valentina admitted, giving him a meaningful look to let him know she was censoring her words. "Dmitri told me about a conversation he overheard that might be related. Two people running deliveries between camps mentioned some weapon shipments were going to the towers. They hadn't been able to reach their contact here for a few days and were concerned. It's possible they were referring to Pavel and didn't know he'd been killed."

Nikolai nodded. "It's definitely suspicious, especially since weapons aren't on the list of approved transport items. If Pavel was involved, it was likely he had accomplices assisting him. It's another lead, but we need more information. We'll start running a trace on his known associates."

Sergei hesitated. "Actually, I might have something else. Jaro mentioned overhearing the name Charles. When I was in Hayden's club last week, a woman approached me. She seemed out of place, so it caught my attention. I spoke with her for a few minutes, and she was looking to meet up with someone from the Coalition. She specifically mentioned the name Charles and how he wasn't able to meet. When she realized my identity, she backed away quickly. It was curious, but I wrote it off at the time."

"That's a fairly common name," Brant said, picking up his tablet from the desk. "We can run it through our system along with similar names, but it could also be an alias. Did Jaro ever see this Charles? Perhaps we can have him watch the security footage."

Sergei shook his head. "No. He overheard some of our people talking, and one of them mentioned they needed to drop something off for Charles. Jaro thought it was strange because all trading with OmniLab must go through official channels. But if you can acquire the surveillance footage from the night I visited Hayden's club, I should be able to point out the woman."

Brant nodded and entered something into his tablet. "I'll have someone pull the video from that night. Hopefully, we can question her about this Charles."

"Perhaps I should visit this club and ask around," Valentina suggested.

Sergei's hand on her back froze as his gaze flew to hers. "What?"

Yuri nodded. "It's not a bad idea. People talk to Valentina. If Hayden will allow her access to his club, she can investigate directly. If someone is distributing weapons, it's unlikely they'll know who she is. I can also go with her to keep an eye on things, just in case something goes wrong."

"The club is closed until we finish our investigation," Brant said with a frown. "I suppose we could expedite things to have it open tonight, but we'll need to have tighter security. We'll probably have a lot of curious people wanting to visit and check things out. It's unlikely this Charles will make an appearance after what happened last night though."

Valentina nodded. "Perhaps, but it will explain my presence more. I can say I heard some rumors and was curious. That's the best time to collect gossip."

"I've been to that club," Sergei began, drawing her attention back to him. "It's... not a place conducive to an interrogation. It's far different from anything we have in our camps."

Valentina frowned and ran her hand down Sergei's chest. "You don't think I should go?"

Sergei sighed, wrapping his arms around her a bit tighter. "I think you'll be very effective there, but I'm not thrilled about it. If you go, I'd like to be there when you do."

"That somewhat defeats the purpose," Yuri said, crossing his arms over his chest.

"Then I'll stay in one of the backrooms where I can monitor things through our bond," Sergei said with a shrug. "I'm not going to sit on the sidelines and let her go into a place like that without remaining close."

"I can also go to keep an eye on things on the main floor," Lars offered. "I'm sure Hayden will want to be there to keep watch too. He has a great deal at stake if we can't get this resolved quickly and his club reopened. There's a security office with monitors in one of the backrooms where you can stay, Sergei. I saw it earlier tonight when I helped retrieve the surveillance footage."

Yuri frowned. "How dangerous is this place? Does Valya need this much protection?"

"It's not exactly dangerous, but there are many Inner Circle members as well as others," Sergei admitted and turned to Nikolai. "Did you watch the surveillance?"

Nikolai nodded. "I understand and share your concerns. In addition to attracting regular attention, Valentina tends to draw energy channelers to her, but that may be beneficial in eliciting information. We've all been practicing suppressing our energy bond to avoid detection, and I believe the potential for exposure will be somewhat limited. I'd feel more comfortable if Hayden allowed both of us in this backroom to monitor things, though, while Yuri stays closer to her and within easy range. Perhaps we can even enlist Alec and Ariana's assistance."

Valentina wrinkled her nose. They were being a little too overprotective, but she had the feeling part of that could be attributed to the change in their bond. Ever since she'd pulled energy through Nikolai and Yuri to heal Sergei, it had deepened their connection to each other. It was much more difficult to separate all the threads of energy between them.

Nikolai's mouth curved in a small smile. "But I'm sure Valentina can handle herself—more so than most of the women there."

Sergei considered it for a moment and grinned. "Actually, I wouldn't mind seeing Ariana dress Valentina for the club."

Her eyes narrowed. "What's that supposed to mean?"

Sergei chuckled and lifted her hand to press a kiss against it. "You'll see."

"It's my understanding this club primarily operates in the evening," Nikolai said, glancing out the window into the interrogation room where they'd brought in the next detainee. "If we're going to pursue this line of investigation, it will have to wait until then. In the meantime, Sergei, you're going to need to finish the interviews. If Valentina and Yuri are going to visit this club, they need to stay away from the rest of the investigation until then. I don't want their identities to become compromised."

When Sergei frowned, Valentina placed her hand on his chest again. "Lars has agreed to pretend to hold the truth barrier for you. It should speed everything up."

Sergei gave Lars a questioning look and the other man nodded. "I doubt I'll be as effective as Valentina was, but you won't have to hide your abilities."

Sergei nodded. "Very well."

"By the way, Valya," Yuri began, darting a quick look at Nikolai. "Your former lover is now assigned to a bunk in our camp and will be put on the work roster beginning tomorrow. He somehow managed to survive the trip relatively unharmed."

"That's a shame," Sergei murmured.

"It is," Yuri agreed. "But whether he continues to survive is up for debate. Accidents have been known to happen."

"That might have possibilities," Sergei mused with a wicked grin.

Nikolai's eyes narrowed. "What the fuck is that arrogant prick doing stationed in my camp? Dmitri was supposed to be transferred out and somewhere on the other side of the world so I don't have to deal with him."

Valentina bit her lip and took Nikolai's arm. "I can explain everything on our way back to Lars's quarters, Kolya. I may have… agreed to certain things." She glared at Yuri over her shoulder, and he just grinned at her. In a low voice, she hissed, "You are such a pain in the ass, Yuri."

He blew her a kiss while Sergei laughed. Oh, she'd definitely pay both of them back for this.

———

VALENTINA WALKED into the bedroom Lars had designated as hers during her stay within the towers. She started to pull off her shirt and paused. Her normal routine was usually to shower, absorbing the water energy to rejuvenate herself, but there was another option. She thought back to the pool Ariana had showed her. Once they'd realized she was a water channeler, they'd given her the access codes so she could use the private pool area as often as she wished.

She headed back out of her bedroom, unwilling to fall asleep until Sergei returned to her. In the meantime, the calming water would help focus her thoughts.

Nikolai was still in the common room and frowned at the sight of her. "Are you all right, Valya? I thought you were going to bed."

She nodded. "I just started thinking about the pool. With everything that's been going on, I thought some clarity might help."

"Ah," Nikolai murmured and walked over to her. He wrapped his arms around her, and she leaned against him and sighed in contentment. It wasn't the same as Sergei, but Nikolai was no less comforting. Each of them provided a foundation she'd come to depend upon. He brushed a kiss against her hair. "I'm going to be up for a bit longer. Do you want me to go with you?"

She shook her head, inhaling his rich, earthy scent. "No, I know you're tired. You've been working longer hours than the rest of us. I'm sorry I haven't been helping you out as much lately."

He chuckled and ran his hand down her back. "You don't give yourself enough credit. I'm glad you've reconciled with Sergei, and you two have needed some private time to reconnect. Over the past few days, you've been happier than I've seen you in a long time, but I understand you still need time for yourself. You haven't gotten much of it lately."

"You haven't either," she said, lifting her gaze to look into his blue eyes. "Sergei said you had another premonition earlier."

He frowned. "It happened as soon as you left the towers. I don't know if it was related to you almost getting caught, or if there's something else that may still happen."

"What's it like?"

Nikolai hesitated. "I'm not sure I can explain. Sometimes it's as obscure as a feeling. Other times, I'll get a flash of a scene, as though I'm watching a video. I think it affected the timeline when our bond changed. The flashes happen more often now, but it's harder to understand."

She bit her lip, sensing his unease. "Is that what happened earlier?"

He absently ran his hand over her back. "Yes. It was only a split second. I saw you, and you were searching for something. I could feel your fear, worry, and a sense of urgency through our connection. But you weren't in any location I recognized. I couldn't see anything except a large, rocky outcropping. Your emotion was the strongest part of that particular vision."

Valentina frowned. "I didn't feel much fear tonight. Adrenaline, maybe a little bit of fear for you if we were caught, but nothing to that degree. Do you think it's something that may still happen in the future?"

Nikolai sighed and tightened his arms around her. "I don't

know, but I don't like it. I wish I could have been able to assess the background more closely. If you didn't experience anything like that tonight, I can only hope the future's been altered." He shrugged. "I want you to be happy, Valya. Anytime you're upset, it affects all of us. More so now than it ever has."

"It affects me too," she whispered, leaning against him and hugging him tightly. "This bond between us has changed in more ways than I imagined. I find myself worried about all of you much more than I ever have before. I probably wouldn't have killed Marek earlier, but I was so focused on Dmitri's potential threat to you, I didn't consider another option. My only thought was, if he was interrogated, you would be held responsible for sending a spy into Ivan's camp. I couldn't let that happen."

Nikolai leaned back, studying her. "Do you regret killing him?"

"I don't know," she admitted with a frown. "I don't regret protecting you, but I wish I hadn't needed to end his life. When you asked me to choose between healing Sergei and killing Viktor, I think it changed something within our bond —within me. I think you were right. If I'm meant to be a healer, killing shouldn't come so easily to me."

"You're too hard on yourself, Valya. Your training taught you to respond in one way, and you've always excelled at that. We're asking you to choose a different path now, and change doesn't come easily to anyone. Be patient with yourself."

"I've never been patient," she grumbled.

He chuckled, lifting her chin to look into her eyes. "No, but I have faith in you. We all have a lot to learn about ourselves, each other, and this bond between us. We were brought together for a reason, and I intend to see it through."

She squeezed her eyes shut. Something about Nikolai

always grounded her, and she nodded. "You're right. I think a trip to the pool will help."

"Good. Will you let me know when you're back?"

Valentina nodded. "I don't think I'll be longer than an hour." Standing on her toes, she kissed him lightly on the lips. "Talking to you always helps. I love you, Kolya."

"I love you too, Valya. Enjoy your time to yourself."

With a smile, she headed out of Lars's quarters and into the hallway. She'd visited the pool area with Ariana several times for training, but she'd never used it alone. Nikolai was right. A little private time was needed, and part of her was looking forward to the opportunity.

The pool was located on the same level as Lars's quarters. Based on her exploration over the past few days with Sergei and Yuri, they'd determined most of the residences on this level belonged to the founding families of OmniLab. They were in one of the uppermost levels of the Inner Sanctum, where the family suites were considerably larger.

She hadn't met many other Inner Circle members, or at least none while claiming herself to be one of them. So far, they'd managed to restrict the knowledge to just a few. Ariana and Alec knew, along with Lars and Brant.

They'd consented to allow Alec to share the information with Seara, the other co-leader of the towers, and also with Kayla, the young woman Sergei had met on the surface. All of them had promised to keep their secret, but once a secret reached this many people, it wasn't much of a secret anymore. One day soon, they'd need to go public, but she worried about what that would mean to their position within the Coalition.

She sighed and entered in the code to access the pool area. The door slid open, and her footsteps echoed softly in the empty room. The stillness of the water called to her, and she immediately pulled off her shoes and unhooked her pants, dropping them beside her. She pulled off Sergei's shirt and tossed it on top of her pants, leaving only her undergarments on. She still felt unsure about going into the deeper areas of the pool, but it was impossible to deny the primal call of the water. Pulling off her weapons, she carefully placed them beside the pool within easy reach and took a step into the calming water.

It was even better than she remembered. She moved deeper into the pool until the water swirled around her waist. Taking a deep breath, she submerged herself below the water's surface and for a moment, her thoughts drifted. A sense of rightness filled her and she reached out, feeling the water's slight resistance against her fingertips, but at the same time, it was a welcoming embrace. She was displacing the droplets, but she was also part of it... as though every molecule of water within her body was reacting with the water surrounding her. It was a feeling of belonging, but there was something more calling to her from beneath the water's surface—

She broke the surface with a gasp, unable to hold her breath any longer.

"Are you all right?" Ariana's voice broke into her reverie.

Valentina turned to find the dark-haired woman standing beside the pool with another woman she didn't recognize. Valentina frowned, studying the petite newcomer. Something about her was familiar, but she didn't know what it was.

Valentina focused again on Ariana and nodded. "You mentioned it would be all right if I came to the pool. I didn't mean to intrude."

Ariana shook her head and smiled. "No, I'm glad you came. Your energy was... unusual just now. I was tempted to reach out, but I didn't want to disturb you if you were practicing."

Valentina stiffened, immediately wary about the

newcomer and Ariana's comment about energy. She hadn't been practicing anything, but she didn't intend to advertise her abilities. "Who is this?"

Ariana smiled and gestured to the dark-haired woman with vibrant green eyes standing beside her. "This is Kayla. She just arrived from the surface."

Kayla inclined her head in greeting. "Hey. It's great to meet you."

Valentina moved over to the edge of the pool within easy range of her weapons, should they be needed. Even if Ariana claimed Kayla to be honorable, she wasn't willing to trust anyone without vetting them first. Sergei hadn't said much either way, but she hadn't really discussed Kayla with him either. Pulling herself out of the pool, she said, "Sergei mentioned he's been working with you."

Kayla studied her for a long time, and Valentina took the opportunity to do the same. Kayla was a few years younger than her, but she carried herself with confidence. It was apparent she wasn't quite as sheltered as Ariana, which made sense given the brief history she'd gathered about her from a few others.

Finally, Kayla grinned. "Wow. You're a lot more like Sergei than I expected."

Ariana laughed. "I thought the same thing when I first met her."

Kayla made a sweeping up-and-down gesture in Valentina's direction. "You're emanating that whole quiet danger thing like he does. It just screams badass. I need to learn how to do that."

Valentina blinked at her, but she couldn't help the smile that spread across her face. Despite her initial reservations, she somehow intuitively knew neither one of these women were threats. Even so, it was always better to remain cautious.

She tilted her head, considering the body language of the

younger woman. Whereas Ariana possessed an almost naïve innocence, Kayla appeared to share more similarities with Valentina. At least, on the surface. "You know Sergei well?"

Kayla shrugged. "I've worked with him quite a bit on the tower construction, but Sergei's always been hard to read. Trying to get any real information out of him is next to impossible, unless he wants you to know something. And trust me, I've tried from almost the moment I first met him. When Ariana told me you were bonded, I had to meet you."

Ariana tucked a small braid behind her ear. "I hope you don't mind me talking about you. We've both known Sergei for a while, and he's always been mysterious. We stopped by Lars's quarters to see you, but Nikolai said you were here."

Valentina nodded. "I've been curious about Kayla too. Lars said our energy was similar."

Kayla took a small step toward her. "I heard that, but you're not a spirit energy channeler?"

She shook her head. "I don't think so. Ariana said I was a water channeler like her."

Ariana smiled. "I don't really understand it. Lars has tested all of our energy and says there's a quality to it that's unlike anything else he's experienced. For some reason, our abilities react differently to Shadows too. None of us seem to have a problem using energy around them."

Kayla straightened. "Oh yeah? So it's not just me?"

Ariana nodded. "When Sergei was hurt, Brant tried to stop Valentina from channeling energy. She'd caused some of the water pipes in the construction tower to burst, but his abilities wouldn't work on her."

"I'm still pretty new to all this," Kayla admitted. "I nearly caused an earthquake in the towers a few months ago, and it took a bunch of the Shadows to stop me. Alec's given me a hard time about not training as much as I should, but it's all a little overwhelming. Did you just find out about your abilities?"

Valentina hesitated and then shook her head. "I knew there was something different about me years ago, but I was never formerly trained like OmniLab's Inner Circle. Many of my people are superstitious or dismissive when it comes to psychics. I thought it best to suppress my abilities to prevent them from learning the truth."

Kayla frowned. "I can understand that. I didn't even know these abilities existed until I met Alec."

Valentina tilted her head, considering the young woman. She seemed sincere and unsure about her abilities. It lessened her threat level on one hand, but anyone wielding a weapon they didn't know how to use could be dangerous. "You had no idea you possessed these powers?"

Kayla shook her head. "I spent most of my time scavenging in the ruins for artifacts. I'd sometimes get flashes or insight into how things used to be, but I always thought it was my imagination running away with me. My scavenging partner, Veridian, used to tell me the ruins spoke to me. I always laughed him off, but now I can't help but wonder if he was right."

Ariana smiled. "Kayla's a true spirit channeler, but in some ways, we're all similar. We each have the ability to tap into all four elements."

Valentina frowned. "Lars said being able to harness all four was extremely rare."

"Yes, and highly coveted," Ariana agreed. "Part of me wonders if Fate's brought us together. It's been centuries since there's been a spirit channeler, and now there are three of us with the ability to tap into all four elements?" She shook her head. "I don't believe that's a coincidence. Neither does Alec."

Kayla wrinkled her nose. "I'm not a big fan of Fate. I prefer making my own path in life."

Valentina couldn't help but smile. "Me too."

Kayla's eyes lit up. "I like you. I was curious about you, but I wasn't sure if I would actually like you. There's something about you though... I get the sense you could seriously kick my ass. I respect the hell outta that."

A laugh bubbled out of Valentina. Maybe she didn't cater to this whole Fate thing, either, but she couldn't deny the strange sense of kinship she felt for both Ariana and Kayla. "I like you too, Kayla."

Ariana smiled. "I had a feeling you two would get along."

Valentina walked away from her weapons and over to the rack where the drying cloths were stored. Perhaps it was her way of testing them to see if her sense of them was misplaced, but they didn't even glance at the weapons on the ground. Valentina wrapped the drying cloth around herself, recalling what Sergei had told her about Kayla.

He spoke of her with some affection, but more so about Ariana. Kayla was skilled with electronics, which was one of the things that had initially impressed him. That same skill had caused several problems when they were trying to launch their invasion against OmniLab. The towers had reinforced their classified archives after Kayla's unauthorized access, which had frustrated Sergei when he'd unsuccessfully tried to hack into them over the past few months.

If Kayla could harness all four elements, Valentina couldn't help but wonder if Kayla shared similar traits to the fire channeler ability of manipulating electronics like the one Sergei possessed.

Wringing the water out of her hair, she said, "I'm still learning about these abilities. Is there any difference between being a spirit channeler and using all four elements at once?"

Kayla shrugged. "I'm not sure, but I don't think so. I

know you and Ariana have access to all the energy types through your bond, but I think that's really the only difference. I don't need a bond to access them, which suits me just fine because Carl is a non-sensitive. I tried the bond thing before and it's just not for me."

Ariana nodded. "Spirit or life energy isn't something we really understand, but I think there's a special quality to us that's different. I don't think just anyone would be able to fuse all four elements together the way we can."

Valentina arched a brow. "What do you mean?"

"There are four elements: earth, air, wind, and fire," Ariana explained. "Until we learned about Kayla, I thought my ability to tap into three elements was incredibly rare. My fire energy is what fuses earth and water together to give me my empath abilities."

"And through Alec, you were able to access the air element," Kayla added.

Ariana nodded. "Yes. But even before we bonded, I noticed I didn't have the same level of discomfort around the Shadows that many Inner Circle people experienced. I always had the suspicion I could circumvent their ability. I was later able to test that theory with Brant to confirm it."

Valentina frowned, considering the implications. "So it's possible I could have avoided a Shadow's ability to negate my powers even before I became bonded?"

Ariana nodded. "I think so, and I believe it's tied to that strange quality Lars detected. I've been giving the whole thing a lot of thought. I have some theories but no definitive proof."

"What are you thinking?" Kayla prompted, her expression more curious than anything.

Ariana clasped her hands together. "We're all very strong in our abilities, much more so than many others within the towers. My last mentor said a few people could tap into two elements, but usually not with equal ability. It's sort of strange that such a rare talent would suddenly emerge at this point in time the way it has."

Valentina frowned. "What do you mean?"

"Maybe it's just a feeling," Ariana hesitated. "I mean, not only are our abilities extremely rare, but the three of us have been put into a position where we'd meet. We each represent three very different cultures."

"But I was born here in the towers," Kayla pointed out.

Ariana nodded. "Yes, but growing up on the surface may have been the best thing for you. Even if your father had survived, I'm not sure your parents would have been able to keep your abilities secret long enough for you to learn how to protect yourself. Back then, your family was too much in the public eye. That's why your father took you to the surface in the first place. He was under extreme pressure to use your emerging abilities to find resources, and you were only a child. It would have only gotten worse as you got older."

Kayla frowned. "I'm not sure I would have been suited for life here in the towers. I've always felt more at home in the ruins."

Ariana smiled. "You're a very strong person, Kayla. I believe your trials on the surface helped shape your identity and prepare you for life within the towers. But now, I find it odd that the three of us have been brought together like this. I can't help but wonder if Fate has something else in store for us."

"I'm not sure I'm willing to go along with whatever Fate has in mind," Kayla muttered. "I'm still getting over the last bruises it left behind."

Valentina made a noncommittal noise. She might agree with Kayla, but she wasn't willing to voice it. She'd always believed every person was the architect of their own fortunes.

Deciding a change in subject was needed, Valentina said,

"Ariana, I was planning to stop by to see you later. I was thinking about going to Hayden's club tonight, and Sergei thought you might have some suggestions on appropriate dress. Some of my people have been patronizing that particular establishment, and I need to check it out."

Ariana nodded. "Yes. Hayden created the club as a way to integrate our respective cultures. I understand one of the Coalition's weapons made its way into the towers and was used by one of our residents. Alec's been dealing with the High Council and their concerns all night."

"Yes," Valentina admitted. "Sergei is interviewing those who were present at the club, but I need to visit the establishment to see if the patrons are willing to reveal more in a less formal setting."

Kayla's eyes widened. "Wait. You're planning to go undercover in the towers to this club?"

Valentina hesitated and then nodded. "Yes. Have you been there?"

"No, but I've got to see this," Kayla replied and grinned. "You've got the same mysterious and sexy danger thing Sergei has going on. The guys in this club are going to be all over you. I don't think they're going to know what to do with you."

Ariana frowned. "Does Sergei know you want to do this? Our kind tends to be very protective. He might have a problem with you going without him."

Valentina arched an eyebrow and remained silent. If Sergei had an issue with her doing this, it was between them.

Kayla laughed. "Yeah, I like her even more. I don't think Sergei's going to say shit to her about it. I really want to see the two of them interact together."

Ariana smiled. "Very well. You're going to need a dress. I'm not sure I have anything that will work quite right on you, but we'll figure something out. Up until recently, I'd never been to a place like Hayden's club. My club attire is somewhat limited."

"My mother would love to help," Kayla suggested. "Seara *lives* to dress people in clothing that's far too uncomfortable. I haven't been to this club, either, but I'm tagging along. I'll tell Seara what we're doing, and she'll be thrilled to find something in my closet."

Valentina frowned, but Ariana's eyes lit up in enthusiasm. "That's a fantastic idea. We should all go. I've wanted to try out my empath abilities more now that I'm bonded to Alec. This will be a perfect opportunity, and we'll have fun in the process."

Valentina's fingers twitched, and she felt the sudden need to scoop up her weapons. These women were crazy. This was an information gathering session to prevent a war between their people, not an informal meeting with girlfriends. Although... Valentina tilted her head, considering the possibilities. It might have potential. Like Ariana mentioned, all three of them represented each of the various groups now present within the towers. Perhaps one of them might succeed where the others had failed.

Just in case, she'd need to bring a few additional weapons with her. Maybe she'd have a chance to convince the two of them to carry their own and show them a few moves before they went. If she stuck around the towers for any length of time, she'd see about arranging more structured weapons training for them. It couldn't hurt.

Inclining her head, she said, "Very well. Nikolai's been reviewing the security feeds, but I haven't had a chance to watch them yet. He indicated we don't have anything like your clubs in our facilities. I admit, I'm not sure what to expect."

"There's some dancing, drinking, and a lot of flirtation," Ariana said and blushed. "I only went once and mainly stayed in the VIP area. My friend Kendra has gone more often, and she frequently picks up men there. What time do you want to go?"

Valentina picked up her belongings. The hour had quickly elapsed, and she didn't want Nikolai to worry. "I'm not sure what time is appropriate. I'll need to speak with Nikolai, Sergei, and Yuri to see what they have in mind. I should get back though. Nikolai's waiting for me."

Ariana clasped her hands together, her eyes twinkling in enthusiasm. "Okay. I'll talk to Alec and let him know our plans. He can help coordinate things with Hayden too. We can all meet at Seara's quarters later this evening or whenever you're ready to do this." She paused and gave Valentina a brilliant smile. "Thank you for allowing us to join you, Valentina. I know you have reservations, but I have a feeling about the three of us together. It feels right somehow."

Kayla nodded. "Yeah, it's weird. There's a connection between us, but it's something different than a regular energy one."

Valentina frowned but more from the sense of foreboding that filled her than the thought of being connected to them. Her life was fraught with danger, but she'd spent years focusing on specialized training to increase her chances of survival. She also had a strong and competent team behind her offering their support.

None of them had counted on Kayla and Ariana also being thrown into the mix. Valentina just prayed she was strong enough to protect not only herself but also these two women who were determined to follow her down that same path. Because the light shining within Kayla and Ariana was something that should never be extinguished.

CHAPTER SIX

VALENTINA LET herself back into Lars's quarters to find him sitting on the couch and studying something on his tablet. She glanced down the hall, but it was empty. Sergei must have finished his interviews and was either in her room or with Nikolai. Lars lifted his head and opened his mouth to greet her, but she pressed a finger to her lips and shook her head. He arched an eyebrow and grinned. When he nodded in silent understanding, she winked at him.

Moving noiselessly down the hall, she paused outside Nikolai's door. She could make out Nikolai and Sergei's voices softly speaking from within. From the sound of things, they were wrapping up their conversation and Sergei hadn't learned much else from the remainder of their people. She glanced down the hall toward Yuri's room, but there wasn't any light emitting from underneath the door. He was most likely already in bed.

Valentina slipped silently into her room, placing her clothing and drying cloth on the dresser. With well-practiced ease, she equipped her weapons and turned off the lights. It only took a few minutes for her eyes to acclimate to the darkness. She moved into place on the far side of the room beside the bed and settled in to wait.

Taking a deep breath, she focused on the bond she shared with Sergei, Nikolai, and Yuri. It had changed when she'd drawn energy from Nikolai and Yuri to heal Sergei. Their bond was stronger than ever, but it reminded her of the early days when they'd first formed their connection and the difficulties they'd faced in learning how to manage their relationships with each other.

In some ways, it was easier to either embrace the entirety of their bond or suppress all of them from her thoughts. The challenge was in isolating each of them, but it was necessary to avoid any problems within their complicated relationship.

Valentina had been treating the task like any other sort of training exercise. Only with practice would she be able to develop a type of muscle memory to be able to quickly pick apart the individual threads with ease. She focused on them now, separating them in her mind. Nikolai was the first one she targeted, reaching out to him and sending a wave of reassuring energy to let him know she was back and safe. She felt his momentary surprise and then a rush of unmistakable tenderness and approval at her efforts. She lowered her head and smiled, returning his affectionate energy with hers before releasing his thread.

This next part was a bit trickier. She reached out to Yuri, wanting to connect with him but not willing to disturb him if he was already asleep. His thoughts were relatively quiet, so she merely wrapped him in a comforting embrace of her energy before releasing him to fall into a deep slumber.

Next, she focused on Sergei and bit her lip in anticipation. This would be more fun. She closed her eyes and opened the bond between them. Sergei immediately filled her thoughts, surrounding her with his blinding heat. Taking a deep breath, Valentina poured every ounce of her desire and love for him through their connection. His immediate response was staggering, matching her energy output with a burst of his inner fire. She cut off the energy, and her door opened less than a second later.

He chuckled into the darkness and closed the door behind him. "Nikolai may not have appreciated such an abrupt departure, but I couldn't resist such an intriguing call from you. Do you wish to play, Valechka?"

Valentina lowered her head and grinned, not willing to risk answering him and revealing her hiding place. He was moving into the room, but he'd found a way to change the temperature of the surrounding air to better mask his movements. She still hadn't learned how he'd managed such a thing, and it put her at a disadvantage in tracking him.

Slipping along the wall, she avoided the area near the bed. He was either moving on the far side of the room or closer to the bed, but she couldn't be completely sure. She waited, making an effort to regulate her breathing and focusing on each of her senses to try to track him. Sergei moved past her, and she knew it was him by his familiar scent. Moving forward quickly, she slid his gun out of his holster and rolled away from him.

His fingertips barely brushed against her leg as she scrambled across the room and out of his reach. Twisting her body, she threw one of her knives in his direction and heard him jump aside to dodge the blade. It was enough to give her an edge. She dove under the bed and out the other side, crouching down and waiting for him to retaliate.

There was nothing. No sound. No hint of movement. No deepening shadows or scents in the air. She frowned, knowing Sergei would never give up but not sure what he was doing. He was sometimes a little too clever, and they were evenly matched. She was usually a bit faster and more agile, but he had more patience. His strength and larger

98 · JAMIE A. WATERS

body mass were enough to give him an upper hand on occasion.

The seconds passed, and her adrenaline continued to soar. Any second, he'd go after her again, but she didn't know from which direction to expect it.

Something fell over on the far side of the floor with a quiet *thump*. Sergei was too graceful to knock something over accidentally, so it had to be a trap. She narrowed her eyes, but a trace of doubt flickered into her mind. He'd been awake as long as her, but he hadn't had the rejuvenating benefits of the pool. It was possible it was a mistake, but he was sneaky. She wouldn't trust it.

Valentina considered the situation. Sergei had two more weapons, both of which would be more difficult to acquire. There was a knife strapped to his ankle under his pants, but the other was a knife on his arm sheath. The one under his pants would be the most fun to remove, so she'd probably leave that one for last.

It was time to get creative.

Opening the bond between her and Yuri, Valentina withdrew some of his air energy threads and used them to trace a pattern back to Sergei. He was exactly where she'd suspected. He'd somehow used his energy to connect with the electrical components of a tablet on the dresser and knock it over. Very sneaky.

Gripping Yuri's air energy tightly, she wrapped it around the hilt of the blade in Sergei's arm sheath and withdrew it abruptly. The knife fell to the floor, and Sergei laughed.

"Impressive, Valechka. Are you finished disarming me?"

She grinned and flicked on the lights. He was standing beside the bed, watching as she prowled toward him.

"Not yet."

Pushing him backward onto the mattress, she climbed on top of him and straddled him. His heated gaze perused her up and down while he tightened his hands on her hips. Valentina unhooked his belt and yanked it off, dropping it to the floor beside her. Grazing the front of his pants with her fingertips, she said, "I think I need to take control of the rest of your weapons first."

Sergei grinned and sat up, and she gripped the bottom of his shirt, tugging it over his head and tossing it aside. He fisted his hand in her wet hair and drew her even closer, scattering her thoughts with his kiss. Valentina met his passion head-on, pushing him back down onto the bed and taking control again. His scent and taste surrounded her, drowning her with need, but she wasn't willing to surrender yet.

She lightly raked her fingernails over his chest before reaching up to unhook her damp bra. Sergei's eyes darkened with desire as he cupped her breasts, rubbing her hardened nipples with his thumbs. Without warning, he sat up abruptly and took one of her nipples into his mouth. She gasped at the erotic sensations coursing through her.

She threaded her fingers through his blond hair as he licked and sucked on one of the most sensitive parts of her body. The feel of his mouth on her breast and his hardened length pressing against her was nearly consuming. As though sensing her impending surrender, Sergei wrapped his arm around her and drew her even closer.

Knowing she needed to regain control now before she succumbed to her desire completely, Valentina grabbed his hands. Using her bra as a makeshift restraint, she quickly bound his wrists together. It wouldn't hold, but she didn't intend for it to deter him for long.

He arched a brow and studied the restraint. "Interesting tactic."

"Stay still or I'll get something you can't escape from," she threatened and nipped at his lower lip.

"Do you have any idea how hot you are right now?"

Valentina crawled down his body, trailing her fingers and lips over his skin until she reached his abdomen. Gripping the edge of his pants, she unfastened them and started to slide them off. "Not as hot as I'm about to make you."

"Fuck," he muttered, looking down at her with unmistakable need. "You'd better hurry because in about two minutes, I'll break out of this restraint, flip you over, and fuck you until you can't move for the next six hours."

She grinned and withdrew the knife from his ankle sheath. Trailing the flat of the blade up his body until she got to his chest, she teased, "Only six, Seryozha? You used to boast much more about your skills. Don't tell me you're losing your touch."

Valentina was tossed on the bed less than a second later. And a second after that, her panties had been ripped off and Sergei was inside her. The knife in her hand disappeared to whereabouts unknown. Gasping at the unrelenting pace he set, she gripped his arms tightly, unable to do anything but hold on as the sensations built within her.

The bond between the two of them flared to life, and her energy rushed outward and into Sergei, and he responded in kind. Energy, emotion, and thought all swirled together in a kaleidoscope of unrestrained passion and need. Everything about Sergei was wild and unpredictable, and it was beyond thrilling.

He'd burned her before, but he'd also taken her to heights she'd never imagined were possible. And after having a taste of him and experiencing everything he was, no one else could ever come close to eliciting the depth of feeling she had for him.

Sergei shifted his angle, and she tossed her head back, scoring her fingernails into his skin as he deepened his penetration. Valentina cried out as energy and ecstasy slammed into her, catapulting her to new heights. Sergei's thrusts became more fervent, and he gripped her hips, yanking her even closer and intensifying the sensations coursing through her.

Wrapping her legs around him, she moved with him, wanting everything he offered. His thrusts became even faster, quickly sending her spiraling toward the peak. It was too much. He was everywhere, surrounding and within her until nothing else existed. Brilliant white energy, a combination of their power, flowed outward and into each other. Every nerve ending was afire and in tune with his. Valentina knew intuitively that he was reading her body as well as his, and he was close too.

"Seryozha, now," she pleaded, arching her back and begging with her energy. He was too much. Too potent. Too everything. She couldn't do it.

"With me, Valechka," he demanded.

"Yes!" she screamed, gripping him even tighter as their bodies and energy climaxed together in a blinding wave of light, color, and sensation. He collapsed on top of her a moment later, breathing just as heavily as her.

Her eyes fluttered shut, too spent to even consider moving. "I may not be able to move for longer than six hours."

Sergei chuckled and pressed a kiss against her neck. Wrapping his arms around her, he rolled over and took her with him. "We'll see. If not, I'll have to try again."

Valentina smiled and nuzzled against his chest. "I've missed you, Seryozha."

He gently threaded his fingers through her hair and whispered, "You hold my heart completely, little dove. You always have."

———

A WARM HAND on her back awakened Valentina. She made a small noise acknowledging its presence but had no intention of moving.

"Are you planning to sleep all day, Valechka?" Sergei whispered in her ear.

She turned her head, burying her face against his chest. He was always so warm. With a sigh, she wrapped herself around him and started to doze again. He chuckled and ran a hand down her naked back. "I've missed this."

"Quit talking," she grumbled, shifting herself so she was sprawled halfway on top of him. He must have already gotten up at some point because he was fully dressed. She slipped her hand underneath his shirt to touch his heated skin.

Sergei placed a kiss against her hair. "Nikolai got a call from Alec earlier. He said you spoke with Ariana this morning at the pool and arranged to visit Hayden's club. I can tell them you changed your mind, if you wish. I rather like the thought of keeping you in bed with me."

She made a noncommittal noise and burrowed deeper against him. He laughed—a deep, throaty laugh that made her blink open her eyes. His gray eyes shone with amusement, and she was momentarily overwhelmed by him. "You should laugh more often, Seryozha."

He smiled down at her and brushed her hair away from her face. "I've been doing much more of that lately."

Valentina shifted, lifting her hand to trace over the features of his face. They were masculine yet beautiful to her. It had always been that way. Everything about him captivated her. He squeezed his eyes shut as she explored his face and then down his chest. In a soft voice, she whispered, "I love you, Seryozha."

He opened his eyes, and the love that filled them was staggering. There was no doubt in her mind how he felt about her. He pulled her tightly against him and kissed her. "Every time you say that, I have to convince myself it's real."

Valentina rested her head on his shoulder and traced a pattern over his chest. "What time is it?"

"Almost five. You've slept most of the day, but considering we got to bed around mid-morning, that's not unexpected."

"Hmm. I met Kayla this morning," she said, partially surprised she'd slept such a long time and so well. Sergei had always had that effect on her though. "Ariana brought her to the pool."

He ran his hand over her arm, the movement a gentle caress. "What did you think of her?"

"She's interesting. They both are. The two of them want to go to Hayden's club tonight with me."

Sergei paused. "I don't think Alec's going to be pleased with that idea."

With a yawn, she sat up and stretched. "I have a hard time imagining he'll be able to stop them. I thought about trying to deter them this morning, but I don't think there's much point. They're both too strong-willed and determined."

Sergei chuckled. "I suspect you're right. I have a feeling that backroom is going to be crowded with people observing all three of you. They should be safe enough."

Valentina stood and lifted her shoulder in a half-hearted shrug. She needed to take a shower and get dressed. Hopefully, Lars still had some of the tea she preferred. "I don't think much will happen. Ariana said there's a VIP area. I may be able to leave the two of them there while I interview people. They're both too recognizable for me to be able to stay by their side."

Sergei stood and wrapped his arm around her from behind. He swept her hair over her shoulder and kissed her neck. She leaned back against him and closed her eyes, basking in his warmth for a few more moments. "Ariana and Kayla are curious about you."

"Ah, yes." He chuckled, trailing his hand over her stomach. "They're most likely just as curious about you. I can't say I blame them though. You're very alluring."

She turned around and wound her arms around his neck. "Does Kayla know about us sharing a bond with Nikolai and Yuri?"

"Yes. She didn't grow up here, though, so she doesn't have the same preconceived notions as many of the Inner Circle members."

Valentina nodded. That's what she'd guessed, but it was always a good idea to confirm such things. She ran her hands down his chest. "Go away before you distract me again. I need to shower and get dressed. We'll never leave this room if you keep touching me."

Sergei grinned and kissed her nose before releasing her. "Nikolai has some of the security footage queued so you can familiarize yourself with the environment in the club before you go. I may be able to offer some suggestions based on my observations while I was there."

She paused. "You have copies of the floorplans?"

"Yes, Yuri is reviewing them now. Brant's on his way here with Hayden to go over the security detail for tonight. They're being cautious in light of what happened last night."

She nodded. "I'll hurry."

He headed out of the room, and she quickly went into the bathroom to prepare for the evening. Whatever they found in the towers would only help them to a certain degree. They also needed to focus on tracing down the supply.

Even though she was still inclined to end his life for harming Sergei, Viktor had the most extensive network of contacts in the area. It would be ideal if she could access his network without involving him. Unfortunately, she knew

Viktor well enough to know he'd guard the identity of his contacts until the very end. For all his other failings, that was one thing she admired about him. It didn't matter though. Sergei, Nikolai, and Yuri would never agree to her working with Viktor again, and she had her own reservations. She wasn't sure she trusted herself not to kill him for trying to kill the man she loved.

With a sigh, Valentina shut off the water in the shower and wrapped a drying cloth around herself. As usual, the water helped focus her thoughts. She'd need every ounce of clarity to ensure the Coalition's weapons stopped circulating through the towers. The sooner this was resolved, the sooner she could focus on finding the people within the Coalition who were responsible for the deception—and prevent Sergei from taking the fall.

CHAPTER SEVEN

VALENTINA TOOK a few experimental steps in her heeled shoes. They had possibilities. She flexed her foot, debating on how much pressure would be required to puncture someone's chest cavity.

"You look stunning!" Seara clasped her hands together.

Valentina blinked at Kayla's mother and managed a demure smile. "Thank you. I appreciate your kindness in helping me dress appropriately. I don't want to cause any offense."

Seara beamed a smile at her. "It's my pleasure. I'm going to see about convincing Kayla to try on a pair of heels. You've taken to them like you were born to wear them."

As soon as Seara left the room, Valentina opened her bag and selected a couple of her smaller knives. The very short, sparkling red dress was made of even less fabric than the last dress Sergei had admired. This one left most of her midsection bare and had even less options for hiding weapons.

She smoothed out the dress and studied her reflection in the mirror to make sure there was no sign of them. Someone knocked on the door, and Ariana entered a moment later wearing a more conservative, pale-blue dress. She smiled shyly. "I think we may need to rescue Kayla."

Valentina frowned. "Is there a problem?"

"Not exactly," Ariana admitted. "Seara pulled out some shoes for her to try on, and I think Kayla's about to panic."

Valentina picked up her bag of weapons and followed Ariana into Kayla's bedroom. Seara had laid out almost a half-dozen shoes and was making suggestions based on the style of her green dress. Kayla's eyes were wide in horror.

"You... you can't be serious," Kayla sputtered. "Those things are deathtraps."

Seara gestured to Valentina. "It just takes a little practice walking in them."

Valentina put her bag on the ground and walked over to Seara, gently placing her hand on the older woman's arm. "The selection you've offered is lovely, Seara. Perhaps Kayla just needs a few minutes to make a decision?" She lowered her gaze a fraction and added, "We're both adjusting to all these new changes. It's quite different than what we're used to on the surface."

Seara nodded and looked over at Kayla with obvious affection. "Of course. If you prefer, I can find some other shoes that might be more comfortable. I'll see what I have in my closet."

Seara headed out of the room, and Kayla fell back onto her bed. "Shoes. The woman is mad over shoes." She gestured toward a closed door on the far side of the room. "She's filled my closet with enough clothes to outfit everyone who's going to be living in this new tower. Every time I open the door, things I've never seen before jump out at me."

Valentina smiled. She bent down and picked up a pair of shoes, dangling them from her fingertips. "You should try these."

Kayla opened her eyes and scowled. "Those are the worst

of the ones Seara brought out. I thought you, of all people, would understand the situation. No one should wear anything like that."

"Mmhmm," Valentina agreed and turned the shoe over, checking the durability of the heel. "But almost anything can be used as a weapon. If you look at these shoes in a different context, I think you'll find yourself much more amenable to your mother's suggestions. For example, the physical impact of the heel in a sensitive area of the body could be quite a deterrent."

Dangling the shoes from her fingertips, Valentina tilted her head and gave Kayla a slow smile in challenge. "Sexuality can be just as much a weapon, especially given the preference for such attire in the towers. Adhering to certain expectations, but understanding you're not confined to them, can be very... disarming. I prefer to embrace all the weapons at my disposal." She held the heels out to Kayla. "What will you decide?"

Kayla's eyes lit up, and she grabbed the shoes. She studied the design and said, "You're a genius! I bet we could even retrofit these shoes to incorporate an actual weapon. Maybe something hidden so only the wearer would know it's there."

Valentina arched a brow, intrigued by the possibility. "You should speak with Yuri. He's designed many of my weapon harnesses, including this one." She lifted her skirt to show them the weapon sheath affixed high on her inner thigh.

Kayla's eyes widened, and she leaned forward to examine it. "I've got to get one of those. I never would have known you were wearing it if you hadn't shown us."

Ariana laughed. "I'm not sure OmniLab is ready for your idea of fashion."

Valentina smiled and smoothed her dress back down. "If you're interested, I could introduce you both to some different unobtrusive weapons."

"Hell yeah," Kayla agreed immediately. "We didn't have access to a whole lot in the ruin rat camps, but we excelled at hand-to-hand and brawling. Mack, a good friend of mine, taught me a lot of different moves."

"Perhaps you'd consider exchanging knowledge?" Valentina asked, curious about the tactics they used in the ruin rat camps. Her training was much more formal, but learning new techniques could be advantageous in a number of situations.

Kayla nodded, sitting down to put the shoes on. "Absolutely. Ari kicks some serious ass in the energy department. Between the three of us, we could be an unstoppable trio."

After taking a few wobbly steps, Kayla practiced "stabbing" someone with her heels. Valentina watched her for a moment with a small smile, but a carved figurine sitting on the dresser caught her attention. She walked over and picked it up, admiring the unusual greenish stone. "This is extraordinary. Where did you get it?"

Kayla paused and lifted her gaze. "Oh, yeah. That's a dragon. I found that artifact when I was scavenging in the ruins. I didn't know what it was at the time though."

Valentina tilted her head. "You didn't know what a dragon was?"

Kayla shook her head. "Nope. I met Alec a few days later and tried to sell it to him, but he gave it to me instead, saying some cryptic thing about how it was suitable for me to have it." She snorted. "Sometimes I think he says vague things like that just to provoke a reaction from me." She looked over at Ariana and winced. "No offense. You guys are great together, but he made me crazy."

Ariana grinned. "None taken. He's said similar things about you."

Valentina ran her finger over the dragon's snout and across its wings. It really was beautiful, and the stone seemed to almost warm in her hand. "My people have stories about dragons."

"We believe we're descended from dragons," Ariana admitted, taking a step toward her. "I'm not familiar with your people's stories though."

Valentina replaced the dragon figurine and turned toward Ariana. "There are several. One of my favorites was a story my *babushka* told me when I was a child. It was about a famous three-headed dragon called *Zmei Gorynich*. It loved the water but could also breathe fire, and it lived either in a cave or atop a mountain."

Valentina smiled at the memory. She used to always ask her grandmother to tell her more stories about the dragons. Curling up on the older woman's lap and listening to her spin fantastic tales was one of the most treasured memories from her childhood.

"Most of our stories revolved around a *bogatyr*, or hero in your language, slaying the dragons. But in some of these stories, the dragons would become friends with them. I liked those the best."

Ariana nodded. "A lot of the folktales in our archives also focus on the hero killing the evil dragons. I think people tend to fear what they don't understand, and the dragons were just one more example of that."

Valentina glanced at the figurine again and frowned. "My grandmother told me some dragons could shapeshift. *Zmei Gorynich* was one of those. If your people believe our abilities are tied to dragons, perhaps the two are connected. It's often said there's some element of truth in every story."

"A lot of the earliest fairytales were passed down by oral tradition. Perhaps they feared putting the truth in writing. The stories could have been a way to preserve knowledge without endangering themselves," Ariana suggested. She was quiet for a moment and then added, "I've always loved books. Until I got a handle on my empath abilities, it was easier for me to cope with the emotions from the characters in the stories. Over the years, I've gotten to know some of the archivists well. They might have some of these stories in our records. It would be interesting to run a check for common themes."

Kayla cocked her head, studying Valentina thoughtfully. She walked over to the dragon figurine, picked it up, and offered it to her. "I think you should have it."

Valentina's eyes widened. "I can't accept that."

Kayla shook her head and continued to hold out her hand. "You need to take it. I don't know why, but one of my abilities is to find lost or missing objects. I have the feeling you're supposed to have this for some reason. When you picked it up, something just sort of clicked into place that it was no longer lost. That feeling went away when you put it down."

Valentina took the dragon figurine again and studied the design. Something about it called to her too, but she didn't know what or why. "It feels warm in my hand."

Ariana frowned and studied the figurine. "That's so strange. There's some sort of energy transference happening. That doesn't usually happen with inanimate objects. Kayla, can you take the object again? I want to see if it resonates with you."

Kayla took the dragon figurine from Valentina's outstretched hand and turned expectantly toward Ariana, who shook her head. "It's not quite the same. There's still a transference, but the resonance is different. I've never seen anything like it."

Kayla offered it to Ariana. "Why don't you try it?"

Ariana bit her lip and took the statuette. She lifted it, studying it in amazement. "This is incredible. The resonance shifted again. But it's different with me too." Ariana turned toward them. "I think both of you need to touch it with me."

Valentina arched an eyebrow. Out of the three of them, Ariana had the most knowledge when it came to energy manipulation. Ariana also struck her as being cautious by nature, so it was doubtful she'd suggest such a thing if it were dangerous. Valentina reached out with her fingertips and brushed against the dragon's wing. Kayla did the same.

The moment they all came into contact with the stone dragon, they each gasped as a sudden awareness filled them. Valentina could sense Kayla and Ariana and knew they felt her too. It was almost as though another bond had formed, reminiscent of the one she shared with Sergei, Nikolai, and Yuri.

Kayla frowned and pulled away. The moment she broke contact, only a lingering trace of the connection remained. "You guys felt it, didn't you?"

Ariana nodded. "Yes. I've never heard of such a thing happening."

Valentina picked up the figurine again and studied it. "I'm not familiar with this mineral. Do you know what it's made from?"

Kayla shook her head. "We didn't do any sort of tests on it. I never considered it until now."

"I suppose we could ask one of our scientists to take a look," Ariana began, looking decidedly uncomfortable. "I'm not sure it should leave our possession though. It seems to resonate with our particular type of energy."

Valentina ran her finger along the dragon's snout. "Perhaps we can take it to them and remain with them while they study it. I don't think it would be wise to have them perform any sort of sampling tests though."

"Hell no," Kayla said, crossing her arms. "No sampling. As soon as you said that, I got chills."

Ariana nodded. "On that, we're all in agreement. I'd be

interested to know if another Inner Circle member has a similar reaction. Perhaps we can ask Lars to try it."

"Or Brant," Kayla suggested. "If it's responding to our spirit energy, I'd like to know how it reacts to him." A wicked grin crossed her face. "He loves it when I ask him to try out these sorts of things."

Valentina placed the dragon back on Kayla's dresser. "We'll need to do it once we return. It's getting late, and the statue will wait until we finish at the club. I'm sure everyone's wondering what's taking us so long."

Kayla glanced over at the figuring again. "You know, if those stories you heard about shapeshifting were true, that could be fun. I wouldn't mind being able to turn into a dragon. At least, provided I could eventually change back."

Valentina laughed. "Ah, but being a human has its benefits. Those shoes you're wearing are just one example. If you're human, no one will know the weapons within your possession. But if you fly around breathing fire, you're suddenly a very large target."

Kayla grinned. "I knew I liked you."

"Come on, *drakonikha*," Valentina teased. "Let's go find some heroes to play with."

"*Drakonikha?*" Kayla asked, saying the unfamiliar word.

Valentina nodded. "Of course. It's what we call a girl dragon. It's not just the boys who can breathe fire. We can do it too."

———

VALENTINA HAD LEFT Ariana in the VIP section with Hayden and navigated her way toward the main floor area where the majority of the people were intermingling with a few Inner Circle members. She would have preferred leaving Kayla behind, too, but the woman was tougher than she'd initially realized. They'd come to an agreeable arrangement, and Kayla and Carl were currently occupying a table on the main floor with Yuri. He had every appearance of socializing with the couple, but Yuri was more focused on listening to her via hidden comms and keeping a discreet eye on her progress through the club.

The last person she'd spoken to had been useless. It had only taken her three minutes to find out he knew next to nothing and was only interested in taking her home with him. After scraping him off, it was time to find a new mark. Fortunately, that wouldn't be difficult.

She walked over to one of the ornately carved barstools and slid onto it, allowing her short dress to hike up even higher on her thigh. Tossing her loose hair over her shoulder, she leaned forward and pretended to study the large array of bottles displayed behind the bar.

"Can't decide?"

Valentina turned to regard a man with sandy-blond hair standing beside her. He was wearing one of the translating devices in his ear, which was promising. If he had enough interaction with their people to warrant such a device, he might have knowledge of their missing supplies.

Tilting her head, she gave him a small smile. "I'd love to hear your suggestions. There are so many choices, and I'm afraid I'm unfamiliar with most of them."

He grinned and ordered something from the bartender. A moment later, she was handed an amber-colored drink. "You're Coalition, right?"

She nodded and took a small sip. It had a nice flavor, but Lars had better liquor in his quarters. "How did you guess?"

"Your accent," he replied, lifting his glass and leaning even closer to her. "I haven't seen you here before, and I would have remembered you. Let me guess... You heard about the excitement last night and wanted to check things out?"

Valentina laughed and leaned forward, mirroring his movements to show her interest. "Is it that obvious? The rumors have been growing since I arrived, but I don't think anyone really knows what happened. I've gotten the impression most of the people here are just as curious as me."

"Yeah," he agreed with a cocky grin. "I overhead the last guy telling you a pretty crazy story. I hope you don't believe a word of it. I wasn't here last night, but my friend David was." He gestured to a man talking to a brunette a short distance away. "We didn't think the club would be open again so soon. We decided to stop in to see what people were saying too."

Valentina took a sip of her drink, smiling over the rim of her glass. She wasn't interested in hearing another outlandish tale, but if this man was a frequent visitor, he might have more pertinent insight. "So the stories aren't true? Lightning didn't strike anyone? The walls in the club didn't collapse?"

He laughed. "No, not even close. Just a minor skirmish, but they found one of your people's weapons."

Valentina frowned and lowered her glass. "I heard that. Just because I'm with the Coalition, I hope you don't think I had anything to do—"

He shook his head and grinned. "No, I don't think you're responsible. Quite frankly, I haven't seen many women from the Coalition here. I was intrigued and had to come over to introduce myself."

She bit her lip and tilted her head. "You're not on the construction crew, are you? I don't recognize you, but then again, I haven't been here long. I haven't met many people yet."

He chuckled. "No, I live here in the towers. I'm Jakob."

"Hello, Jakob. I'm Valentina." She held out her hand and he took it, squeezing it gently.

"Gorgeous name," he said, sliding into the seat next to

her. "You don't strike me as the type to work a construction site."

She shook her head and smiled. "I don't. Not really. I mostly do some administrative-type duties. You know, inventory of nails and tools. I'm afraid it's not very exciting."

"Oh yeah?" Jakob put his elbow on the bar and leaned in closer. "There was a guy who used to come in here who did that too, but I haven't seen him in about a week or so. I think his name was Pavel. You work with him?"

Valentina lowered her gaze. "No. I'm sorry if he was a friend of yours, but I believe Pavel was in some sort of accident. I've been temporarily assigned to take over his duties." She sighed wistfully and looked around the club. "I never imagined your home was so beautiful. I'm grateful for the opportunity to experience it, even if the circumstances surrounding my promotion are less than ideal."

Jakob paused, studying her for a long time. She finished her drink and put it on top of the bar. When he didn't say anything, Valentina inwardly smiled. Something was telling her Jakob knew something, and his silence only helped reinforce that opinion. She glanced at him. "So what do you do here in the towers?"

Jakob waved over the bartender and ordered her another drink. "I manage a store a few levels down."

"Do you enjoy your work?"

"It's all right," he said with a shrug, glancing toward the dance area. It was clear he wasn't thrilled with his job and didn't want to discuss it. "What do you think of the club?"

"It's much different than anything we have on the surface," she admitted. "I never imagined anything like this existed. You're very fortunate to live in such a place."

He turned back toward her and arched a brow. "Yeah? If you like it, there are a bunch of places around here that are even better. I don't think they're open to your people yet, unless you have an escort."

Valentina blinked up at him. "Really?"

"Oh, sure," Jakob said, puffing out his chest a bit.

She resisted the urge to smirk and took another sip of her drink, pretending to hang on his every word as he described some of the other clubs and restaurants in the area. He seemed to enjoy the idea he could introduce her to a world she'd never experienced. Fine. If this was his game, she'd play along.

Valentina sighed wistfully. "It sounds wonderful. Some of my people were talking about this club, and I thought they might have been exaggerating. That's part of the reason I wanted to come here tonight."

He rubbed the back of his fingers up her bare arm. "I could show you a lot of things."

She bit her lip and lowered her gaze. "I'm sure you could."

"I thought you might brush me off like the last guy," he admitted. "You've been doing that all night."

She tilted her head and gave him a small smile. "You were watching me?"

He chuckled. "Most of the men in here have been watching you all night, even a lot of the Inner Circle people."

Running a hand down the front of her dress, she used the gesture to subconsciously draw his attention to her figure. It was highly effective as far as distractions went. He wouldn't be quite as fixated on her questions if he were too focused on getting her into bed. "I guess the dress was worth it."

"Definitely," he agreed, his gaze roaming over her curves.

Valentina smiled. "Men from the Inner Circle don't usually look at women?"

He hesitated, his expression darkening. "They do on occasion, but they mostly stick to their own kind. It's better that way. Sometimes, women come in here specifically hoping to get their attention. Is that what you're looking for?"

Valentina frowned, understanding the need to navigate carefully. For whatever reason, this was a sensitive subject with him. "My only agenda was to explore a little bit of the towers and see what life was like here." She shrugged. "I don't know much about this Inner Circle. I've heard a few rumors about them, but I haven't paid much attention. I'm still learning my way around."

Jakob relaxed a fraction. "Sorry. It's just a touchy subject. If you've only been here a short time, it makes sense you wouldn't know much about the political stuff."

"What political stuff?"

He waved off her question. "Oh, it's not important. Why don't you tell me more about yourself? I'd like to get to know you better."

Valentina frowned. It was time to step things up a notch or they'd be sitting here exchanging small talk all night. He was hinting around to something but leery about letting her in on whatever it was.

Tucking her loose hair behind her ear, she leaned forward to give him a view of her cleavage and then brushed a light kiss against his cheek. "Actually, it's getting late. Thank you for the drink, Jakob. I really enjoyed meeting you. Maybe I'll see you again soon."

His eyes widened. "You're leaving already? Don't you want to dance?"

She glanced toward the dance floor. "Oh, I don't know if I'm much of a dancer."

Jakob took her hand. "I'll show you. It's too early to leave just yet. Besides, I want you to meet someone."

Valentina followed him to the dance floor, immediately intrigued. "Your friend David?"

"Nah," he said and put his arm around her, pulling her

close as he began to move to the music. "Another friend of mine was wondering what happened to Pavel. They'd gotten to be good friends. I'm sure he'll want to know what happened."

"Oh," Valentina murmured, running her hands up his chest and winding them around his neck like some of the other women were doing. "I don't know if I can tell them much. I only met Pavel twice, and I don't know many details. Who's your friend? Would I know him?"

He ignored the questions. "Hey, you're a pretty good dancer."

She smiled up at Jakob, debating whether to suggest Sergei plant him in a chair and try out his truth detection abilities. The only problem was that she didn't quite trust Sergei to not kill or maim him in the process. "I think I have a pretty good teacher."

He slid his hand down her back and cupped her backside. "I bet we could teach each other a lot of things."

"That might be fun," Valentina agreed, wondering whether Sergei would leave any of Jakob's bones intact by the end of the night. She hoped Nikolai was keeping him distracted. At least he'd agreed not to listen in on her comms. Only Nikolai and Yuri were doing that.

Jakob pulled her even closer, and she softened her body against his. "You know, after you meet my friend, we could go back to my place. You mentioned wanting to see more of the towers."

She bit her lip and teased, "I'm not sure how much of the towers I'll see if we end up at your place."

He chuckled. "Well, maybe I can show you the towers some other time. What do you think? Do you want to get out of here?"

She arched her brow. "You sure you want me to meet this friend of yours?"

He swept his gaze over her and hesitated. "No, but he'll kill me if I don't introduce you. Come on. I'll call him and have him meet us outside. My place isn't far away. We'll head there afterward."

Valentina giggled and leaned into him as he led her off the dance floor. She caught Yuri's gaze on the way out, and he inclined his head, indicating he'd heard everything and would follow them.

They headed outside the club into a busy commercial district. She looked around, pretending to be amazed by the sights, but she was studying the layout of the area as well. She'd entered through a side entrance with everyone else and hadn't seen the main entrance. "Your friend doesn't want to meet us in the club?"

Jakob glanced over at her. "Not until things settle down after last night. Have you been to many of these shops?"

Valentina shook her head. "Just a few places on the way to the club. A lot of the areas are still off limits to my people. Will you get into trouble for bringing me here?"

"Nah," he said, waving off her concerns. "It's mainly the Inner Circle who are uptight about those things. None of us are permitted in their tower. You're allowed in ours, provided a resident is with you."

She gave him a small smile. "Thank you for escorting me."

He grinned and puffed out his chest. They walked a bit further down the corridor and halted outside a small store. It was still open, but there weren't many people inside. He put his arm around her and pulled out his commlink, holding it to his ear. "Hey, Maggie, it's Jakob. Can you let Charles know I have someone new he should meet?" Jakob paused to listen for a moment. "Yeah. Oh, really? That long?" He frowned, indecision clearly warring on his face. Valentina leaned into him again and ran her fingertips across his chest. Biting her lip, she let him see the invitation in her eyes.

He swallowed, his eyes darkening with lust as his looked down at her. "No, that won't work for me. I'll be busy later. Where is he? I'll take her to him."

After another lengthy pause, Jakob disconnected the call. "Okay, change of plans."

Valentina blinked up at him. "Is everything all right?"

Jakob swept his gaze around the area. She knew without looking that it was mostly deserted with a few idle stragglers. Yuri would hang back to avoid detection and only intervene if she needed assistance or if she stopped responding.

"Yeah. Everything's fine. My friend's just tied up. We're going to stop by to see someone else really quick. My friend will meet up with us afterward."

"Oh," she murmured, tucking her hair behind her ear. "I'm not sure about this. You haven't explained why you want me to meet with your friend. I thought you wanted to spend some time alone with me."

"Trust me, I do. At this point, I'm ready to say to hell with my *friend*," he admitted, putting his arm around her waist and pulling her closer. "But it won't take long. They're just a few levels down from here, and it's close to my quarters."

Valentina looked up at him and gave him a small smile. "Good. I'm really looking forward to getting on with the rest of our evening."

"You and me both."

———

SERGEI GRITTED HIS TEETH. He'd kill the fucking bastard.

He glared at the security tablet Brant was holding. Valentina was in the elevator with that *mudak*, and he kept putting his hands all over her. Jakob started to slide one of his hands under her very short dress, and she tossed back her hair and laughed, moving away from him as the elevator door opened.

"It looks like they're exiting on the ninth level," Brant said and pressed a button to switch the view from the security feed to the outside corridor where Valentina was walking.

"Good," Sergei said and entered the floor number on the panel in the priority elevator. That particular level connected to the construction breezeway. If Valentina ran into a problem, she'd have easy access to escape, though he didn't intend to let her go far without him. They'd been following her since she left the club, using the tower's surveillance system to avoid detection.

"This is why she didn't want you on comms," Yuri said, leaning against the wall of the elevator. "You worry too much. Valya can handle herself."

"I'm not worried about her handling herself," Sergei retorted, staring at the numbers displayed overhead as they descended. "I'm worried about how much *handling* he's doing. I'd simply like to kill him before she does. She'll do it far too quickly for my liking."

Brant frowned and looked up from the tablet. "If you don't mind, I'd rather not have to explain any more bodies in the towers. We still have a mess from last night."

Sergei arched an eyebrow. "Who said anything about a body being discovered?"

"I'm not helping you clean up the blood," Lars advised him.

"We could take him out of the towers first," Nikolai said, studying Brant's tablet with a frown. "My recruits have gotten quite skilled at cleaning up."

Sergei's eyes narrowed on the video again. *Fuck.* Jakob practically had her pinned up against a wall and was trying to kiss her. Valentina was brushing off his more overt advances with a small smile, but he knew she was getting irritated. Her fingers were flexing as they did when she wanted to draw a weapon. He cocked his head and considered it. If Jakob pushed her too far, Valentina might get creative with him when this was over. The possibility had merit.

Kayla leaned over Brant's shoulder to look at the screen and laughed. "I knew it would be more fun coming with you guys than sitting in the club. Valentina looks like she can handle herself."

Carl wrapped his arms around her waist. "I'd probably have a similar reaction if that guy touched you like that."

She lifted her head to look up at him and grinned. The door opened and Sergei walked out, heading in the direction Jakob had taken Valentina. Brant slowed and said, "Hang on. They're going into one of the distribution centers."

Brant spoke quietly into his commlink, most likely ordering his people into position and alerting Alec to their location. Sergei was surprised when Valentina agreed to leave the club with Jakob, but Yuri said the guy was acting suspicious and mentioned the name Charles. Unfortunately, it was the best lead they had regarding how the weapons were being funneled into the towers.

Sergei turned toward Brant. "Is there another entrance to the distribution center?"

"Yes. I'm having the rest of the team stationed nearby. They'll move in on my command."

"This guy is persistent, I'll give him that much," Yuri said with a chuckle and pressed his finger against his earpiece as though he was being thoroughly entertained.

Sergei frowned. He was going to have to start ignoring Valentina's requests not to listen in on her comms. While her concern about him possibly losing control was understandable, not knowing what was happening was chiseling away at the last of his patience. Reaching into his pocket, he plugged in his earpiece.

Nikolai shook his head. "Valya won't be pleased if you interfere in this, Sergei. She specifically didn't want you to listen."

"I don't give a damn," he snapped, pulling out his comm-link and threading his energy through the electronic device to connect into Yuri's earpiece. With a snap and crackle, Valentina's voice sounded in his ear.

Nikolai sighed and turned toward Brant. "Is your building adequately protected against fire?"

Brant nodded and frowned. "Yes, we're still cleaning up the mess from Kayla's last fire suppression incident in the lower warehouse."

"At least you know what to expect," Nikolai muttered. "This isn't going to end well."

———

VALENTINA WALKED into the distribution center and swept her gaze over the area. There were dozens of workers operating various consoles while automated robotic mechanisms moved large crates to various areas of the cavernous room. Shelving units reached nearly to the ceiling, creating towers of supplies where stolen weapons could easily be hidden. This was definitely promising.

"Impressive, huh?" Jakob asked, his arm still wrapped around her. At least it wasn't on her ass anymore. His hands had gotten a little too close to one of the knives strapped to her inner thigh while they were in the elevator. "I bet you don't have anything like this on the surface."

Valentina smiled sweetly and made a small noise of agreement, but she was ready to shove her knife in his throat to keep him from talking. He seemed to have the remarkable delusion that the Coalition primarily lived in dirty, run-down huts on the surface. While their existence wasn't as posh as life in the towers, their people controlled a vast expanse of the viable territories around the globe.

He led her to another door and knocked.

"Whose office is this?" she whispered loud enough for Yuri to overhear on her hidden comms.

Before Jakob could respond, the door opened to reveal another man estimated in his early thirties with long, dark hair tied at the nape of his neck. He was wearing some sort of gray uniform, similar in style to those in the outside room. But his bearing led her to believe he was in some sort of supervisory position. His eyes narrowed, but he stepped aside to allow them to enter the small office.

Valentina followed Jakob inside, not bothering to hide her curiosity as she looked around. It was some sort of administrative office, but there was only one door in and out. Other than a large desk, a few consoles with security feeds being displayed, and a few shelves and bins in the corner, there wasn't much to it. She turned back to the man to find his eyes on her and not appearing very friendly.

"What are you doing here, Jakob?"

Jakob hesitated and then gestured to her. "This is Valentina. She's Pavel's replacement. I thought Charles would want to meet her, but he's busy for a while. I thought you could meet her instead."

"You're an idiot," the other man snapped. "You bring some woman here you don't know anything about?"

Valentina frowned and leaned closer to Jakob. "Um, Jakob, are you sure he's a friend of yours? I know you wanted me to meet him, but maybe this wasn't a good idea."

Jakob put his arm around her again. "Don't worry, Valentina. It's fine. Walter's just a little uptight."

"For fuck's sake," Walter muttered, pinching the bridge of his nose. "How many more of our names are you going to give her?"

Jakob released her and grabbed Walter's arm, pulling him a short distance away. In a quiet voice, but still easily overheard, he said, "Look, I met her at the club tonight. We started talking, and I found out she's taken over the construction inventory for Pavel. He's gone, man. We need to find another source. She can help us."

"That's a little convenient, don't you think?" Walter demanded, still eyeing her suspiciously. "They find a weapon yesterday and suddenly she's there tonight?"

Valentina bit her lip, doing her best to appear uneasy. "Jakob, maybe you should take me back to the club. I don't want to cause any problems."

Jakob blew out a breath and didn't respond. Instead, he focused on Walter again. "I was the one who approached her. There were a ton of people there tonight. Most of them I've never seen before. They were all curious about what happened yesterday. I saw plenty of Omni security there, but she's not one of them."

"Look at her, Jakob," Walter argued. "Quit thinking with your dick. Ask yourself what someone who looks like her is doing with someone like you. I'm surprised half the Inner Circle wasn't hanging all over her dressed like that."

Jakob sputtered an objection, but Walter ignored him and approached her. "I need to search you. I'm sure you understand. We don't know you, and we need to be cautious."

Well, dammit. The knives and microphone might be a little hard to explain, and she didn't want to kill anyone without getting some answers first. Feigning fear, she backed away from him. "Jakob told me he wanted to stop and see a friend. I don't know what's going on, but I want to leave. I didn't agree to any of this. Jakob, please don't let him touch me."

"Walter, knock it off. Look at that dress. There's no way she's hiding anything."

Walter hesitated, scanning her up and down and making her glad she'd chosen two of her smallest knives to bring along. She lowered her gaze, trying to appear as nonthreatening as possible.

Jakob walked over to her and draped his arm around her shoulders again. "Don't worry. Walter's mostly harmless. Come on, I'll take you out of here."

She leaned into him and whispered, "Thank you."

Jakob started leading her to the door, but Walter stopped them. "Wait. Just... bring her back."

When they turned around, Walter leaned against his desk. "Valentina's your name, right?"

She bit her lip and nodded.

"How well did you know Pavel?"

Valentina tucked her hair behind her ear. "I didn't. Not really. I was transferred here a week ago, and I only met him twice. If you were friends with him, I'm sorry. But I don't know much about him."

"Where did you transfer from?"

She frowned, allowing her fingers to rub against the hem of her dress in a gesture of unease. These questions were more pointed than she expected, but Sergei had helped her craft a plausible explanation for her presence within the towers. The trick was weaving enough truth into a story to lend believability to the lies.

"I managed inventory accounts for two of Chairman Nikolai Berkutov's camps. When I heard about the new tower being built, I submitted an application requesting a transfer. Someone told me my chances of being accepted would be higher if I joined the construction crew, so that's what I did. I was hoping to become Pavel's assistant. But after he died, I was asked to temporarily fill in for him since I have experience with inventory management."

Walter studied her for a long time. "You want to live in the towers?"

"See?" Jakob said, not bothering to hide the smugness from his tone. "I told you she's perfect. Even better than Pavel."

Walter glared at him. "Would you shut up?"

Valentina bit her lip, looking back and forth between them. "Why are you asking me all these questions?"

Walter turned back to her and frowned. "I'm happy to explain, but I need you to answer just a few more questions. Okay?"

"All right," she said quietly. At least Walter appeared to be buying her unsure and demure routine.

"What do you know about the Inner Circle?"

She blinked at him, thoroughly confused. "What?"

"Have you heard of them?" Walter prompted again, watching her reaction.

Valentina frowned, deciding to stick as close to the truth as possible. She had no way of knowing if this Walter had ways of verifying her information. "Yes. I know they live in the other tower, and it's closed to everyone else. Your leadership is made up of Inner Circle members, right?"

Walter nodded. "A few of them lived amongst your people. Did you know any of them?"

She shook her head, getting the impression he was looking for any holes in her story. His caution was promising. "None of them lived in any of the camps I was stationed in. I've seen one or two in the construction tower and some in the club tonight, but I don't really know any of them."

"Some of our people made an arrangement with yours," Walter began, taking a step closer to her. "We expect some rather dramatic changes to be happening soon, and we'd like to continue the deal we originally struck with Pavel. He was acting as an intermediary and helping us with... a sensitive project."

Valentina tilted her head, pretending to misunderstand. "Intermediary? Oh, you must be talking about Sergei Sokolov. I believe Pavel reported directly to him." She frowned. "I'm not familiar with any sensitive projects though. Have you been working with Sergei on this?"

Walter waved off her comment. "No. He's not important. Not yet, anyway." He straightened and pushed off the desk, walking over to her. "If you'd be willing to take over Pavel's arrangement with us, we could make it worth your while."

She frowned. "I don't understand. What do you mean?"

Jakob turned toward her. "Valentina, we need your help moving some equipment into the towers. If you're handling the inventory now, you can help us."

Valentina bit her lip. "Into the towers? But I oversee our construction materials. What could you possibly need from our supplies?"

Someone knocked at the door, interrupting them. Valentina buried her irritation as Walter walked over to open the door. She caught sight of a dark-haired woman wearing a similar gray uniform. The woman leaned close to Walter and whispered something fervently in his ear. His body tensed, and he spun around, slamming the door behind him.

He walked over to his desk and yanked open a drawer. Withdrawing a gun she recognized as belonging to her people, he pointed it directly at her. Unfortunately, this wasn't one of the more harmless electrolaser guns. She knew this particular weapon well—it was designed to kill.

Walter took a step toward her. "Who are you? Why is OmniLab security all over this level? Start talking or I'll shoot."

Dammit. This was why she hated working with amateurs. They were always so quick to pull out the weapons, even when they weren't proficient with them. To make matters worse, she really wanted both of them alive to find out what they knew. Five more minutes and they would have confirmed the presence of weapons, without her needing to look down the barrel of one.

Jakob took a step toward Walter and glanced over at her. "Are you sure security's outside?"

"One of you led them to us," he snapped, still aiming the weapon at her. "Are you with OmniLab security?"

She held out her hands to show they were currently empty. Walter's hands were slightly unsteady, indicating he didn't really want to harm her. He was just afraid and needed a little reassurance. Even so, caution was warranted. Some of the most dangerous individuals were those who were nervous and handling a weapon.

"No, I swear it. I don't understand what's going on outside, but I told you the truth. My name is Valentina, and I have spent my life working for the Coalition. I am loyal to my people." She lowered her hands and repeated the same thing, but this time, in Russian. With Jakob wearing the translating device, he would understand what she was saying.

Jakob turned back to Walter and shook his head. "It's got to be a coincidence. They wouldn't be working with her, and no one would have been able to learn their language that well in such a short amount of time. Maybe they're conducting searches on this level. We were worried something like this would happen."

Walter hesitated and then lowered the weapon. He walked over to a nearby grate that was partially obscured by a shelving unit, pushed the furniture aside, and quickly unscrewed the cover. Walter gestured for them both to climb inside. She glanced into it and frowned. The minute she started climbing, either of them could look up to see the knives strapped to her inner thigh. She also needed to let Yuri know where they wanted to take her. Gesturing to the small duct, she feigned shock. "You want me to climb through that grate? In this dress?"

"Let's go," Jakob said and pulled her toward it. She pretended to stumble on her heels and fell to the ground with a pained cry.

Walter cursed and walked over to her. He scooped her up into his arms and said, "It's not far. There's a larger duct only a few yards away. You can scoot your way down. If you are who you say, you don't want them to find you here."

Valentina blinked at him and nodded. He carried her over to the grate and gently put her down. She slid backward into the duct, waiting until Walter was inside and busy replacing the shelving unit and grate cover behind them before crawling the rest of the way.

As soon as she reached the cross juncture, Jakob pulled her up the rest of the way into what appeared to be some sort of narrow service area. Pipes, electrical cabling, and wiring ran along the exposed walls illuminated with dim emergency lighting. She looked around, noting the lack of surveillance, and wondered how Sergei, Nikolai, and Yuri were going to follow her through here. From all appearances, she was likely on her own. They weren't going to like that one bit.

CHAPTER EIGHT

SERGEI'S EARPIECE SQUELCHED, and he yanked it from his ear. Something in the area where those two men had taken Valentina was causing too much interference for him to pick up on her dialogue. He glanced over at Yuri, who was also scowling.

Nikolai took a step toward Brant. "You need to locate her immediately. The signal's completely gone. We've lost all contact."

Brant entered a few commands on his tablet. "She's not appearing on any of our security feeds. They must have entered an area of the towers that's not monitored. You said she mentioned a grate?"

Sergei crossed his arms over his chest. "Yes. Can you find her?"

"I'm working on it. We have thousands of cameras in the towers."

Yuri glanced down the corridor. "What do you know about these two men she's with?"

"Nothing remarkable. Jakob manages a retail store on one of the lower levels. It appears Walter handles the distribution of merchandise and supplies for six different levels, including the store Jakob manages. If they've been smuggling weapons through that distribution center, Walter could have doctored the records to hide them."

"That's not enough," Sergei said, trying to resist the urge to go after her right away. He'd give Brant five minutes to locate her, but that was all. "I want access to their personality assessments, arrest or detainment records, or anything else that can help us determine their propensity for causing her harm. Otherwise, I will damn this entire operation and go in after her."

Brant frowned, typing furiously. "We've already pulled it up. There's nothing out of the ordinary. They both stay under the radar. Jakob had one minor infraction for public intoxication, but that was over a year ago. It's going to take more time to go through all their messages and electronics."

Yuri glanced down the corridor toward the distribution center. "What about known associates?"

"A list is generating now," Brant said, still studying the screen. "I'll cross-check all names of associates for both men and focus on those first. That'll help speed things up."

Kayla frowned. "If you're bonded to Valentina, can you pick up on anything? Alec was able to communicate with me telepathically when we shared a connection."

Sergei shook his head. "No. She's suppressing our bond to avoid detection. If she were in trouble, she would take the risk. Although, I can tell she's irritated."

"She's not hurt," Nikolai said, staring down the corridor with a faraway look in his eyes. He shook his head as though to clear it. "But Sergei's right. She's annoyed. I believe she's walking through some sort of service area with them. I saw cabling and pipes. I didn't see any distinguishing landmarks though."

Kayla's eyes widened. "You can see her?"

Nikolai shook his head. "My ability's erratic. I occasionally get glimpses of future events, but I have them more often when it comes to Valentina. She'll be walking down that area in the next few minutes."

Yuri moved closer to them. "I don't like it. We need to get into that office and find out where they took her. Even if she's okay right now, they pulled a gun on her. She doesn't know the layout of the towers, and if she comes into contact with anyone from the Inner Circle, we're going to have a problem."

Sergei nodded. "Brant, clear out the distribution center. We need access to that office but can't risk anyone knowing that's our focus."

He nodded and barked out instructions on the commlink.

Kayla stepped closer. "I'm going with you guys."

"Kayla," Carl began, putting his hand on her back, "you may be familiar with the construction tower, but you don't know this one very well. You won't be able to help them navigate the area."

"That's true, but I can find lost or missing objects. Right now, Valentina's missing. I might be able to help find her."

Sergei cocked his head and studied Kayla for a long moment. He inclined his head and said, "I'd appreciate your help. Leave your shoes behind. It sounds as though we'll need to crawl through a duct."

Kayla huffed. "Are you kidding? Your girlfriend showed me how these could be used as a weapon. Check out the heels. I'm armed and dangerous. If she's rocking her shoes, I'm doing the same thing."

Sergei arched his brow. He should have known Kayla and Valentina would immediately have a sense of kinship with one another. Valentina seemed to like Ariana just as much. It was an interesting friendship between three very different women, but he wasn't sure how far it would go. Valentina tended to be wary of letting anyone past her defenses. Anyone other than him, Nikolai, and Yuri, that is.

They waited another ten minutes until the distribution center was cleared out before they were able to enter. By that time, all of them were uneasy and their sense of urgency was growing. Valentina could be anywhere by now.

Sergei swept his gaze over the small office where they'd taken Valentina. There wasn't much to it, and no grate was easily within sight. He grabbed a shelving unit leaning against the wall and shoved it to the side. Yuri started on the opposite side of the room. Nikolai opened drawers and began digging through the contents.

Kayla studied one of the shelving units and pointed to it. "Behind that one."

Sergei immediately pulled the furniture to the side, exposing a metallic grate. Bending down, he withdrew one of his knives and used the edge of the blade to quickly unfasten it. The cover came off easily. It was narrow inside, but Valentina would have been able to navigate it easily. He continued climbing and paused at a small intersection, debating which direction to take.

"Go straight," Kayla said from behind him.

"No good," he replied. "It's sealed. Left or right only."

Kayla blew out a breath. "Then try going to the left. Everything's getting confused in here, but she definitely went this way. Or at least her shoes did."

Sergei took the left tunnel and continued climbing. "What do you mean?"

"I'm tracking her shoes," Kayla retorted. "I don't know how to track people."

Sergei opened his mouth to respond, but Kayla interrupted him. "Don't you dare start bitching to me again about training and not practicing with my *weapon*. I'm working on it. Speaking of which, you guys could lessen up on your intensive training with all this woo-woo shit. You're making me look bad. Alec's been giving me grief again."

He didn't bother replying, too focused on finding Valentina than criticizing Kayla. Pulling himself out of the duct, he stepped down into a narrow service area. Something sparkling and red caught his attention and he walked over to investigate. Frowning, he bent down to pick up Valentina's discarded shoes.

"Well, shit," Kayla muttered. "I seem to have crap luck when it comes to people keeping on their shoes when I'm tracking them."

Nikolai approached them and cursed. "She most likely left them as a marker to indicate the direction they were traveling."

Sergei nodded, staring down the corridor in the direction the shoes had been pointing. There was no way to know how far it went or where they'd stopped. Valentina probably didn't realize how far behind they were.

This whole thing made him uneasy. Valentina knew how to handle people, but she was in an unfamiliar environment with people they didn't know. Even if she needed to use lethal force, OmniLab security didn't know her identity. They could easily determine she was a threat since they were already on edge after the attack last night.

"Can you see her through our bond, Nikolai? Even an approximate location?"

Nikolai shook his head. "No, Sergei. I can't sense her right now. Valya's still suppressing our bond."

Yuri swore under his breath. "I don't like this. Let's keep going. Maybe she'll leave another clue up ahead. I don't want to stay this far out of range. If she runs into trouble, she'll need backup."

Sergei glanced over at him. "I agree. Let's go."

"Hang on. I think I know how we can find her," Kayla said

and pressed a button on her commlink. Nothing happened. She frowned and glanced around at the wiring running up the walls. "Is there some sort of interference in here?"

Sergei nodded. "That's why we lost communication with Valentina. It may reconnect once she leaves this area, but there's no way to know."

"I need to make a call," she said, heading back toward the duct.

Sergei plucked the commlink from Kayla's hand and ran a trace of his electrical energy through the device. "Go ahead. You have only a few minutes to talk before the energy fails."

Her eyes widened. "That is a seriously cool trick. You're going to have to show me how to do it."

Without waiting for a response, Kayla pressed a button and said, "Hey, Alec. Are you with Ari? I need her." She paused. "Yeah. Valentina's missing. Can you run to Seara's quarters and get the dragon? I have an idea of how to find her." She paused again, listening. "Right. We're with Brant. Hurry."

She closed the device. "Okay. They'll be here in a few minutes. We tried something a little earlier when we were getting dressed for the club. If my hunch is right, we should be able to track her with another type of connection."

Nikolai shook his head. "We can't wait. Sergei, you and Yuri should go ahead. I'll stay with Brant and his team to continue searching the office. If I learn anything from his messages or pick up anything from Valentina, I'll try to reach you."

Sergei nodded. "I don't know where this corridor goes. We don't have the maps on it, but I'll periodically enable the power on my commlink to check in with you. See if you can get the floorplans from Brant and send them to me."

"I'm going with you," Lars said, moving forward through the narrow hallway. "I might not have a tie to Valentina, but you're still technically Coalition. If either of you run into a problem, I can help."

"You have a weapon?"

Lars nodded. "Always. My time living with you taught me better than to walk around unarmed."

"Good," Sergei replied, moving forward. "Let's go."

———

VALENTINA CONTINUED FOLLOWING Jakob through the narrow service area with Walter right behind them. They'd passed several ducts, but based on Walter and Jakob's confident footsteps, they were extremely familiar in navigating these tunnels. They were most likely using these service areas to transfer the weapons to various locations within the towers.

"Where are we going?"

"Just keep walking," Walter said from behind her.

Valentina blew out a breath. She still hadn't seen any surveillance cameras since they entered the tunnel, and it was starting to worry her. She didn't know where she was, and even once she escaped, it would be challenging to get back to the Inner Sanctum without being identified. The dress she was wearing was far too conspicuous. At least she'd lost those shoes. Kayla had a point; they really weren't very practical.

It was time to start demanding some answers before they took her much farther. At the very least, it would give Yuri a chance to catch up.

Halting in her tracks, she spun around and wrapped her arms around herself. "No. Jakob wanted me to meet you for some reason, and you pulled a weapon on me. Now I'm being dragged through the service alleys of the towers. Security is after us, and you expect me to just continue to follow you blindly? How do I know you're not planning to kill me anyway?"

Walter frowned at her. "I scared you earlier, didn't I?"

She hesitated and then nodded, slowly softening her expression. "Please tell me what's going on or take me back to the construction tower."

With a sigh, Walter pulled out the weapon and showed it to her. As she suspected, it was one of the Coalition's weapons, but this was a newer model with a slightly modified design from previous versions. They'd only begun testing it in the past year, and distribution was still limited to high-ranking officials. This time, her surprise wasn't feigned. It was a clear indicator they'd been right—one of their leaders was involved in the distribution of weapons to OmniLab's residents.

Valentina frowned and looked up at Walter. "That's a Coalition weapon. Why do you have it?"

"I'm not going to hurt you, Valentina," Walter said, putting the weapon back into his pocket. "Your people have been supplying us weapons. We're planning something, and the Coalition has agreed to help us."

"Who's 'we'? Why would you need our weapons when OmniLab has their own?"

Jakob sighed. "Just tell her and let's get the hell out of here. These tunnels smell weird."

Walter ignored him. "Only certain people have access to weapons, and they're strictly regulated. The Inner Circle is in control of the highest tiers of our government. We don't even have a voice amongst the High Council. It's time we forced a real change, and your people have agreed to give us the opportunity."

Aha. That explained why Pavel was so willing to help them. According to what Sergei had shared, Pavel didn't trust the Inner Circle's abilities.

She cocked her head and frowned. "You want us to help overthrow your government?"

Walter nodded. "It's been a long time coming. Between everyone living in this tower and your people, we far outnumber the Inner Circle. They'll have to step aside."

Valentina glanced back and forth between Walter and Jakob. "I've heard rumors about them. I don't know what's true."

"They have different abilities," Jakob began, his expression hardening. "They use them to control us. That's why this needs to be done. They need to know we're not defenseless."

She bit her lip and lowered her gaze slightly. "I don't know how I could help you. I only manage the inventory for the construction materials. If one of my people made this arrangement with you, would I get the weapons from them? Who would I need to contact?"

"Let's keep going," Walter began and motioned for her to keep walking. "Security might already be searching these tunnels, so we can't stay here. Let me take you to Charles. He can explain the rest to you. We already have a system in place to move the items into the towers. We just need someone to alter the inventory records so no one becomes suspicious. Pavel used to do it for us, but it's been held up since he disappeared. We'll be there soon. It's just a little farther now."

She nodded and turned back around, continuing to follow Jakob. At least some of their questions had been answered, but most likely, she'd need to speak directly with this Charles to find out which of their people was orchestrating this smuggling operation. Until she had that answer and Sergei was cleared from any involvement, his life would continue to be at risk.

———

VALENTINA CLIMBED down the ladder behind Jakob. Thankfully, his focus was on the ground below him, so she was in little danger of exposing the knives strapped to her inner thigh. Unfortunately, they were still in an area without surveillance, and she didn't have a way to let Yuri know where they'd taken her. She'd left her shoes behind as a marker, but the only other clothing she could risk removing was her panties. Even though she was quite creative, she couldn't think of a plausible explanation for slipping them off.

They'd gone down at least six levels, and she guessed they were probably near the main level, close to where one of the breezeways connected with the construction tower. Valentina stepped off the ladder and walked over to Jakob, who was studying another duct.

He turned around and gave her a sheepish smile. "Not your idea of the best first date, huh? I'll make it up to you. I swear it."

Valentina arched an eyebrow. He couldn't seriously be thinking he still had a chance of getting lucky, could he? Based on his cocky grin, he was. No way in hell was she parting with her panties now. It would only encourage him. With a sigh, she gestured to the duct. "How much farther?"

Walter approached from behind her. "We're almost there. Just stay close."

He bent down and unfastened the cover grate. Jakob went first and Valentina followed, tugging down on her dress as much as possible to keep her weapons concealed. Fortunately, Walter was busy moving the grate back into place and securing it once more.

The duct was short and stopped abruptly. Jakob crouched down in front of yet another grate, where she could make out a large room through the thin, metal slats. She sat beside him, curling her legs up underneath her. Walter crawled up to them a moment later and passed his utility tool to Jakob.

He pushed out the grate, holding on to it to keep it from falling. Valentina scooted the rest of the way out and stood, noting they were on the second floor of a huge warehouse. This location was even bigger than the distribution center. Most of the activity on the lower level appeared to be handled by robotics, their whirring and buzzing almost symphonic. A few surveillance cameras caught her attention, but their positioning probably prevented them from capturing them on their feed.

"It's quiet this time of night," Jakob whispered, placing his hand on her lower back. "Only a few people are here, and most of them are ours."

Valentina clenched her teeth. If his hand crept any lower, she'd cut it off. Making an effort to ignore him, she followed Walter across the walkway and over to a stairway on the opposite side of the warehouse. Apparently, he knew where the cameras were placed because he skillfully managed to bypass them.

They navigated their way through a maze of shelving units and robots until they came to a much smaller storage area. Valentina could make out the sound of voices from within, and she hoped this would be the elusive Charles.

Walter opened the door, and Valentina halted in her tracks, gaping at the man in front of her.

"Uncle Grigory?"

He spun around, ignoring the other three men he'd been speaking to. His expression was both shocked and downright pissed. "Valya, what the hell are you doing here?"

She glared at him. "I should be asking you the same question."

Walter's eyes narrowed. "You two know each other?"

"She's my niece," Grigory snapped. "And she shouldn't be here."

"You shouldn't either," she retorted, her temper starting

to spike. If Grigory had anything to do with supplying weapons to the towers, she'd strangle him herself.

An older man approached them and gestured toward her. "Walter, Jakob, how did this young lady come to join you?"

"I met her at a nightclub earlier tonight," Jakob began, warily eyeing her and Grigory. "She's taken over Pavel's position handling some of the inventory for the towers. I thought she might be a suitable replacement. Although, I thought her name was Valentina."

"Valya is a nickname, usually reserved for only close friends and family," she said, glaring at Grigory and seriously doubting whether he still fell into that category.

Grigory frowned at her and shook his head. Valentina paused for a moment, wondering if she might be misreading his presence. She hoped so, anyway. The thought of Grigory having a hand in these treasonous actions was unconscionable.

"I see," the older man murmured. "Is this true, Grigory? Is your niece handling the tower inventory?"

"In truth, I don't know what she does," Grigory admitted. "I saw her yesterday and encouraged her to get married and have some babies. Based on her current attire, I'm wondering now if she decided to take my advice."

Valentina glanced down at her dress and shrugged. For now, she'd play along and assume he was innocent. "You didn't specify *how* I should find a husband. I thought my options might be better in the towers. Unfortunately, things didn't quite go as planned. I seem to have stumbled into something."

Grigory's mouth twitched in a smile, and he nodded. "Indeed."

"I find it interesting your niece just *happened* to appear tonight," the other older man said, considering her and Grigory for a long moment. "Assuming this was a remarkable coincidence, her position may prove to be helpful. Tell me, young lady, do you feel like working with your uncle?"

Valentina took the opportunity to study him in return. He appeared to be somewhere in his late fifties, maybe a little older than Grigory. On the surface, he had a certain polish with his trim goatee and neat suit. But underneath, she detected a coldness within him that was unsettling. He didn't exactly emanate evil, but Valentina suspected something in his past had twisted him beyond most acceptable standards of morality.

Understanding the need to be careful how she handled him and the situation, she debated her options. Until she understood more about Grigory's role here, she couldn't count on him as an ally. She was vastly outnumbered, and it was impossible to know how far away Yuri was from the warehouse.

If his unbalanced stance was any indication, the older gentleman was carrying some sort of weapon. One of the other men with him was, too, but the third appeared unarmed. As far as she could tell, Grigory wasn't carrying, which wasn't necessarily a guarantee of his innocence. He could have been searched and his weapons confiscated before he entered this tower.

Crossing her arms over her chest and praying the comms were working, she said, "I'm not agreeing to anything. I've had a rough night. Walter pulled a gun on me, threatened me, dragged me halfway through the towers through service tunnels, and brought me to this warehouse. No one has bothered to tell me anything except you need someone to alter inventory records so you can smuggle contraband into the towers. They assured me someone named Charles would answer my questions." She paused and arched an eyebrow. "I'm assuming you're Charles?"

"You may call me that," he agreed, observing her a little

too critically for her taste. It was unlikely he'd respond to the damsel in distress routine or be taken in by her sex kitten persona. Dammit. She was going to have to adopt a new role.

"Your uncle here somehow got wind of our little trading operation. Supposedly, he wants a cut. We're having some problems verifying his identity though. Can you help with that?"

She frowned. "I don't know what to tell you. We've never worked in the same camp. Up until yesterday, I hadn't seen him for several years."

Grigory sighed. "It's like I told you. Ivan wants in on whatever deal you have going. We have no interest in your rebellion or plot to overthrow your government, but Ivan wants to run the new construction tower. We can help provide you with supplies, and in exchange, you make sure he's put into power when the time comes."

Valentina tried to keep her body relaxed, but her heart was hammering in her chest. She was starting to believe Ivan had instructed him to investigate the thefts. Although, she was very curious to learn how Grigory had found out about Charles.

Before she could say anything, a strange awareness filled her and she gasped. Kayla and Ariana once again swirled through her mind, but this time, there was something else. Thoughts, foreign and alien, filled her head, the chaotic brand of energy almost threatening to drown her with its weight. Her world tilted, and she reached outward, trying to stabilize herself.

The bond with Sergei, Nikolai, and Yuri surged wide open, shattering her earlier efforts to suppress them. Sergei's warm energy wrapped around her, and all three of them converged in her mind, grounding her and calming the tumultuous storm. She blinked open her eyes to peer into Grigory's worried face. She started to push herself up from the ground, but Grigory stopped her. "Shh, Valya. Are you all right? You lost consciousness for several minutes."

She frowned, shaken and alarmed. "Yes."

"She had a lot to drink earlier," Jakob volunteered, taking a step toward her.

Grigory arched an eyebrow at her, letting her know he didn't believe that. For whatever reason, though, he wasn't going to dispute Jakob's claims. Valentina merely nodded, willing to accept Jakob's excuse so she didn't have to invent her own.

"I'm not familiar with your drinks in the towers. They must have affected me more than I realized."

"Unlikely," Charles said, studying her thoughtfully. "You would have felt the effects long before now, and it doesn't explain your weapons."

Valentina inwardly cursed, trying to keep her body relaxed. She was still too shaken to play this game, but maybe her confusion would help lend believability in this situation.

Grigory looked up at the other man. "I explained that to you already. Most of our people are armed. A young, attractive woman alone in a strange place would be remiss in not carrying some sort of weapon on her."

"It doesn't explain how she managed to smuggle the knives into the towers or how she acquired such an expensive looking harness," Charles replied, holding up her thigh sheath. "OmniLab security would have scanned her for weapons before she entered our tower."

"No," she said softly, scrambling to come up with a plausible lie while Grigory helped her stand. She was still a little lightheaded, making her wonder if she'd hit her head. "They didn't search me. I wanted to visit the club I'd been hearing about, but I was worried about not being able to protect myself if there was a problem. I saw Ambassador Sergei's calendar and knew he was meeting someone in the Inner

Sanctum. I timed it so I could discuss some inventory lists with him and go through their entrance. He's allowed to carry weapons within the towers, so I wasn't searched either."

The slightest trace of a smile crossed Grigory's face. "Very industrious of you, Valya."

Charles's eyes narrowed. "How well do you know the Coalition's ambassador?"

Something in his tone caught her attention, and she frowned. "Up until a week ago, the last time I saw him was three years ago. So, as well as can be expected."

"Your hair color is very distinctive. So are your eyes. Someone matching your description was seen going into his private quarters a few days ago."

"Of course I went into his quarters," she argued, letting a trace of her temper filter through. "I've been handling the inventory for the construction tower. Sergei keeps his notes and instructions for me on his desk or in his office. He did the same with Pavel."

Charles nodded. "That would make sense, but it doesn't explain why you were taken to a medical ward a week ago for treatment. Nor does it explain why the Inner Circle, including Alec Tal'Vayr and Ariana Alivette, has such an interest in you. A security officer also reported seeing you in their offices with the Coalition's ambassador this morning while he was conducting some interviews."

Fuck. Valentina tensed, her heart hammering in her chest. Walter withdrew his weapon and pointed it at her. "Still think someone who looks like her would be interested in you, Jakob?"

"Fuck off," Jakob muttered, crossing his arms over his chest.

Grigory moved to stand in front of her and held up his hands. "I don't know what you're accusing my niece of being involved in, but she was injured when one of those Inner

Circle members was taken captive. They brought her back to the towers for treatment. If she's working that closely with Sergei doing inventory, it makes sense she would have accompanied him to various locations."

"We're better informed than you give us credit," Charles said, the chill in his voice leeching the warmth from the room. "I happen to know she arrived here again after the Coalition's ambassador was shot. I heard she was more than a little distraught. One of the medics mentioned she works closely with one of your leaders."

Valentina frowned. Charles had already convinced himself she wasn't who she claimed, so there wasn't much point in protesting. The situation might still be able to be salvaged though. Straightening her posture, she moved to stand beside Grigory.

"You're right, but so is Grigory. We were both equally surprised to see each other tonight. I don't know why he's here, but my original purpose in coming to the towers was for medical treatment. I returned here again because supply shipments are being stolen from my people and being sent to the towers. I have no interest in your rebellion or your purpose here in the towers. My only intention is to locate those supplies so my people don't continue to suffer. In addition to weapons, we're also missing food and medical supplies."

"I'm afraid that's going to be something of a problem," Charles said, taking a step toward her. "You see, we have no intention of returning your supplies. But aside from that, I happen to know you're lying. You're an Inner Circle bitch, just like the rest." Without another word, he pulled out one of the Coalition's weapons and fired at her twice.

Valentina staggered, falling backward onto the ground. It felt like a metal pipe had slammed into her stomach. Burning pain seared through her a moment later, and she winced, clutching her stomach. It wasn't the first time she'd been shot, but it still hurt like a bitch. At least Charles had bad aim. As painful as being shot in the gut might be, it took longer to die from such an injury.

"Valya!" Grigory shouted, dropping down beside her and pressing his hands against her midsection.

Valentina cursed and pushed him away, needing to focus on the others. Bleeding out slowly was preferable to allowing herself to be executed. Charles was stalking toward her, his stance telegraphing his intention to fire at her again. She'd never survive at this range.

Grabbing Yuri's energy threads, she whipped the gun out of Charles's hand. It slid along the floor toward her. She snatched it up, gripping it tightly, and fired at Walter just as he pulled the trigger on his weapon. The bullet ricocheted off the floor near where she was still lying but missed hitting her. Walter's weapon clattered to the ground and he collapsed, either dead or dying from a fatal shot. Either way, he was no longer an issue.

"Valya, ten o'clock!" Grigory yelled.

Valentina turned and fired at the other man who was starting to draw his gun. It hit its mark, executing him. With this many potential threats, she couldn't risk simply wounding him.

Jakob turned and ran, and Valentina fired a shot in the back of his leg. He yelped, falling to the ground, howling with pain as he clutched his thigh. She couldn't risk him escaping and bringing back more people.

Grigory pushed off the ground and reached down to pull her up to a standing position. The pain in her abdomen was a sharp, burning pain, but she ignored it and trained the gun on Charles. "Interlace your fingers on your head. Now."

Charles glared at her but made no move to follow her instructions. "You'll need to kill me first."

He reached down to make a grab for Walter's abandoned

weapon, and Valentina shot his hand. Blood spurted from the wound, but he tried to grab it with his other hand. Valentina advanced, firing again into that one. With a wordless scream, he rushed her.

She narrowed her eyes, firing into his kneecap. He collapsed on the ground, wailing in agony. The other unknown man dove for the weapon, but she shot him too.

"Bastard," Valentina muttered, pressing her hand against her stomach. She was starting to feel lightheaded and had the suspicion the bullets had done far more damage than she'd first realized. The gun fell out of her hand, clattering to the floor. It was just as well. She'd used up all the ammunition in the chamber.

Grigory secured the weapon near Charles, and then walked back over to pick up her empty one. Wincing, she stumbled over to her knives and tried to bend over to pick them up. The movement was too much, and she pitched to the side, hitting the ground hard.

Grigory dropped the weapons beside her and pressed his hand against her abdomen. "Stop moving, Valya. You're just making it worse. Do you have a commlink? They confiscated mine before they brought me to this location."

"No," she managed, wincing and reaching into the front of her dress to pull out the microphone she'd hidden earlier that evening. She opened her hand to show Grigory and said, "One-way only. Yuri is almost here. Nikolai is... on his way."

Grigory took the microphone and spoke into it, "Nikolai, she's taken two shots to the abdomen. One exit hole. She's already lost a lot of blood." He glanced around the warehouse area. "We're on the lower level of a two-story warehouse somewhere off the construction tower breezeway. If you have access to Sergei, tell him we need a medic here immediately."

She grabbed Grigory's arm. "Don't... don't let Sergei know how bad it is."

Grigory frowned. "Forgive me, Valya, but if Sergei can get a medic to you in time, I don't give a damn what he knows or doesn't."

She blinked up at him, part of her wishing she'd hurry up and pass out so the pain would lessen. That was one thing they never told you about being shot: it took way too long to lose consciousness. "Why are you here?"

"Stay quiet and I'll tell you," he ordered, glancing over at the two other men who were injured and wailing. "At least Nikolai will be able to find us quickly with all that noise. It figures, the only woman here and you're the only one not making a fuss."

She managed a pained smile. Grigory sighed and said, "I saw your face when you first walked in. You thought for a moment I'd possibly betrayed our people. I haven't. I told you yesterday that Ivan's shipments have been going missing. I reached out to Peter and found out some of his supplies have also disappeared."

She nodded and squeezed her eyes shut. "I heard that."

"Shh. You promised to stay quiet."

When she fell silent again, he continued, "All signs pointed to Sergei, but I don't believe that to be true. He's a bit of a bastard, but he's too honorable to steal from his own people."

"It's not him," she whispered. The pain was beginning to lessen, which wasn't a good sign. The cold chill within her was growing stronger.

Through their bond, she could feel Sergei and Yuri nearby. They were almost there. Nikolai was rapidly heading toward her too, but she didn't know if he'd make it there in time. She reached out to them psychically, embracing them with her energy one last time before slipping into darkness.

———

TERROR FLOODED through him when he felt Valentina slip away from him. Sergei shouted her name, running in the direction where her energy had originated. A maze of crates towered in front of him, and he shoved them aside with a fire blast, intent on his destination. He had to reach her before it was too late.

He ran around the corner to witness a grisly sight. Blood was everywhere, covering the floor and splattered on some of the crates, the overhead lights making it appear more black than red. Two men lay on the floor whimpering in agony, while three more lay still. But Sergei only had eyes for the woman on the ground.

"Valechka," he whispered, dropping to the floor and pulling her into his arms. She was so cold. Her skin was normally cool compared to his, but there was an unnatural iciness that should never be allowed to touch her. Pouring his fire energy into her, he tried to eliminate the frozen chill from threatening to steal her away. He couldn't lose her. Not like this.

Lars pulled out his gun and held it on the two injured men, making sure they remained secure. Sergei barely spared him a glance, trusting him to do whatever was necessary. If not, well, he'd deal with them soon enough.

Valentina murmured his name, and his heart thudded in his chest, threatening to break free of its restraints. His fire energy sparked, and he struggled to focus it on her to continue chasing away the chill. "You must stay with me, little dove. Can you open your eyes?"

Blue eyes fluttered open, but they were filled with so much pain. If he could trade places with her right now, he'd do it in a heartbeat. He'd give anything for her to keep breathing. From almost the moment he'd first met her, he'd wanted her. She'd captured his heart—all their hearts—within days after that. She was the one person in this world he'd sacrifice everything for.

Valentina started to reach for him, but her hand fell back to the ground as though she couldn't manage the effort.

Yuri knelt beside her, his face equally stricken, and took her hand in his. "Valya, we need you to hold on just a little longer. Ariana and a medical team are on their way. Nikolai is bringing them."

She nodded, and her eyes closed again.

"One of the bullets passed through," Grigory said, keeping his hands tightly against her abdomen to staunch the bleeding. Yuri pulled off his shirt and rolled her on her side to press it underneath her. Sergei fought against his growing panic. Dammit. She'd already lost too much blood, and that didn't account for the internal damage.

"You must stay awake, little dove," he urged, holding her close. "If you do, it's your turn to choose. I'll tell you one secret or grant one favor."

Valentina managed a small smile, but he could tell the effort cost her. "I don't think I like this game anymore, Seryozha."

"Me neither," he whispered, surrounding her with his heated fire energy in a gentle embrace. "After this, we're going to stop playing it. But in the meantime, it's still your choice. I need you to keep talking to me."

"A secret then," she whispered.

Sergei brushed her hair away from her face, debating what to tell her. There was one thing, but it might not go well for him later. It would be enough to get a reaction from her, though, and that's what he needed to keep her awake. Although, if he lost her... He swallowed, unable to consider the possibility.

"I intend to marry you, Valechka," he began, watching as she blinked up at him with confusion in her eyes. "Three years ago, before we launched our offensive on the last facility, I told Nikolai I planned to persuade you. He asked me to wait until after we returned. He suspected you'd take it poorly, and we weren't sure I'd have enough time to heal from any injuries you might inflict if I pushed you. I agreed to wait and have regretted it ever since. I should have made you mine back then."

He trailed his fingers over her cheek, accompanying the gesture with his energy. He'd broached the subject of marriage once before, years ago, but she'd avoided the conversation and slipped away before he could pin her down.

Sergei suspected she was worried about how it would affect their bond and relationships with each other. That's why he'd gone to Nikolai in the first place. Nikolai had agreed with his assessment, but like so many other things with Valentina, it would take perseverance and patience to convince her. But nothing worth having was ever easy, least of all the woman he loved.

Yuri pulled out his commlink again and spoke urgently into it, most likely to Nikolai. Sergei needed to focus on keeping Valentina awake and talking. Looking down at her again, he said, "Shall I try to persuade you now, little dove? I don't believe you have the strength to lift a knife or run from me this time."

"You're cheating again," she whispered.

He smiled and leaned forward, pressing a light kiss against her lips. "There have never been any rules between us. Even if there were, I would break all of them to keep you."

"I'm cold, Seryozha," she said, her voice growing fainter.

Sergei tensed, amplifying his energy output to try to stabilize her. He lifted his head and snapped, "Where the fuck is the medic?"

"A few minutes out," Yuri retorted, placing the commlink

beside him to better hold the compress in place against her back. "Hang on, Valya. Nikolai and Ariana are almost here."

He looked down at Valentina again, but she was unconscious. Their time was running out. Sergei cursed, his arms tensing around her. Grigory was still applying pressure to her midsection, but it wasn't enough. She wasn't responding to his energy output anymore.

Panic flooded through him, and several nearby crates burst into flames. Grigory stared at the fire in shock before looking at him. Sergei took a deep breath, once again focusing on keeping his chaotic energy directed toward Valentina and willing her to respond. A hissing noise came out of the mounted fire suppression equipment mounted on the ceiling and a moment later, foaming fire retardant was ejected over the area.

Yuri grabbed his commlink and spoke briskly into it. "Tell them to get someone down here now, Nikolai. We're losing her."

Yuri pressed his fingers against Valentina's neck, feeling for a pulse. Sergei frowned as a strange awareness went through him. When Yuri pulled his hand away, it disappeared.

Sergei's gaze flew up to meet Yuri's eyes. "Touch her again."

Yuri did so immediately, and they both stared at each other. Sergei sent his energy into Valentina, and Yuri did the same. Somehow, she was acting as a conduit. He'd never been able to sense Yuri before, but he could now. But more importantly, he could feel Valentina's energy beginning to rise to the surface. Whatever they were doing was helping to stabilize her. It might buy her a little more time.

"Nikolai," Yuri spoke into the commlink, holding it to his ear with his other hand. "I need you to focus on Valya." He paused and said, "Yes. Do it."

Sergei tensed as Nikolai's energy flooded through their

connection. It wasn't as strong, but that was most likely because he wasn't touching her.

Footsteps sounded behind them a moment later. Sergei turned his head to see Nikolai racing into the room with Brant right behind him. Kayla, Ariana, and Alec were with them, along with a host of other personnel.

Nikolai dropped to his knees beside Valentina and reached over to touch her arm. Awareness surged through Sergei the moment Nikolai's hand came into contact with her again. The last time they'd all touched Valentina with their bond wide open had been when they'd formed their connection. They stared at each other for several heartbeats and simultaneously began sending their energy into her.

Ariana sank to the ground beside them. "I can feel all of you. Keep doing whatever you're doing. It's helping her." She looked over at Grigory. "Remove your hands, please. I need to take over."

Grigory hesitated for a fraction of a second before moving away. Ariana placed her hands over Valentina's abdomen and closed her eyes. Sergei watched Ariana's healing energy, so similar to Valentina's, as it enveloped the woman he loved. The High Council leader reached over and placed his hand on Ariana's shoulder, and Sergei knew the minute Alec's energy flowed into the mix, strengthening Ariana's already remarkable power.

Alec's eyes widened, and he frowned at them. "How is this possible? It's almost as though Valentina's bonded to Ariana."

Kayla held up a strange, green figurine. "It happened earlier, too, and I think it's because of this. It's tied to all three of us somehow."

Ariana looked up at Kayla. "Place the dragon on her skin and touch her, Kayla. Keep one hand on the statue. She has too much damage, and I can't heal her fast enough. I think the dragon will help connect all our power together."

Kayla cocked her head. "Um... You're glowing, Ari."

Sergei turned to look at Ariana, and his eyes widened. An aura of gold light was emanating from the healer, and Valentina too.

Ariana nodded. "I know. Use the dragon, Kayla. Hurry."

Kayla dropped to her knees and did as she was instructed. Ariana reached out, keeping one hand on Valentina's abdomen, and touched the figurine with the other. The same light surrounded all three women and encompassed the dragon figurine.

Sergei looked down at Valentina in his arms. The glow surrounded him as well, at least the part of him that was touching her. He glanced over to find it wasn't affecting any of the men the same way as it was affecting the women though. The dragon statue, on the other hand, no longer appeared green, but was now an iridescent gold—the same color as the aura around them.

Sergei was dimly aware of the gasps of surprise from the security team and everyone else, but he was too busy focusing on Valentina and the power building within the room. A moment later, Valentina's eyes fluttered open. Relief flooded through him, and he tightened his arms around her.

"Valechka," he murmured, searching her face. Her eyes were still somewhat unfocused, but she was awake. Her energy was stronger too.

Nikolai frowned. "Her injury isn't healing."

Sergei looked down at her abdomen. He could see *something* happening, but he didn't know what. Nikolai was right. She wasn't healing. Or at least, they couldn't see what was being healed.

"Can you hear it?" Valentina whispered, her voice strained with pain.

Yuri nodded. "I do, Valya, but I don't understand it."

Sergei frowned and glanced around at everyone else.

Ariana and Kayla were concentrating on something with their eyes closed.

"What do you hear, Valechka?" Sergei urged, wanting her to keep talking.

"Listen, Seryozha. You too, Kolya," she said softly. Her eyes fluttered closed again, but her cool water energy embraced him once more and extinguished the threat of the flames. A moment later, he heard—or rather, felt—something else within their bond. It was a type of sound, but the resonance was different from anything he'd ever heard before. He couldn't even call it a sound.

It was a vibration, for lack of a better description. He closed his eyes to better concentrate and was immersed in different colors. They pulsated in a rhythmic dance that resonated within him but was beyond his understanding. It was strangely familiar, though he couldn't place it.

Somehow, through Valentina, he could sense everyone around her. He was most aware of Nikolai and Yuri's presence, understanding intuitively they were just as aware of him. Valentina was reaching out to them with her energy, and they were channeling theirs toward her in return. Ariana and Kayla, however, were just as potent as Valentina but slightly different. Now that he was more focused on the energy, he noticed they all shared the same gold aura but with slight variations in color. Together, the sight was almost blinding.

"Excuse me, Master Tal'Vayr," someone spoke from behind them. "We're getting reports of a strong electrical storm happening outside the towers. The elements are all going haywire—rain, lightning, dark clouds, and high winds. The towers are issuing an alert right now."

"It's not just there," Carl said from off to the side. "The river's rising and flooding the cavern. I just got an urgent message from our people there. They're evacuating right now."

A second later, Sergei's commlink began vibrating in his pocket. He frowned, suspicion growing in his mind that whatever was happening between these three women was tied to the strange phenomenon outside the towers. He withdrew his commlink, careful not to jostle Valentina. The message was from one of his men in the construction tower.

"We've lost contact with some of our outlying camps. Before communication was disconnected, they reported a possible earthquake," he said and focused on Valentina again. He couldn't tell if her injury had healed yet because her body was swathed in that gold light.

"Valya," Nikolai said, his voice worried. "Our people are in trouble."

She took a deep breath, and the light surrounding the three women immediately dimmed. The dragon figurine, however, retained that unearthly golden light. Valentina's eyes opened again, but this time, they held concerned look. "Our people? What's happened?"

Ariana pulled her hands away, blinking in confusion. Sergei looked down at Valentina's abdomen and there wasn't even a trace of a scar.

Nikolai's expression was equally shocked. He laid his hand over her abdomen, careful not to touch the dragon figurine, and said, "How do you feel, Valya?"

She frowned and tried to sit up. Sergei helped her, watching her carefully. She shook her head, looking down at the dragon figurine that had tumbled into her lap. It still retained that strange gold coloring. "I... I don't know. I don't hurt, but I feel different somehow."

Ariana bit her lip. "I didn't heal you. At least, not completely. I'm not sure what we just experienced, but something happened. To all of us. It's tied to that statue."

Kayla curled her fingers into fists. "You're freaking me out a little bit. If you don't know what just happened and you're supposed to be the expert, we're probably pretty much fucked."

Alec pulled Ariana up and into his arms. "I've never seen or felt anything like that before either. May I see that dragon statue?"

Kayla shook her head and crossed her arms over her chest "Hell no. It doesn't want to go to you." At Alec's puzzled expression, Kayla waved off his confusion. "Look, don't ask how I know. I can't explain it. But that dragon wants to stay with Valentina. It'll go to me or Ariana, but it *really* likes *her*."

"We should check the archives," Ariana suggested. "There's got to be some record somewhere of what just happened. We need to find out more about the dragon figurine."

Carl frowned. "Kayla, that was the one you found in the ruins, right?"

Kayla nodded. "Yeah. Although, it's not so green now."

Valentina cradled the statue in her hands and closed her eyes. In a soft voice, she said, "If I listen closely, I can still hear it. It's quieter though." She opened her eyes again. "Are our people all right, Kolya?"

Nikolai pulled out his commlink to contact his camp. Sergei pulled out his communication device too and angled the screen so she could see it. Valentina curled up against him as he typed in a message asking for the current status of the situation outside the towers. A response came in almost immediately that everything appeared to have calmed down. They were running an analysis on all systems to check for damage and would keep him advised.

Nikolai closed his commlink. "Everything appears stable again in my camp."

Alec kept his arms around Ariana and looked over at one of the men who had accompanied them. "What's the status of the storm outside?"

"It's gone, Master Tal'Vayr. The sky cleared up almost immediately. Everything is normal again."

Alec looked over at Carl. "What about the river?"

Carl frowned, studying the screen on his commlink. "Our people down there are out of danger, but the water level is still high. They've had to evacuate the area, and one of the nearby buildings collapsed. Hopefully, the water will recede soon. Until then, everything is at a standstill. They're running a stability check now on the other ruins in the area."

Sergei kissed her. "Will you agree to allow the medical personnel to check you out?"

When she frowned, Nikolai gave her a sharp look. "Valya, do not argue on this. There was only one exit wound. We do not know how much internal damage was caused, and the bullet needs to be extracted."

"I'll go to the medical ward," she agreed.

Yuri stood and held out his hand to help her up. He wrapped his arm around her and pressed a kiss against her hair. "Get checked out and then you can deal with Sergei's latest secret. You need to be healthy to keep him in his place. Or you'll end up married and having his babies before you know it."

Valentina froze, turning around to narrow her eyes on him. Sergei glared at Yuri who was smirking at him safely behind Valentina. She put her hands on her hips, those gorgeous blue eyes filled with temper. God, she was beautiful... and absolutely irresistible. He'd gladly take her ire over seeing her in pain any day.

"You intended to *persuade* me? Waiting until I'm bleeding out on the floor?" she demanded, tapping her foot in irritation.

Taking a step toward her, he gave her a disarming smile. "Come now, Valechka. You cannot blame me for trying."

She jabbed her finger against his chest. "I most certainly can. That was cheating, Seryozha."

He grabbed her finger and wrapped his other arm around her waist. Pressing a kiss against her lips, he said, "I intend to resort to as many devious tricks as necessary until you agree. I love you, little dove."

She softened against him and looked up into his eyes. The tenderness and love in her expression made his heart skip a beat, and he pulled her closer. He loved this woman beyond all reason, and it terrified him how close he'd come to losing her again.

The culprits still needed to be dealt with, and he intended to make them suffer a thousandfold for every moment of pain they'd inflicted on her. Sergei glanced over at Nikolai, catching sight of the medics working on the two people on the ground. "Nikolai, why don't you escort Valentina to the medical center?"

Her eyes narrowed, but before she could object, Nikolai put his arm around her and pulled her away. Brushing a kiss against her temple, he said, "Please, Valya. It would make me feel better if you allowed me to go with you."

Valentina scowled. "You're all manipulating me."

Yuri chuckled and picked up her knives. He offered them to her and said, "Get checked out. Otherwise, you won't be able to keep any of us in line."

She snatched her weapons from him. "Fine. But don't kill them yet, Sergei. They have information we need."

Sergei made a noncommittal noise, staring at the two men. He wouldn't make any promises. They'd hurt the woman he loved and had nearly taken her from him. Even if he left them alive, by the time he was finished, they'd wish they weren't.

Yuri glanced over at him and grinned. "I'm staying too."

He nodded. "I had a feeling you might."

CHAPTER NINE

VALENTINA DIDN'T bother to look back. Sergei and Yuri would do what they must, and she suspected Lars would intervene with OmniLab on their behalf. But quite honestly, she didn't care. If Charles or Jakob knew who was responsible for providing them with weapons, Sergei and Yuri would find out.

Ariana and Alec approached them, along with Kayla and Carl. Ariana smiled and said, "I'll go with you. If there's any additional damage, I can heal the remainder without surgical interference. If the bullet is still embedded somewhere, Alec may be able to help remove it."

Nikolai put his arm around her waist, and Valentina leaned against him.

Grigory walked over to her and said, "I would like to accompany you, if you don't mind."

Nikolai frowned and glanced at her. "Valya?"

"Please, Uncle Grigory. Come with us. I'd like to speak with you about what happened and why you're here."

Alec's eyebrows rose. "Uncle?"

"Not by blood," Grigory said and fell into step beside her.

Valentina glanced down at the gold dragon in her hand. "You weren't surprised when I pulled Charles's weapon out of his hand. How long have you known about me?"

"I only suspected until now," he said quietly. "I knew your parents for a number of years, Valya. They were discreet, but you can't be in a unit for long without knowing every detail about another person. That's one of the reasons I tried to keep track of you, but you managed to hide your abilities well. I'm assuming your grandmother warned you against the dangers of being discovered."

"Yes," she admitted. "Then Ivan knows as well?"

Nikolai tensed beside her, and she couldn't blame him. Nikolai and Ivan weren't at odds, but they weren't allies either. Ivan and her parents had been in the same unit together years before she was born, but Grigory had always remained closer to her family. Several years after her parents had died, Ivan had been awarded his current leadership position.

Grigory sighed and nodded. "Yes. Ivan would have offered you a place within one of his camps, but we knew you were loyal to Nikolai. Years ago, Ivan and I promised your parents we would look after you and Nadiya if anything ever happened to them. You've always been independent though. We respected that and decided to keep our distance."

Now it was her turn to stiffen at the mention of her sister. Valentina darted a glance at Alec, and he was regarding her with a question in his eyes. With a sigh, she said, "Yes, Alec. Nadiya is my sister. She's an energy channeler, too, but she was too young to come into her abilities when I left. My grandmother would have taught her the same restraint she taught me." She paused and looked over at Grigory again. "That's why Nadiya is sworn to Ivan's service and not in your camp?"

"Yes," Grigory replied with a frown. "She was safer

remaining in one of his other locations. Otherwise, she would have needed to travel with me to areas that were more dangerous. I know she'd like to see you again. She misses you and asks after you often."

Lowering her gaze, Valentina nodded. She had avoided reaching out to her sister for years. If people believed the two of them were close, they could try to use Nadiya against her or Nikolai. It had pained her to do it, but it was necessary to put distance between them. "I miss her too. Thank you for keeping her safe."

"I would do the same for you, if you would let me."

Nikolai trailed his thumb along her side in an agitated gesture. She leaned against him again and said, "I appreciate that, Uncle. But I won't leave Nikolai, Yuri, or Sergei."

Grigory nodded. "I didn't make the offer before now because of that reason." He paused, darting another glance at her. "Although, until today, I thought you and Sergei had broken ties."

"They've been mended," she said with a shrug, not willing to explain everything that had happened.

All of them entered the priority elevator, and Alec programmed it to take them to the medical ward. Grigory stared out the glass wall, which overlooked an expansive gardenscape, complete with a cascading waterfall. He watched it for a long moment and then said, "A fire broke out in the warehouse when you lost consciousness."

Valentina started to stiffen but forced her body to remain relaxed. She hadn't been aware, but she wasn't surprised. Sergei had gotten much better with his control, but the circumstances today had sorely taxed his limited training.

"Perhaps there were some combustible materials nearby," Nikolai mused, staring overhead at the floor indicator screen. "A weapon misfire could have triggered something."

Valentina sent a wave of thankful energy toward Nikolai.

The accidental fire in the last facility wasn't public knowledge. If people believed Sergei had caused it with supernatural abilities, the result could prove to be disastrous. Nikolai had covered for him then, too, claiming it was an effort to expedite the surrender of the residents within the facility.

"Perhaps," Grigory agreed with a small smile. "Although, the same thing tended to happen whenever your mother was injured. Your father didn't take it well either. Ivan and I became quite accustomed to putting out fires caused by... misfiring weapons."

Everyone's gaze flew toward Grigory.

"Holy shit," Kayla said and snickered. "It's nice to know I'm not the only one with impulse control problems when someone they love is in danger."

"I think a fire is a little easier to contain than one of your earthquakes," Carl said, pulling her closer.

"You're probably right," Kayla said with a grin. "But Sergei's always giving me shit about training. It's nice to know I'm not the only one who needs it."

Nikolai frowned. "What do you intend to do with this knowledge, Grigory?"

Grigory's eyes softened, and he smiled at Valentina. "Nothing. I won't betray your secret, Valya. Your parents saved my life more times than I can count." He glanced over at Nikolai. "Although, I am curious about you and Yuri. Something was happening with you two."

Valentina stiffened. "Sergei and I have powers, yes. But Nikolai and Yuri have been my brothers for over ten years, Grigory. Just like you were close with my parents, they are also my family. I don't know what you suspect or believe you witnessed, but Nikolai brought me here so I could learn more about my abilities."

She lifted her chin, daring him to contradict her. She might agree to let him know about her talents, and even

Sergei's powers since he'd witnessed such a thing, but hundreds of lives depended on Nikolai retaining his position.

"I see," Grigory murmured. "I won't ask any questions, but I want you both to know you can trust my discretion. I agreed to operate a camp under Sergei's command in the hopes I might learn more about OmniLab's abilities. I wanted to know if they were similar to the talents your parents possessed. Once Sergei helped form an alliance with them, Ivan moved into this area too. We were planning to bring your sister here once things settled down. Our goal was to make sure she had a place within the new tower if they proved to be likeminded people who would embrace her skills."

The elevator opened, and they all filed out. Alec led the way down the hall to the medical ward and showed them into one of the empty rooms. Kayla and Carl agreed to wait outside while the doctor conducted an examination.

Ariana motioned for Valentina to sit on the bed. "Alec will be right back with a doctor. Why don't you go ahead and lie down? I can do a preliminary evaluation while we're waiting."

She nodded and laid back, and Ariana placed her hands over her abdomen. Valentina paid careful attention to how Ariana was using her healing ability to assess for damage. It was fairly straightforward, and Valentina suspected she could duplicate the process if necessary.

Nikolai turned to Grigory. "Perhaps you should explain why you're here in the towers."

"I find your presence here curious too, Nikolai," Grigory said, watching Ariana standing over Valentina.

"Uncle, I've heard a friend is often found in times of misfortune," Valentina said, quoting an old, pre-war proverb and one of her late father's favorite sayings. "I know you weren't responsible for the missing weapons, but if we're going to get to the bottom of this, we need to work together."

Grigory's mouth curved upward. "You're correct, darling girl. Very well. Ask your questions. I will share with you what I know."

Alec came back into the room with the doctor. Valentina studied the woman, but she didn't see the translation device. Alec was still wearing one, but she wouldn't object to him overhearing this conversation.

Switching to her native language, she asked, "How did you come to meet with Charles?"

Alec's gaze flew to her, and she gave him a small smile and tapped her ear to let him know she knew. Grigory arched a brow and said, "Interesting. I see you've made allies for yourself, haven't you?"

"They've agreed to keep my secret and train me," she said, watching as Ariana moved away and the doctor began running a scanner over her midsection. Valentina gestured to Alec. "This is Alec Tal'Vayr, leader of the High Council."

Grigory gave him a brief nod in acknowledgment before focusing again on her. "I'll share with you what I can, but some things need to wait until we're alone."

Valentina nodded. If she were in his position, she'd do the same.

"When you showed up in Ivan's camp yesterday, I mentioned he's had shipments go missing. However, what I didn't tell you is that we intentionally allowed another smaller delivery to disappear... but we made some slight adjustments first."

Her eyes widened. "You set a trap."

"Clever," Nikolai murmured.

Grigory nodded. "We attempted it, but I'm afraid it didn't exactly work out. We confirmed Pavel was the one moving the supplies into the towers, but we didn't know who else was responsible. Unfortunately, Sergei killed Pavel before he could be questioned."

"That's why you suspected Sergei's possible involvement," she guessed.

"Ivan did, yes," Grigory agreed. "I've had more opportunities to work with Sergei. I had difficulties believing he could have been close to you for so many years and been that type of man. I didn't know why you had a falling out, but I had my doubts about his involvement."

The scanner beeped, and Valentina looked over at the doctor, who was frowning.

Nikolai took a step forward. "Is she all right?"

The doctor hesitated, glancing at everyone in the room before turning back to her. "You were shot?"

Valentina nodded. "Yes. Twice."

Nikolai moved to stand beside her and took her hand. "There was only one exit wound."

The doctor glanced over at Ariana. "I know you're skilled, but I can't find any trace of an injury. If she weren't covered in blood, I would have doubts she'd ever been injured."

Nikolai ran his thumb over the back of her hand. "There's no bullet?"

"No. There's nothing."

Valentina frowned. "Where could it have gone?"

"With your permission, I'd like to do a more thorough scan," the doctor suggested. "It may be that it's lodged in an area not displaying on my handheld scanner. We can give you a mild sedative first. The more intensive scanner can be slightly uncomfortable."

Valentina frowned as the doctor headed out of the room, presumably to set up the scan. Other than being tired, she felt fine. If they needed to sedate her for this test, she wasn't interested in having it done. "I don't believe a scan will be necessary."

"Valya," Nikolai began, his expression growing concerned, "perhaps it would be for the best. I don't want to risk anything happening to you."

Valentina turned toward Ariana. "Can you detect foreign materials?"

Ariana hesitated. "Usually, yes. I was trying to check before the doctor came in, but I didn't sense anything either. It's possible I'm not picking up on it for some reason."

"Did it melt?"

Valentina looked over at Grigory, surprised by his question. "What? What are you suggesting?"

Grigory shrugged. "Your father could melt metal. If Sergei was generating enough heat to cause a fire in the warehouse, he may have melted the bullet."

"That would have caused a great deal of damage to Valentina," Nikolai said with a frown.

Ariana shook her head and smiled. "No, not to her. Sergei would never hurt her, even accidentally. Even if he didn't realize what he was doing, he subconsciously would have taken care to only affect the bullet while keeping the rest of her from harm."

"I've never heard of such a thing," Alec said with a frown. "It's possible, especially since they're mates. We don't usually use lethal weapons within the towers, so our experiences are somewhat limited."

Ariana nodded. "I'm inclined to believe she's fine. And I have to agree with her. I don't think a full scan is necessary. Other than picking up her exhaustion, I don't sense anything else wrong. But I can stop by Lars's quarters to check on her in a few hours, or have one of the medics do it, if it makes you feel better."

Nikolai ran his thumb over Valentina's hand. "Yes. Thank you. I'd rather not take any chances."

Ariana smiled. "Valentina, if you want to shower and clean

up, you can use the facilities here in the medical ward. I can have someone bring you a change of clothes."

"No. I appreciate the offer, but I'll shower when I get back to my room."

Valentina climbed off the table, stretching her body to check for any twinges. There was nothing, and it only reaffirmed her belief. She bent down to reattach her thigh holster, immediately feeling better by the comforting weight of her weapons.

When she straightened, she noticed Grigory watching her thoughtfully. Part of her was curious why he had never shared information about her parents' abilities before now, but she suspected it most likely had to do with the fact she'd kept her talents a secret. If she'd never given him any cause to suspect, it made sense he wouldn't volunteer the information.

"You want to ask me something?" he prompted.

Valentina hesitated. She wanted to know more about her parents, but such things could wait for another time. While he was here, they needed to focus on the stolen supplies. "If you knew enough to use one of Ivan's shipments to set a trap, he must have had others go missing."

Grigory nodded. "Yes, two others disappeared. This would have been the third."

"We've lost two," Nikolai admitted with a frown. "Peter's claimed to have lost some too."

"Yes. I've heard that, but I believe Peter's under the impression Sergei is responsible."

Valentina picked up the dragon carving and absently ran her fingers over the curves of its wings. "I met with Viktor, Peter's second-in-command, a few days ago here in the towers. He mentioned Peter's hoping to take control of the new tower. He's made a bid to have Sergei removed as ambassador. I can't help but wonder if he could be the one responsible for framing Sergei."

Grigory rubbed his chin. "It's possible, but I don't see Peter as the type of man who would provide arms to Omni-Lab's residents. He wouldn't want to risk alienating a potential ally. However, if his goal is to control OmniLab, toppling its current regime might make sense. It's much easier to wrest control away from people if they're experiencing open rebellion."

Grigory looked over at Alec and added, "You've made it clear certain items cannot enter into your towers. Most of us respect that decision, with the exception of a few rogue agents. I apologize for entering your towers under this subterfuge, but we need to ascertain the identity of the individuals responsible."

Alec nodded. "I appreciate your efforts in trying to trace down the source of the problem. You're welcome to conduct your investigations, but I would ask you contact me personally if you need to access certain areas of the towers. I can keep your presence quiet, but this will help avoid any future incidents."

Grigory nodded.

Valentina looked down at the dragon statue again, turning over everything in her mind. "Who has a vendetta against Sergei? Someone is obviously framing him, but why? Other than his position as ambassador, what hope would someone have to gain in discrediting him?"

"Perhaps you should ask Sergei that question," Grigory suggested.

"We will," Nikolai agreed, resting his hand against her back. "But I'm curious about something else. Valentina mentioned she saw Lena at Ivan's camp yesterday. Do you know if she's had shipments go missing?"

Grigory hesitated. "She claims some have disappeared, yes. All the leaders in the area are claiming that."

Valentina tilted her head. "You don't believe her?"

The older man sighed. "I don't know. The only one I'm absolutely sure of is Ivan." He glanced over at Nikolai and added, "With all due respect, I don't know you very well, and there was some question about your involvement until now. It was suggested you might have an interest in framing Sergei for a possible rebellion. That's why I didn't tell Valya all of this sooner."

"I assumed as much," Nikolai said.

Valentina frowned. "Nikolai has supported Sergei's efforts here publicly, even against some of our other leaders."

Grigory smiled. "Yes, he has. But if you look at it from a more personal standpoint, Sergei's sudden split from your group was quite surprising. Shortly after that, rumors began spreading about you and Nikolai. It was safe to assume there were some tensions between all of you." He paused for a moment. "Matters of the heart can cause people to do unexpected things, Valya."

Nikolai brushed a kiss against her temple, and she leaned against him. She'd agreed to act as Nikolai's lover so she could remain close and help safeguard him, but people had been gossiping and speculating for years. It had never been her intention to involve Sergei in those rumors though.

"Love does make people do strange things," she agreed with a sigh. "Speaking of which, you insinuated Ivan and Lena were lovers. I happened to see her while I was in Ivan's camp and overheard a curious conversation. She mentioned having one of her people check Ivan's shipping manifest. It was strange she didn't ask Ivan for them herself."

Grigory's eyes narrowed. "What else did Lena say?"

"That was all. Ivan appeared almost a minute later. I wasn't aware they had a close relationship until you mentioned it."

Grigory frowned. "Close may be too strong of a word. Ivan does not trust Lena or her motivations. We're uncertain about Peter too. Viktor, his second-in-command, has been something of a pain lately. He's been trying to investigate Ivan's interests in the area."

"I'm not particularly fond of Viktor either," Nikolai said, his expression darkening.

When Grigory arched an eyebrow, Valentina shrugged and said, "Viktor offered me an invitation to join Peter's camp. Or rather, a place here in the towers once Peter took over Sergei's command. But our mutual dislike for him aside, Viktor shared some detailed information about Peter's missing shipments."

"Such as?"

"Specific cargo information, amounts, tracking information from point of manufacture up until they learned of the disappearance," she explained, recounting the unpleasant conversation. "My gut is telling me Viktor was being honest, but that doesn't necessarily mean Peter isn't involved."

Alec nodded. "We questioned Viktor under a truth barrier before we released him from the towers. There was no deception."

"That technology is easily fooled," Grigory began, but Valentina shook her head and smiled.

"Trust me, Uncle, this is one of their abilities. It cannot be easily fooled." She paused, considering their options. "Viktor believed one of our leaders had a hand in this. If we give Peter the benefit of the doubt, we should probably investigate Lena first. Unfortunately, I don't have any reliable contacts within her camp. I think Viktor might, but I don't know how close they are to Lena."

Nikolai stroked her side with his thumb. "No. You're not working with him again, Valya."

Valentina blew out a breath but didn't argue. She wasn't particularly interested in dealing with Viktor either, but more importantly, Sergei and Yuri would also lose their minds.

Grigory rubbed his chin. "Ivan prefers a more straightforward approach to things, so it's unlikely he can help you in that department. The only thing I may be able to offer you is information regarding when Lena will be visiting Ivan next and her primary camp's location. Her security will be lax once she leaves. In exchange, I would make a request."

Nikolai tensed. "Such information would be mutually beneficial, but we would hold the majority of the risk. Yet you still wish to ask for payment?"

Grigory's mouth twitched in the barest of smiles. "Indeed. A few things, actually."

Nikolai's eyes narrowed. "What?"

Grigory studied Valentina for a long time, and his gaze softened. "I would ask Valentina to visit with her sister at the earliest opportunity. Nadiya will be moving to the area in the next week or two."

"You don't even have to ask, Uncle," she said softly. "I wanted to bring her here as soon as I learned about Omni-Lab's abilities."

Nikolai relaxed. "Was there something else?"

Grigory nodded and approached her. "Yes. I will not try to stop you from going because I remember your stubbornness well. But I would ask that you do not go to Lena's camp alone. At the very least, take Sergei and Yuri with you."

"She will not go alone," Nikolai promised.

Valentina tilted her head to regard Grigory. All the requests so far had been reasonable, but she had the impression he wasn't finished. "There's something else, isn't there?"

He hesitated. "Yes. Although, this last request isn't dependent upon my cooperation, but it would mean a great deal to me if you would consider it."

"What is it?"

Grigory smiled. "Once Sergei finishes persuading you, I'd like to be there when you marry him, Valya."

Her mouth dropped open, and Grigory chuckled. "It's only a matter of time before he does. Sergei has always been just as stubborn as you. Anyone can see how much he cares for you." Grigory paused and regarded Nikolai thoughtfully. "How much they all care for you. You've been very fortunate, Valya."

"I know," she agreed, resting her head against Nikolai's chest. They'd all enriched her life so much, it was impossible to imagine her existence without them. "I'd still like to have that dinner with you to catch up, Uncle Grigory. Now that you know about my abilities, I'd like to hear more about my parents. There's so much I don't know about them. My grandmother only told me a few things."

"I'd enjoy that. Let me know whenever you're available," Grigory said and glanced over at Alec. "Charles and his people took my commlink and weapons before I entered the warehouse. Is there any chance I can get those returned? I need to check in with my camp to see if they have any damage from that storm."

Alec nodded. "Of course. I'll arrange to have someone escort you back."

Valentina walked over and hugged Grigory. "Thank you, Uncle Grigory. For everything."

He returned her hug and shook Nikolai's hand. "Thank you, Nikolai, for taking care of Valya. There are few people who wouldn't have taken advantage of her connection to me or Ivan for their own benefit. It speaks well of you that you never made any demands."

Nikolai inclined his head. "Valentina is family. By extension, that makes you mine as well."

Grigory nodded. "I see good things in the future between us. Take care, both of you. I'll be in touch."

———

VALENTINA LIFTED HER HEAD, allowing the water from the shower to wash away the blood. She poured some of the foaming cleanser into her hand and soaped up her body. A noise at the door caught her attention.

She turned to look over her shoulder at Sergei and gave him a teasing smile. "Are you here to wash my back, Seryozha? Or are you just admiring the view?"

He chuckled and approached her, pulling off his blood-stained shirt in the process. Dropping it on the floor, he unhooked his pants and said, "I wanted to join you the last time you asked me that."

She turned around, watching as he removed the rest of his clothing, and bit her lip in appreciation. "You're not the only one."

As he stepped into the shower, she placed her soapy hands against his well-defined chest and looked up into his eyes. "Will you tell me what you learned?"

"Later," he murmured, bending down to kiss her. "I'm having a hard time thinking about anything other than you at the moment."

Winding her arms around his neck, she said, "I can tell."

"You've always been very perceptive," he teased with a grin, wrapping his arms around her and pulling her close. His expression became more serious. "How do you feel? Any pain?"

"I'm not hurt," she said, her heart aching at the worry in his eyes. "I went to the medical ward. You managed to remove the bullet. Grigory thinks you melted it."

"Nikolai told me," he said, cupping her face and tracing his thumb over her cheek. "I didn't stop to talk to him though. I wanted to see you for myself."

She ran her hands over his muscular chest, following the movement with her eyes. The water pelting over his skin was washing away some of the blood, but not all. There had been so many occasions over the years when they'd been injured, but each time seemed to hurt worse than the last. They'd been fortunate, but their lives were too unpredictable. She needed to treasure every moment with him.

He lifted her chin, the small flame around his iris flaring brightly with emotion. In a low voice, he said, "I love you, Valentina Golubeva. You're the most precious thing in the world to me, and I intend to spend the rest of my life proving it to you."

She swallowed and said, "Show me, Seryozha. No more words. I want to feel you inside me."

Sergei lowered his head, pressing his lips gently against hers. His kiss was as light as a whisper but as unyielding as the promise behind it. Her body softened against him as his heated fire energy swirled around her. This was Sergei in his purest form—raw, primal, and elemental, but also achingly tender and gentle. He was multi-faceted—like the flicker of a flame, but he was the only one who had ever been able to burn away all her subterfuge to reveal the truth of her emotions for him.

He caressed her skin, the heated path of his hands marking her like a brand. She surrounded herself with him, their hearts beating in time with each other as they explored each other's bodies with gentle touches and soft kisses.

The care he was taking with her was almost reverent. She never would have allowed this tender lovemaking with anyone else. But this was Sergei, the man she had spent her entire life loving. He understood her in a way no one else ever had, touching the most vulnerable parts of her spirit and cherishing her heart.

When he finally pressed her against the wall and slid inside her, Valentina gasped at the sense of rightness that filled her. His movements were slow, drawing out their love-making and the exquisite sensations he evoked. His energy caressed every inch of her skin, their bodies moving together in an impassioned dance. Fire and water collided, his heat and her coolness blending together in an explosive union that had them both crying out their release.

Sergei held her tightly for a long time, and she lowered her head against his chest, panting softly. The room had filled with steam, a merging of fire and water, and her limbs felt boneless. If it weren't for him holding her up, she wasn't sure she'd be able to stand just yet. After a long moment, he withdrew from her body, and she whimpered at the absence of him.

Sergei's voice was gentle as he asked, "Are you all right?"

She nodded and wrapped her arms around him, unwilling to let him go yet. "I am now."

He rested his forehead against hers. "I was worried I might lose you tonight, little dove."

"I knew you would make it to me in time," she whispered. "I felt you and Yuri coming for me."

Sergei cupped her face and searched her expression. "I know you have reservations still, but I'm not going to live another lifetime of regret in not making you mine. I'm going to marry you, Valechka. And soon."

She blinked at him. "You're bringing this up *now*?"

He was quiet for a moment and then nodded. "You tend to be very agreeable when you're relaxed. I intend to take advantage of that."

Her eyes narrowed, and she pulled away from him. He chuckled from behind her, but she ignored him and grabbed a drying cloth. Wrapping it around herself, Valentina stomped into the bedroom and over to the dresser. She pulled one of Sergei's shirts over her head, listening to his footsteps entering the bedroom.

"How much time do you think you'll need before you

realize it's inevitable? We could get married by the end of next week. Maybe sooner, if you prefer."

She clenched her jaw. Picking up one of her throwing knives, she spun around and threw it in his direction. It embedded itself into the wall with a *thump*. He eyed it appreciatively and grinned.

"Well, you didn't hit me. That's not a no. In fact, I'd go so far as to say it's promising."

She huffed and pulled on her panties. Ignoring Sergei, she grabbed more of her knives and headed into Nikolai's bedroom. He glanced up from his desk and cocked his head. "Sergei trying to convince you to marry him again?"

Valentina didn't answer. Instead, she crawled into Nikolai's bed, placing her weapons strategically around her. With a yawn, she said, "I'm sleeping here tonight. I'm tired, and he's annoying me."

Nikolai made a noncommittal noise and put down whatever he was working on. "Go ahead, but he'll come in and remove you shortly."

"Then I'll sleep with Yuri," she grumbled into the pillow. "He snores, but he won't let Sergei take me away."

Nikolai chuckled. "I beg to differ. It'll only take a few days' worth of training for him to agree." He stood and walked over to her. Leaning over, he pressed a kiss against her hair and said, "Goodnight, Valya. I'm glad you're safe."

"I love you, Kolya," she whispered. "Come to bed soon?"

"Soon enough," he agreed, pulling the blanket over her. "But I don't think Sergei will wait that long to take you back to his bed. Get some rest while you can."

———

SERGEI RAN a hand through his overly long hair, irritated by its length. He needed to cut it soon now that there wasn't much point in keeping it this way anymore. Glancing at the closed bedroom door, he debated how long it would take Valentina to fall asleep. At least she was only next door with Nikolai and he could easily retrieve her. He wanted her with him tonight, and every night afterward, if he were honest with himself.

He smiled and pulled on some clothes, remembering the fire in her eyes when he'd provoked her. Catching her off-guard was the quickest way to get her to agree. He'd wear her down eventually. Although, he might actually have to take a few knife wounds before that happened. Those wounds would easily heal. The possibility of not having her in his life, however, was something from which he'd never recover.

Deciding to give her some time to fall asleep, he headed out into Lars's common room to find the former exile and Yuri drinking together.

"Better, but you need a small bite of something to accompany it," Yuri argued. "None of this dainty sipping shit."

Lars chuckled and lifted his glass. "That's one thing I'll agree with. Your pickled vegetables are quite enjoyable."

Sergei paused for a moment, watching the two of them. Yuri could be dislikable and abrasive on occasion, but he'd seemed to develop a fast friendship with Lars. The training Lars had been doing with him on his air abilities had only helped strengthen their camaraderie.

With a grin, Sergei said, "I've been trying to get Lars to learn how to drink properly for years."

Lars grimaced. "I've never had to watch you cut off a man's hand before. That changed my perspective. I plan to drink until I can erase that image from my mind."

Sergei shrugged and walked over to the bar. "If he doesn't have a hand, he won't be able to raise a weapon in Valentina's direction again." He poured himself a drink and recapped the bottle. "Besides, Yuri took the other hand."

Yuri scowled. "Brant said they were going to reattach them."

"That's a shame," Sergei said, picking up his glass and walking over to the couch.

Yuri sighed. "It is."

"We can always cut them off again," Sergei suggested.

Yuri brightened considerably. "There is that."

"Scary motherfuckers," Lars muttered, tossing back the rest of his drink.

Yuri grabbed the bottle from the nearby table and refilled his glass. "Valya ran out on you again?"

"Mmhmm," Sergei said, swirling the liquor in his glass. "Threw a knife at me too. Only one, though, so she's not really angry."

"Is she in Nikolai's bed?"

Something in Yuri's tone caught his attention, and his eyes narrowed. "Yes. Why?"

Yuri chuckled. "You're a fool. You think you know her so well, but you're going about this marriage thing all wrong."

Sergei paused, lowering his glass to study Yuri. "You know something?"

"I know a lot," Yuri agreed with a grin and downed his beverage. "I could help convince her, if properly motivated."

He hesitated. Yuri was playing with him, but it was possible he knew a way to get Valentina to agree. "One month of training."

Yuri scoffed. "One month in exchange for a lifetime with Valya? Pathetic."

Sergei leaned forward. "Three months. Two training sessions a day."

Yuri leaned back and grinned. "Keep going and I might consider it. Although, right now, it's far more enjoyable watching your frustration and knowing she's throwing knives at you."

Sergei's jaw clenched. "Six months."

"Keep going. I'm listening," Yuri said, reaching over to splash more liquor into his glass.

"A whole fucking year. Twice a day."

"Keep your mouth shut, Yuri," Nikolai warned as he walked into the room. "Do not get involved in this matter between them. Valentina will carve you into pieces if she finds out. Then I won't have anyone to train my recruits."

"Spoilsport," Yuri grumbled.

Nikolai's only response was a dark look. He walked over and sat on the couch, pinching the bridge of his nose. "So what happened tonight?"

Lars snatched the bottle from Yuri's grasp. "They each cut off one of Charles's hands. Jakob only had his hands broken for grabbing Valentina's ass, but both of them have been carted off to the medical ward. They're reattaching Charles's hands and regenerating Jakob's bones. Brant's downright pissed about the whole thing. He threatened to arrest Sergei and Yuri."

"That's a shame," Nikolai murmured. "Why would they reattach them? Now you'll just have to cut them off again."

"Exactly," Yuri agreed, lifting his glass in salute. "And these Omnis claim they don't condone torture."

Sergei grinned as Lars shook his head in exasperation and poured another drink. Lars wasn't quite as squeamish as he pretended. He'd seen the former exile handle himself in far worse circumstances than what he'd witnessed tonight.

Leaning forward, Sergei said, "There were some benefits to us remaining behind."

Nikolai's expression turned curious. "Such as?"

Sergei picked up the abandoned bottle and topped off his glass. "I had an opportunity to try out my version of a truth barrier on them. That, coupled with losing a hand or two, and Charles became quite cooperative."

"Sergei's mastering the art of paralyzing people while interrogating them," Yuri said with a trace of envy in his voice. "It was a beautiful thing to witness."

Nikolai arched his brow. "That has possibilities. I'd like to see a demonstration at some point. Did Charles mention any names?"

"No," Sergei admitted. "I don't believe they knew who they were dealing with on the surface. Pavel was their main contact, and he could have handled everything. That's why they were so quick to try to pull in Valentina. Their supply dried up when I killed him."

"At least the infusion of weapons has stopped," Lars said, refilling his glass. "Brant and the rest of the Shadows are trying to chase down everyone involved with the possible rebellion. They're also conducting searches to locate the weapons that have already made their way into the towers. It'll take time, but at least we're that much more ahead."

Yuri scowled. "The halt is temporary. We still need to find out who's responsible. Otherwise, they'll just find another distributor."

Nikolai drummed his fingers on the edge of the couch. "Yuri's right. Based on what Grigory said, we can most likely narrow it down to Peter or Lena. I'm inclined to rule out Ivan as a possible suspect. I believe he's only in the area out of respect for Valentina's parents' last wishes. Nadiya is sworn to Ivan's service, and she's going to be arriving in his camp soon. Grigory wants to secure her a place in the towers."

Sergei paused in surprise, a slow smile spreading across his face. "Well, that's somewhat unexpected but very welcome news. Nadiya was the main reason Valentina was reluctant to risk alienating herself from the Coalition. But if her sister is living here, Valentina will be more inclined to stay in the towers. I know she wants a relationship with her again."

Lars's eyes widened, and he leaned forward. "Wait. What? Valentina has a sister? I need more details."

Yuri snorted. "If you want to find out what it's like to lose a body part, go ahead and touch Valya's little sister. I dare you."

Lars grimaced and reached for the bottle again.

Sergei grinned and turned back to Nikolai. "We know Peter has ambitions to take over control of the new tower, but I don't know Lena's motivations for being here. She's been in the area for the past two months but hasn't had much of an interest in the construction. Some of her people have been helping with resource acquisition and the river excavation though. It's possible Pavel was working with her as a connection to the construction, but I don't have any knowledge of it. He never mentioned her while he was acting as my second-in-command, and she never requested any construction progress reports from me. But that may be an indication he was already providing that intel."

Lars frowned. "When Pavel abducted Ariana, he took her to Sofia's camp. Maybe Sofia's the connection instead."

"Possibly," Nikolai admitted, drumming his fingers on the edge of the couch. "Valentina can make some discreet inquiries about Peter and Lena's relationships with Sofia. To be honest, I personally don't know much about Lena. I only know she's been an adamant objector to Sergei's position within the towers. Does she have a problem with you, Sergei?"

He shrugged. "I've met her a few times, but nothing happened out of the ordinary. She's not fond of me, but I've never troubled myself over it. I'm not Peter's favorite person either."

"Speculating about why Sergei pisses people off isn't going to be helpful," Yuri muttered, placing his glass on the nearby table and reaching for the bottle. "With the exception of

Valya, more than a few of our people wouldn't mind seeing him prematurely expire."

"The same goes for you, Yuri," Sergei reminded him. "You're just as much of an unlikable bastard."

Yuri snorted and lifted his glass. "There is that. We'll leave being likable to Valya and Nikolai."

Sergei grinned as Yuri downed his drink. It was true. Neither he nor Yuri had ever cared what people thought of them. In some ways, it worked to their advantage. They were able to accomplish their tasks without worrying about dancing around people's sensitivities. Nikolai and Valentina had always stepped into those roles with remarkable skill, frequently smoothing over any issues he and Yuri had caused.

Unfortunately, since Sergei had left them three years ago, he'd been operating without Nikolai or Valentina's softening influence. Nikolai had stepped in to assist him every now and then to support him with their leaders, but Sergei had made more enemies than friends over the years. The list of people with possible vendettas against him was considerably long.

Nikolai was quiet for a moment. "Before he left the towers, Grigory offered to let us know when Lena visits Ivan's camp next. He suggested we use the opportunity to investigate her camp to see if she's responsible since security will be lessened. Although, I'm thinking a change of plan might be in order."

Sergei arched a brow. "What do you have in mind?"

"I know you've been practicing, but can you hold your truth barrier for an extended period of time?"

He nodded. "Yes, but if you're thinking about having me interrogate Lena, there will be serious challenges with that. If she's innocent and Peter's the one who's responsible, it could jeopardize your leadership position. Ivan could also have some fallout for his involvement."

"I'm aware," Nikolai said, motioning for Yuri to pass him

the bottle. "But the alternative is far deadlier. We need to stop our supply shipments from being stolen. We're already hard-pressed to meet the demand for resources, and these thefts are endangering our people. I'm going to ask Alec if he'll accompany us to Ivan's camp so we can interrogate Lena. If we're wrong on this, he may be able to use his ability to influence her to forget what happened. It worked well enough on Viktor after he stabbed you. I don't see why we can't utilize the same tactic now."

Sergei frowned. "It has potential, but I'm not sure how Valentina will feel about involving Grigory in this plan. They aren't that close, but she still respects their familial relationship."

Yuri snorted. "Valya will agree. She's been going out of her mind thinking someone will target you again. She wants the person responsible for these thefts caught and your name cleared."

Sergei couldn't help but smile. God, he loved her. She was so passionate and fiery. Her sense of loyalty and protectiveness was only part of the reason he was enamored with her. He'd have to keep working on convincing her to marry him sooner rather than later, even if it meant agreeing to whatever outrageous demands Yuri suggested.

He glanced toward the hallway again, remembering how she'd felt in his arms while he made love to her. She didn't let many people see that softer side of herself, and it only made him treasure those moments that much more.

Nikolai chuckled and shook his head. "She's most likely asleep. If you want to collect her from my bed, you should probably do it now. Otherwise, I'll keep her with me tonight."

"Not a chance," Sergei said and stood. After three years without her, he was determined not to go another night without her by his side.

Nikolai smiled. "I had a feeling you'd say that. Come find

me when you wake up. I want to plan as much of this as possible so Valya can coordinate with Grigory."

"Of course," Sergei agreed and gestured toward Yuri. "You might want to hold off on going to bed until Yuri tells you the rest. We're going to have more challenges beginning tomorrow, and you'll need to decide how you want to handle it."

When they both nodded, Sergei turned and headed into Nikolai's room. Valentina was curled up underneath the blankets, appearing almost angelic in her repose. The hilt of a knife poking out from under her pillow was the only hint of the fire that burned brightly within her.

Walking over, he pulled down the blanket and lifted her into his arms. She murmured his name on a sigh and snuggled against him. With a smile, he said quietly, "Shh. Go back to sleep, little dove. I'm just taking you back to bed."

He carried her into their room and placed her on the bed. She made a noise of protest when he pulled away but otherwise didn't awaken. Sitting on the edge of the bed beside her, he trailed his fingers over her soft skin. He'd come so close to losing her again, and that possibility just wasn't acceptable.

"I'm going to keep you safe, Valechka," he promised, leaning down and pressing a kiss against her hair. "No one will ever hurt you again. They'll have to go through me first. I swear it."

CHAPTER TEN

VALENTINA WOKE up encased in Sergei's arms. She relaxed against him, enjoying his warmth. She wasn't surprised to find herself sprawled all over him again; he made a fantastic heater.

"You undressed me," she murmured against his chest.

He stroked his hand leisurely down her naked back, tracing his heated energy along the same path. "Mmhmm. I like to feel you pressed against me."

"You took my weapons too," she guessed, not bothering to check.

"I did. I even considered tying you up so you couldn't run away again, but I thought you might not miss next time you threw a weapon at me."

"Very wise of you," she said, still not moving from the heated cocoon.

"I have my moments," he agreed with a chuckle.

Lifting her head, she smiled up at him. "You're such a troublemaker, but I love hearing you laugh."

He grinned and kissed her nose. "I love you, Valechka."

Her eyes softened as she gazed at him. She really did love

him beyond all reason. Laying her head back against his chest, she traced a pattern over his chest. It was tempting to stay in bed with him for the rest of the day, but it would only postpone the inevitable. "Will you tell me what you learned last night from Charles and Jakob?"

Sergei stilled his hand on her back, and she lifted her head again. His expression was dark, a silent fury emanating from him. She frowned, guessing the source of his irritation.

"They're still alive?"

"For now," he replied.

Valentina slid her body over his, sitting up so she was straddling him. Placing her hands against his chest, she looked down at him. "They aren't our people, Seryozha. I already killed a few of them in self-defense, and we may face some repercussions for my actions. But we don't have any right to take the rest of their lives or demand recompense. We haven't acknowledged our place amongst them yet, but I appreciate the sentiment."

Sergei didn't respond. Instead, he ran his hands up her thighs and rested them on her hips, tracing the edge of her panties with his fingertips. He studied the material for a moment. "I probably should have removed these too when I brought you to bed. I'll have to do that next time."

She narrowed her eyes. "Am I wrong? Have we acknowledged our place here?"

He winced. "I'm afraid our secret's out, Valechka. Too many of their people followed Alec and Ariana into the warehouse to find you. We had reports of the storm coming in from too many outside locations. Even now, gossip is running rampant through the towers. You, Ariana, and Kayla were all glowing with that strange light. Everyone witnessed it, even those who don't possess any abilities. I also managed to cause a small fire when you lost consciousness. The fire suppression equipment kicked in, but not before a few people witnessed it."

She felt all the blood rush out of her head. Grigory had mentioned Sergei causing the fire, but she'd been so out of it that she hadn't remembered the gold light or the storm. Climbing off Sergei, she grabbed her discarded shirt off the floor and pulled it over her head. "Did you tell Nikolai?"

"Yes. Yuri knows too."

Valentina swore and started digging through the bag near the dresser. Pulling out some weapons, she quickly began strapping them on. This was a disaster. Nikolai had to be in a panic. They didn't have a contingency plan firmly in place, only the beginning of one. They'd left too many things open-ended because they'd thought they had time. She should have known better.

"Dammit," she muttered, grabbing another weapon as an afterthought. Yuri would probably comment on all the knives, but she wasn't about to limit her options. The golden dragon figurine on the dresser caught her attention, and she scowled as she equipped the last knife. "Of all the stupid... That damn dragon was what made me lose consciousness and why I didn't have any weapons when Charles shot me."

"We knew it would eventually come out," Sergei said gently.

"Yes, but not *now*," she argued, leaning against the dresser for support as the weight of this new reality crashed over her. "Nikolai's going to lose everything over this. They're going to divide and reassign his territories amongst the other leaders. People who depend on us are going to have to merge into new camps, lose whatever standing they've gained with Nikolai, and we won't have any way to make sure they're properly taken care of."

"Valechka," Sergei began, his footsteps sounding behind her, "it's going to be fine."

She squeezed her eyes shut and took a deep breath. "You can't know that, Sergei. They may have to split up families if their new camp can't support them. I don't know if it's possible to prevent that from happening. I don't want to be the reason a child doesn't have the chance to grow up knowing a loving family member."

He sighed. "I know you entered the training program to make sure your sister was able to remain with your grandmother, but you once told me you believed that was for the best."

"Yes, but I wasn't with her when our grandmother passed away," Valentina whispered, her heart aching. "My sister had to deal with it alone. I didn't find out for more than a month, and it took me another month to get back."

"Your sister understood," he said, placing his warm hand against her back. "You made a sacrifice for your family. That's what families are supposed to do."

Valentina nodded, leaning against him as he wrapped his arms around her. "I know, but I wish I had been there to help shoulder her burden."

She turned around, cupped his face, and searched his expression. Her sister wasn't the only reason she wanted to keep families together. In a soft voice, she whispered, "Sometimes I think about the boy you were, and it breaks my heart a little to know you didn't have that sort of family as a child. I wish I could have saved you from that."

His gaze softened. "Everyone's damaged in some way, but not everyone is fortunate enough to have found what we've discovered in each other. You've given me a real family, Valechka. I don't have any regrets."

Valentina swallowed, tracing the lines of his jaw with her fingertips. "You're right. I've never regretted accepting the offer for the training program. It kept my sister with my grandmother, and it also led me to you, Nikolai, and Yuri. I love you, Seryozha. I love all of you. I wouldn't trade being with you for anything, but not everyone was so fortunate with their units. It just as easily could have gone the other way. I don't want that to happen to any of our people. They should have a choice."

Sergei didn't respond, but she didn't need him to say anything to know he understood. His reasons for joining had been different. For him, the training program had been an escape. But for her, it had offered her family a future together. At the time, Grigory hadn't yet been in a position to help them. So she'd done what was necessary to ensure Nadiya could remain with her grandmother.

She pressed a light kiss against his lips before turning away and heading into Nikolai's bedroom. She'd expected to find him pacing—or worse. Instead, he was quietly sitting at his desk, reading something on a tablet.

Nikolai lifted his head and smiled at her. "Valya. You're awake. How are you feeling?"

Valentina paused, studying him in surprise. He appeared tired, but more rested than she expected. At least he'd gotten some sleep. She frowned, glancing back into her room at Sergei who was calmly pulling on a shirt. Neither of them appeared overly concerned or frantic.

She turned back to Nikolai. "I'm worried about you and our people, but now I'm wondering if I need to be. Are you all right, Kolya? You don't seem as upset as I expected."

Nikolai sighed and motioned for her to come to him. She did, and he pulled her into his lap. Wrapping his arms around her, he said, "I guess Sergei told you our secret's out?"

Valentina nodded, laying her head against his shoulder. "I thought we'd have more time. I can reach out to some of my contacts in the area to see if they've heard any rumors. Even if the truth has spread outside the towers, some of our people are going to want to follow you. We can negotiate with Ivan or some of the other leaders to make sure families can stay together."

She frowned, thinking about the logistics. They couldn't bring all their people here, but maybe they could barter some of their supplies in exchange for certain concessions.

"It's going to be fine, Valya," Nikolai murmured, placing his hand on her knee. "We knew this was a possibility. We'll do whatever is in the best interest of our people. It'll require some adjustments on our part, but it's inconsequential compared to your life. We'd all rather have you with us than the alternative."

"Nikolai's right," Sergei said from the doorway. Valentina lifted her head, and he took a handful of steps toward them. "You're the most important thing to all of us, Valechka. Nikolai mentioned you told Grigory about us but nothing about him and Yuri. We can still try to spin this, if that's what you wish, but this may be a good opportunity for us to embrace a new beginning."

She frowned and placed her hand on Nikolai's chest. "Is that what you want, Kolya?"

"What I want is to make sure you, Yuri, and Sergei remain safe." He lifted her hand and pressed a kiss against it. "Everything else is secondary, including our position within the Coalition. I'll renounce my position before I will risk losing my family."

Valentina bit her lip. "What about everyone in your camps?"

"We're going to move some of them into the towers," Sergei said, closing the distance between them. "We spoke at length about this while you were asleep. Even if Nikolai's removed from his leadership position, he has the skills and allies needed to run the new tower. He also has us. No one besides the four of us can adequately understand the Coalition's needs and those of OmniLab. Just as Kayla straddles the line between the ruin rats and the towers, we can do the same with our people. The spirit of our people will thrive in the towers, Valechka, especially under your guidance. It's not just Nikolai they follow."

"Sergei's right," Nikolai added. "Our people know you love them, and they respond to that. Their loyalty is just as much yours as it is mine. In some cases, I'd say they'd follow you first."

She frowned. "This is what you both want? To stay here? What about Yuri?"

"He fell asleep a few hours ago," Nikolai said, giving her a gentle squeeze. "But Yuri has made it clear he will defer to whatever we all decide. He doesn't particularly care either way, provided we stay together."

Valentina sighed. "I don't want to walk away from our people completely, but if they turn away from us, we won't have a choice. Provided we can resolve this situation with our alliance, staying in the towers might be the best option. We'll need to return to our camp and make some final arrangements for our people, just in case. Perhaps we can go by there before we investigate Lena's camp."

"There's been a change on that too," Sergei said, holding out his hand toward her. Nikolai released her, and she climbed off his lap. Sergei drew her back into his arms and added, "We need you to contact Grigory to set up a meeting. We're going to hold a paralyzing truth barrier over both Peter and Lena to get to the truth. One of them is responsible for the thefts, and this is the quickest way to resolve the situation. We've already spoken with Alec. He's agreed to travel there with us. He'll try to influence them to forget, if it's necessary."

She peered up at him and frowned. "That's very risky. They won't go to a meeting without armed escorts."

"We'll limit it to one guard. I'll also be there to explain

the incident at the nightclub and how one of our weapons was discovered in the possession of a tower resident. That'll lend believability to my reasons for being there. With your energy, I should be able to extend the truth barrier to encompass several people simultaneously. You can go as Nikolai's agent and help me hold the truth barrier, but Yuri will need to remain out of range. Peter will most likely bring Viktor. I believe Lena's second-in-command is Roman. Unfortunately, we need to call the meeting tonight."

Her eyes widened. "You can't be serious. We need at least a day to put together even a rudimentary plan."

Nikolai shook his head. "It must be tonight, Valya. Omni-Lab's High Council is holding a vote in the morning to close the towers to our people and terminate our alliance. They discovered a large cache of weapons in that warehouse, but it's not enough to account for all the missing weapons. Some of our weapons are still out there, but the damage has already been done. The High Council believes these weapons are evidence of our plans to launch another assault on OmniLab to retake the towers by force."

Valentina blew out a breath. "This problem originated from an unequal representation within their government. They need to clean up their own damn house. Brant said this resentment has been going on for fifteen years."

"I agree," Nikolai said, drumming his fingers on the desk. "Alec is taking steps to appoint a non-Inner Circle representative to the council, but the High Council is somewhat resistant. It will take time for changes to happen, but in the meantime, they're all pointing their fingers at us."

Sergei nodded. "We also can't give Lena and Peter time to prepare. This is our best chance to resolve the situation from our end and keep our people safe. You know what will happen if this alliance falls apart."

Valentina squeezed her eyes shut. The loss of life on both

sides would be extraordinary. It seemed they didn't have much of a choice. Most likely, they could rely upon Grigory and Ivan to act as Nikolai's allies, but there were too many other unknowns. They'd need to go over everything carefully, searching for any and all exploitable vulnerabilities.

With a resigned sigh, she lifted her head. "You've made a lot of plans. How long did you let me sleep?"

"Most of the day, but we've already started running different scenarios," Sergei admitted and kissed her nose. "We let you sleep as long as possible, but you always have a different way of looking at things. Your unique perspective will help tremendously."

Valentina relaxed against him. The three of them had probably already done most of the heavy lifting. Despite Sergei's claims, she'd always found them to be more skilled at this type of planning and strategizing. "I got to be lazy in bed while you three did all the work? That doesn't seem fair. You should have woken me."

Nikolai smiled. "I told him to let you sleep, Valya. A medic stopped by earlier to check on you, but he said sleep was the best thing for you. As long as we were monitoring you, he suggested we leave you alone. Apparently, Kayla and Ariana have been sleeping most of the day too. Whatever energy you three generated must have exhausted all of you."

She paused, remembering a dream she'd had. "Kolya, you told me you had a bad feeling when I left to meet with Dmitri. How do you feel now?"

Nikolai frowned at her. "I'm not worried right now, but that doesn't necessarily mean the danger has passed. The thought of you going off alone bothers me more than I'd like to admit, but I don't know if that's because of my premonition. It might be because we almost lost you last night. Either way, you're going to have to suffer my unwillingness to let you out of my sight for a while. Why do you ask?"

"I had a strange dream last night," she murmured, trying to recall the different elements. "I saw a rocky outcropping, like the one you described from your vision. But there was something strange about it... I think Kayla and Ariana were with me too."

Sergei arched his brow. "Ariana doesn't leave the towers. Could it have been just a dream? Perhaps prompted from Nikolai's description?"

It was possible, but she didn't think so. With a shrug, she said, "I don't know what happened between the three of us in that warehouse, but I think we need to find out what that dragon figurine is made of. There's something significant about it."

Nikolai frowned. "Is it still that gold color?"

She nodded. "Yes. I saw it on the dresser when I woke up."

Nikolai stood. "Do you mind if I take a closer look at it?"

Valentina led him and Sergei back into her room. She picked up the dragon and offered it to him. Nikolai turned it over in his hand, studying the intricate details. "Remarkable. It feels like stone, but it's unlike anything I've ever seen before."

"I saw it in Kayla's room when we were getting dressed for the club," Valentina admitted as he ran his fingertips over the small statuette. "When I picked it up, she had the impression it belonged with me. Apparently, one of Kayla's abilities is finding lost or missing objects. It somehow responds to my energy. It actually reacts to all three of us, but in a different manner."

Nikolai raised his head to look at her. "With all the commotion, I hadn't given much thought to Kayla or Ariana. When you disappeared from the surveillance cameras, Kayla tried to track you using your shoes. I wonder if she can track other objects too."

Valentina paused, mentally kicking herself for not making the connection earlier. "Yes. I don't know what sort of range she possesses, but she might be able to find the missing weapons and other supplies."

"It's a possibility," Sergei admitted and picked up a tablet she'd left on the dresser. "You mentioned that only a partial shipment of weapons was missing. If we pull one or two guns out of the existing shipment, Kayla might be able to track them for us." He studied the tablet for a moment and tapped on the display. "It looks like some of them are still in your camp waiting for distribution."

"Go ahead and contact Kayla to see if she's willing to help," Nikolai said and handed her the figurine. "If so, we can take her to our camp when we go back to the surface tonight."

Sergei frowned. "The missing weapons and supplies are only part of it. We still need to call this meeting with the other leaders to find out who's responsible. Otherwise, there's a chance it will continue. Alec said the only way he can stop the vote tomorrow is if he can assure the High Council the smuggling has stopped. Ariana's father is also on the council, and he's agreed to pull in favors to back our position too. But only if we can end this before tomorrow morning."

"Kayla will need to be a backup plan," Nikolai said and kissed her forehead. "There's no guarantee Peter and Lena will show up to this meeting, but we'll do everything we can to protect our people. Unfortunately, time is very much against us right now. We won't have long before the rumors spread to our people and my standing is called into question."

Valentina frowned. "If OmniLab votes to end our alliance, we'll have to stand with them against our own people. Otherwise, we'll run the risk of being cut off from both groups. OmniLab is the only one we know who will accept our abilities."

Nikolai nodded. "Let's not worry about that right now. We need to focus on getting through tonight first. Go ahead and get dressed. I'll go wake up Yuri."

Nikolai headed out of the room, and she gazed down at the dragon statue. She was grateful Ariana and Kayla had been able to use it to save her life, but the cost had been so high. Dealing with the threat of their alliance falling apart was worrisome enough, but it still saddened her to know she might need to say goodbye to a lifetime with the Coalition. The only bright spot was knowing she'd be able to keep Sergei, Nikolai, and Yuri with her.

"All this trouble over a little dragon," she murmured. "It's strange these Omnis believe we're related to them."

Sergei chuckled and placed his hand against her back. "Shall I start calling you my little dragon instead?"

Valentina looked up at him and smiled. "I'm not sure that will strike fear into anyone's heart."

"Fear, no," Sergei agreed, drawing her closer. "But you've definitely captured my heart, little dragon."

She softened against him, telling him with her eyes that he'd done the same to her. "You shouldn't say such things right now, Seryozha. Not when we have people to hunt."

Sergei reached up to cup her cheek. "I *am* going to marry you, Valechka. I intend to spend the rest of my life saying these things to you."

Valentina started to pull away, but he held her tightly. Fine. If he wanted to force this here and now, she'd play along. Lifting her head in challenge, she said, "You don't think I should have a say in this?"

He grinned. "Only if it's your agreement in becoming my wife."

She arched a brow. "I don't recall you asking me. How can I agree if there's no question on the table?"

Sergei pressed a kiss against her lips. "And give you the

opportunity to refuse? Not a chance. You're far too crafty. You'll find a way to wriggle out of such a question or disappear on me."

A laugh bubbled out of her. He knew her too well, but she'd never admit he was right.

Valentina unsheathed a knife and ran the flat of her blade down his chest. He tensed at the gesture but didn't move away. If anything, he seemed almost intrigued. "Maybe, just maybe... if you *ask properly*, I'll give you the answer you want."

Leaning close to him, she gave him a mischievous smile and added, "But it wouldn't be wise to keep trying to dictate to me, Seryozha. I've always been a woman who knows her own mind. It's best you accept that before we discuss any other... future arrangements. Let me know if I need to make my *point* a little clearer."

Without waiting for a response, Valentina sauntered into the bathroom. She closed the door behind her and bit her lip to keep from laughing aloud. He really was adorable and so much fun to tease.

She'd definitely marry him, but she'd make him work for it first.

———

VALENTINA BENT down to check her speeder for any damage or maintenance issues. They were going to be traveling quite a bit tonight, and it was too risky to have one of their vehicles break down. She was also checking for any tracking devices that may have "accidentally" been left behind while her speeder was unattended in the OmniLab garage.

Pulling out a multi-purpose tool, she tightened a few of the bolts. Sergei walked over with some hydrating packs and opened her storage compartment. He paused and glanced down at her. "You're bringing the dragon?"

She nodded and stood. "I'm not leaving it here. I lost consciousness last time someone touched it. I decided it was better to keep it with me until we discover more about it."

"That's probably wise," Nikolai said, picking up his helmet. "When we get back, we should have it analyzed."

Sergei placed the hydrating packs in the compartment of her speeder, taking care not to disturb the statuette. "I don't like the idea of you leaving it in here either. Would you prefer one of us carried it for you?"

"I'll put it in my pocket once we arrive," she said and zipped up her jacket. "It doesn't seem to react poorly to any of you, but I don't think anyone else should touch it."

"How long are these people going to take?" Yuri said in a low growl, pacing the small area around their vehicles. "If they aren't down here in the next three minutes, we're leaving without them. I'll send the coordinates for them to catch up."

"Alec's on his way now," Lars said, glancing down at his commlink. "It looks like we're going to have a few extra people joining us."

Valentina frowned. Other than Lars, only Alec and Kayla were supposed to be joining them. "Who? We're going to have enough challenges masking Alec and Kayla's presence."

The priority elevator opened a moment later, and Valentina inwardly cursed as Alec and Ariana stepped out, along with Kayla, Carl, and Brant.

Sergei frowned and took a step toward them. "Ariana, I do not think you should accompany us. We're going to meet with four of our leaders in a highly volatile situation. We will not be able to protect you from harm."

"She understands," Alec began, glancing at his fiancée with worry in his eyes. "I'm not particularly happy about this, either, but Ariana insisted. I've been trying to talk her out of it."

Ariana gave Sergei a small smile. "I appreciate everyone's

concern, but I need to go. Alec mentioned Yuri is going to be monitoring from another location. Perhaps I could wait there with Brant?"

Sergei hesitated. "That's the plan, but we're still going to be within a Coalition camp. Someone other than Nikolai controls it, so these people will not be loyal to any of us. It would be best if you don't accompany us on this trip."

Valentina put down her multi-purpose tool. Her dream from the other night briefly flickered through her mind. She'd pushed it aside when Sergei had assured her Ariana never traveled to the surface, but now Valentina couldn't help but wonder if Fate was guiding them again. Something had changed to cause Ariana to want to travel with them, and she needed to discover the reason.

Valentina took a step toward the two women. "Ariana and Kayla, may I speak with both of you privately for a moment? Nikolai and Yuri, why don't you two head out to secure the location? I'm going to be a few minutes. Sergei can wait with me."

Yuri frowned. "Don't take long, Valya. We'll need you to help coordinate with Grigory."

Valentina nodded and led Ariana and Kayla to a corner of the garage. She studied Ariana thoughtfully for a long time, trying to figure out her motivations. From what she knew of Ariana's history, she'd been remarkably sheltered for most of her life. She suspected this wasn't just an excuse to explore life outside the towers.

"You know this will be dangerous. I have no intention of talking you out of it, but I will ask you to tell me the truth. Why do you wish to accompany us?"

Ariana bit her lip. "Part of me is worried about Alec. He's skilled when it comes to influencing people, but his ability is subtle. When he used it on Viktor to make him forget the fight with Sergei and the use of your abilities, Alec needed my energy to amplify his power. If your people resist him again, it would be best if I remain close to him. The greater the distance between mates, the more difficult it can be to share energy."

Kayla frowned. "I know what you mean about wanting to stay close, but Alec's pretty good at taking care of himself. I don't think he'd want to be the reason you put yourself in danger."

Valentina considered Ariana for a long moment. "You said that's only part of the reason. What is the rest?"

Ariana lowered her gaze and sighed. "I should have known you'd catch that."

When she lifted her head again, there was a fierce look of determination in Ariana's eyes. "This is something I need to do, Valentina. When Pavel abducted me and took me to Sofia's camp, I thought I might die. I've never feared for my life before, and it changed something inside me. I'm still afraid, and I don't like it. I don't want to be that person. When I walk into that Coalition camp tonight, it will be *my* choice. It wasn't before, but it will be now."

Valentina arched an eyebrow but remained quiet, waiting for Ariana to finish. Sometimes, voicing one's thoughts and worries helped to focus them. She had the impression Ariana needed that more than anything right now.

Ariana stared at the wall for a long moment with a faraway look in her eyes. "Our people made an agreement to acquire weapons from yours because they were afraid of us and our abilities. When Pavel abducted me, I felt his fear too. He thought I was weaker because he read Sergei's notes about how I didn't possess any traditional offensive abilities. But I'm not weak. I've never been weak. You told me I was stronger than I believed, and you were right. But if I'm strong, I can't let my fear rule me. I need to face my fears and overcome them. I won't allow them to control me."

Valentina tilted her head and smiled. "You're correct. It's not your power that makes you strong, Ariana. It's the spirit that lives within you. I've seen children who are stronger than some adults because the adults allow their fears to govern their actions. It can cripple them from moving forward. That's why so many children don't realize the dangers around them. Fear is taught and a learned behavior."

Ariana nodded, and her eyes lit up. "That's it exactly. I knew you'd understand. I can't ask anyone to set aside their fears when I'm not willing to do the same. I know your people are good and honorable, Valentina. You, Sergei, Nikolai, and Yuri are proof of that. You set up this meeting tonight to eliminate the threat to our people, even though it puts all of you at risk. If I can help protect you all by amplifying Alec's abilities, I intend to do it."

Kayla cocked her head and grinned. "Well, shit. Go, Ari. I knew you weren't as mild-mannered and sweet as you appeared."

Ariana smirked at her. "Keep it up and you'll go for another dunk in the pool."

Kayla laughed. "Yep. You've definitely got some spunk. It's a good look for you."

Ariana smiled and focused on Valentina again. "I know you've been hesitant to let your people know about your abilities. I understand your reasoning, but I'm starting to wonder if we've all made a mistake by keeping our powers quiet."

Valentina tilted her head, intrigued by the direction of Ariana's words. "What do you mean?"

"If fear has brought us to this place of conflict, maybe transparency is the key," Ariana suggested. "Your people don't trust us because our abilities are new to them. The people in the towers don't trust us because we've kept ourselves isolated. I'm starting to think we've handled this wrong."

Valentina regarded Ariana in surprise. "What are you suggesting?"

"Maybe we should begin breaking down the walls dividing our people and cultures. If our people had accepted our abilities, they could have helped your people adjust too. Instead, we have two groups who are working together to oppose us. It doesn't have to be this way. Only through understanding will we begin to overcome these fears of the unknown."

Kayla frowned. "You know, it's not just the people in the towers. The ruin rats are uneasy too. I think they're a little more accepting because they know me, and I don't know shit about these powers. I'm not quite as threatening or mysterious. They ask me questions and I answer them."

"You may have a point," Valentina agreed, glancing over at Sergei, who was leaning against his speeder and watching them. "When we return, we may want to discuss a plan to slowly begin sharing this information with our respective groups. If we focus on the good things and opportunities these abilities can provide, we may end up having more allies than we anticipated. At least, it's something to consider."

Ariana beamed a smile at her. "Then you're okay with me joining you?"

"Only if you agree to something," Valentina began and pulled off both of her arm sheaths. She took a step toward Ariana and fastened one over the arm of her UV jacket. "I want you to keep this with you. Yuri will help to watch over you, but if you feel threatened at all, I want you to use this. No hesitation, Ariana. I want your promise."

Ariana's eyes widened. "I can't take your knife. I don't know how to use it."

"I have more on me and another bag of weapons on my speeder," Valentina said, waving aside her concerns. "If you need to use the knife, consider it an extension of your arm. The trunk of the body is the best place to puncture or stab."

She pointed to the area on her chest. "If you need to make a slashing motion, the face or neck can be good targets. Do not worry about accuracy. Your only goal is to get away. Do whatever is necessary to protect yourself. Once we arrive, Yuri will show you some basic maneuvers. I'll also have him give you a gun that doesn't require you to be close to your opponent."

When Ariana frowned and her gaze became wary, Valentina touched her arm. "Ariana, you must agree to this or I will not allow you to accompany us. You need to remember you are a healer. If necessary, you can heal your assailant later. But you cannot heal yourself."

Ariana's eyes widened, and she slowly nodded. "I never considered it like that. I promise I'll do as you say."

"Good," she said and handed her other knife to Kayla. "The same goes for you. Although you're already wearing one in your belt, a woman can never have too many knives."

Kayla gaped at her. "You knew I had a knife?"

Valentina nodded. "When you get uncomfortable, you touch your belt. Most of your other equipment and clothing is newer, but it appears as though you've had your belt for a number of years. I also noticed the thickness was a little excessive. Given your comment about hiding a blade in your shoes, I assumed you had other hidden weapons. The belt was a logical place."

Kayla laughed. "Okay, I'm impressed. No one else has ever known unless I showed them."

Valentina grinned. "We will have to set up some time to do a bit of training. I can show you how to tell if someone's carrying a weapon."

Ariana touched the hilt of the knife on her arm. "Can I join you too?"

"Absolutely," Valentina agreed. "Now come. Let's go find some people to hunt."

———

VALENTINA SHUT off her engine and climbed off the speeder. They were running late. She muttered a curse and pulled off her helmet just as Sergei parked beside her. She barely spared him a glance as he directed everyone where to store their speeders in the abandoned building they were occupying.

The room was fairly crowded with people and their vehicles. In addition to Kayla and Carl, Brant and Lars had accompanied them. Ariana had never ridden on a speeder, so she and Alec had doubled up. Based on her flushed cheeks and the excitement in her eyes, Valentina surmised she'd enjoyed herself.

Yuri walked over and said, "You have less than fifteen minutes to get into position."

Valentina nodded and pulled off her jacket, tossing it over the seat of her speeder. Dammit. She needed weapons. Before she even had a chance to ask, Sergei dropped a bag in front of her. He winked at her and casually brushed his hand against her ass as he moved away. "Your weapons, Valechka."

Shaking her head in exasperation at his teasing, she yanked open the bag and pulled out a few more knives to replace the ones she'd given Ariana and Kayla. With one hand, she began fastening her arm sheaths in place.

Grigory approached her and frowned. "Are you out of your mind, Valya?"

"I've thought that on more than one occasion," Yuri muttered and handed her a miniature listening device. "I still need to calibrate the audio properly. "

She nodded at him and slipped it into her arm sheath. "Did Peter agree to meet with us?"

"Yes," Grigory admitted, running his hand over his hair. "He'll be here shortly with Viktor. He refused until I told him you and Nikolai were going to be joining us too. He sounded... intrigued."

"Good," she murmured, accepting a hydrating pack Nikolai handed to her. Yuri walked over to the control system he'd set up and began adjusting some of the controls. He nodded at her, acknowledging he'd started the calibrations.

"This plan of yours has the potential to be disastrous, Valya," Grigory said, crossing his arms over his chest. "You nearly lost your life yesterday, and now you're running straight back into danger. This was not what we agreed upon."

"It wasn't her plan." Sergei walked back over, checking the clip on his gun. "She argued against it initially. It's not ideal, but if we don't take drastic action, our alliance won't survive. All our people will be in danger then. How many will die if it comes to another war?"

Alec nodded. "The High Council is voting in the morning about terminating our alliance. Right now, most are in favor of ending our agreement. We searched the warehouse and discovered a large cache of weapons your people helped smuggle into the towers. Given our recent obstacles, I'm not sure I can persuade them otherwise unless we can provide them definitive proof that your people are not a threat."

"That's what Nikolai said," Grigory admitted with a frown. "I suppose we don't have much of a choice."

"Uncle," Valentina softened her tone, "I appreciate your concern, but I need to be by Nikolai's side in that meeting. With you and Ivan working with us, we'll have more allies in that room than possible enemies."

Nikolai nodded. "As much as I hate to say it, Viktor also has a soft spot for Valentina. I believe Peter does too. She's likely to be the safest one in that room."

Valentina finished her hydrating pack and dropped the empty container into the compartment of her speeder. "What about Lena? Have you heard from her?"

Grigory sighed. "We did not tell her about the meeting. She's supposed to meet with Ivan in about thirty minutes. We decided to tell her then."

Sergei arched his brow. "She may not agree to join us."

"No, but it's far more likely if she's already here. She may end up being curious or annoyed enough to want to join us," Grigory said, his eyes narrowing on the weapon at Sergei's side. "You're not going to be able to bring a gun into the meeting."

Sergei nodded. "I wasn't planning on it. But if I don't go in with one, they'll question it."

Alec's expression became confused, his gaze focusing on the knives she was carrying. "Why are you able to carry weapons?"

Valentina smiled. "I'm going as Nikolai's bodyguard. I'm permitted to carry certain weapons to keep him safe, but Sergei is... independent, I suppose you could say. He works as an agent of the Coalition, but he doesn't follow any specific directives, save those of our collective leadership."

Yuri snorted and added, "And until we find out who's framing him for supplying weapons to your people, they're not going to want to meet him while he's carrying a gun. He's still a suspect in most of their minds."

Sergei shrugged. "We will find the truth about who's responsible soon enough."

Valentina frowned. She wasn't thrilled with Sergei going unarmed, but Yuri was right. They'd never agree to meet with him unless they searched him first. Even so, Viktor's attempt at killing Sergei was still too fresh in her mind. She swallowed, staring at Sergei and wondering if this was the best thing to do. If they even *perceived* him as a threat, they could be within their rights to kill him.

Sergei's eyes softened as he returned her gaze. "It will be fine, little dove."

"Cheer up, Valya," Yuri said with a grin. "If Viktor stabs Sergei again, you get to heal him. I can't help but wonder... if Viktor cuts off a body part, can you reattach that too?"

Valentina glared at Yuri, tempted to throw something at him, but Nikolai placed his hand over hers and shook his head. "Hold on to your weapons, Valya. We need Yuri until after the meeting." Nikolai turned toward Yuri and added, "I trust you are finished with your calibrations and that's why you're provoking her?"

Yuri chuckled and nodded. "She needed a distraction."

Sergei leaned in close to her. "If you agree to marry me, Valechka, I'll hold him down any time you want to hurt him."

She blew out her breath and decided it would be best to ignore both of them. Yuri's distraction had been right on target and helped turn her worry into something more manageable. It was imperative she focus on what they were about to do and not allow her fears to be the guiding force of her actions. Ariana had said it plainly to her before they left. She'd be a fool not to do the same.

"We should go," Grigory said, glancing down at his commlink.

Valentina started to turn away, but Sergei stopped her. "This will be the last time I agree to keep my distance from you, Valechka."

Without waiting for a response, Sergei pressed his lips against hers in a heated kiss that sent her senses reeling. The fire within him swirled around her, scorching her with his heat. Unable to resist him, she gripped his jacket tightly and met his power head-on with hers, deepening the kiss and demanding more. He wrapped his arm around her, pulling her tighter against him.

"Wow," Kayla said from the other side of the room. "You weren't kidding about the energy."

Ariana laughed. "I told you. Water doesn't always put out a fire."

They broke the kiss, and Valentina blinked up at Sergei, staring into his passion-filled eyes. His gaze roamed over her features, and he murmured, "You're mine, Valentina Golubeva. I don't give a damn who knows it after this."

She swallowed, finding it difficult to argue with the truth. But it went both ways. If she belonged to him, he'd also always been hers.

Nikolai placed his hand on her back. "Come, Valya. It's getting late. Let's go clear Sergei's name before he completely distracts you from duty."

She frowned and darted another quick glance at Sergei, whose mouth had curved in a knowing smile. Nikolai was right; he was too distracting and far too appealing. Sergei also knew exactly how he affected her. Dammit. He was going to wear her down sooner than she intended.

Determined to focus on the task at hand, she turned away. "I'm ready."

Grigory grinned and led them out of the abandoned building. "You two remind me of your parents more and more. You complement each other well, Valya."

She made a noncommittal noise, unwilling to say anything that might encourage Grigory to start talking about marriage and babies again. "Where is the meeting being held?"

"The building is right up this hill," Grigory said, gesturing further down the alleyway. "I'll show you into the meeting room, but then I must go meet up with Ivan. Once Lena arrives, and if she agrees, we'll bring her along. Our people have already been put on notice to escort Peter directly to the meeting room."

Nikolai nodded. "We appreciate you orchestrating this."

They stopped outside a modest-sized, pre-war building that was in relatively decent shape. From all appearances, some of Ivan's people had reinforced areas of the structure. Two guards were stationed outside the door and stepped aside to allow them entry.

"Help yourself to whatever you'd like," Grigory offered, gesturing toward a table on the far side of the room with a few refreshments. "I'll be back with Ivan shortly, and hopefully, also with Lena."

Valentina nodded and watched as Grigory walked back outside. Once he was gone, she turned back to assess the room. It was bare, with the exception of an elongated table and some seating. In accordance with their request, the location they'd chosen appeared to be fairly secure with only one entrance. The building was far enough away from Yuri and everyone else that they wouldn't be detected if Peter or Lena decided to scan the area.

The only window had been sealed, which served their purposes well. They didn't need any witnesses to observe what they were attempting tonight. Supposedly, the guards outside were amongst those most loyal to Ivan and would keep their silence. Their endeavor would still be risky, but it was better than any other alternatives.

Nikolai approached her. "How are you feeling?"

"I should be asking you that," she said softly, aware the outside guards might be able to hear them. The room was most likely being monitored. Even with Grigory and Ivan claiming to be allies, it would have been foolish for them not to have listening devices planted.

Nikolai kissed her forehead. "It will be good to get all this cleared up. A chance for a future is what we've always wanted for our people."

Valentina looked up at Nikolai and smiled. He had one of the best hearts of anyone she'd ever known. "We'll make this alliance work, Kolya."

Footsteps sounded from outside, and she turned toward

the door to see Peter enter, followed by Viktor. Peter was more charismatic than attractive, and it was his allure and boldness that had helped secure his position and retain it. People believed the promises and assurances he made, and he'd developed a wide following in a short amount of time.

Nikolai gave Peter a nod in greeting. "It's good to see you again, Peter."

"You as well," Peter replied, reaching forward to shake Nikolai's hand before turning to Valentina with a warm smile. She offered him her hand, and he took it, squeezing it gently. "It's a pleasure to see you too, Valentina. You're lovelier every time I see you."

"That's very kind of you to say," she said softly, giving him a small smile. Peter was a handful of years older than Nikolai but still close enough in age compared to some of their other leaders. The two of them were the youngest of their leaders to acquire their position and one of the reasons they'd been friendly with each other. They'd both faced certain challenges in proving themselves, and it had created a sense of camaraderie.

However, Nikolai's opinion of Peter had chilled considerably ever since Viktor had tried to recruit her on Peter's behalf. Although she'd vehemently refused Viktor's invitation, Alec had used his powers to "encourage" Viktor into remembering events somewhat differently. As far as Peter and Viktor knew, she was still considering the offer. Unfortunately, it hadn't affected Nikolai's recollection or his irritation about the whole experience. Through their shared connection, she could sense Nikolai's aversion to allowing Peter and Viktor near her.

Peter wasn't a particularly bad man, but Valentina wasn't quite sure about his agenda. She had a few contacts in his camp, but no one particularly close to him. For all his failings, Viktor had always managed to keep Peter's camps fairly secure. That was part of the reason she'd agreed to work with Viktor in the past. He, and by extension Peter, had always been more forthcoming with her. It made sense if they sincerely hoped she'd join them, but she'd never abandon her family.

Peter released her, and Viktor took her hand instead. The memory of him plunging his knife into Sergei's chest was still too vivid, and it took every ounce of her self-discipline not to betray her anger or draw a weapon.

Lowering her gaze until she managed to control her emotions, she said, "Viktor, I wanted to thank you again for meeting with me the other day. Your information was very helpful."

Viktor's eyes warmed as he regarded her, and it still managed to catch Valentina by surprise. He really didn't seem to have any memory of what happened. "It's always enjoyable to work with you, Valentina. I hope to do more of it in the future."

Nikolai moved beside her and placed his hand against her back. Viktor immediately released her, and she sent a silent thank you to Nikolai for his intervention. It was only possible to hold a mask in place for so long, especially when her emotions were so close to the surface.

"Thank you for agreeing to join us," Nikolai began and gestured toward the table. "I believe Ivan and Grigory will be here shortly, if you'd care for some refreshments."

"Perhaps in a bit," Peter said, studying the room. "I was intrigued by the invitation to join you, Nikolai. I wasn't aware you had a friendship with Ivan."

Nikolai's mouth formed a thin line. "These shipment thefts are worrying all of us. Valentina spoke with Grigory the other day and learned Ivan's been having a similar problem. Given your previous agreement to work together, I thought it would be best for all of us to come together and share information."

Peter nodded. "I see."

The door swung open, and Grigory entered, along with Ivan, Lena, and her second-in-command, Roman. Lena was a striking woman in her fifties with dark hair that had only begun to gray in the past few years. In fact, Valentina was mildly surprised by the changes that had happened since then. The lines around her mouth and eyes had deepened, drawing attention to the cold chill within them. She'd never been an overly pleasant woman, but the hostility in her mien was staggering.

"What's the meaning of calling such a meeting, Nikolai?" she demanded, pinning him with her gaze. "You do not have any right to summon us. The last time I checked, you were little more than a junior chairman. Your arrogance and impudence will not be tolerated."

Valentina's eyes narrowed at the insult, but Nikolai put his hand on her arm in a warning. Her jaw clenched, but she remained in position beside him. It wouldn't serve their purposes to respond, but such a slight couldn't go unanswered.

Apparently, Ivan agreed. He took a step closer to Lena. "That's enough, Lena. You will not insult my guests. I told you that you were under no obligation to attend this meeting. If you don't intend to work with us to resolve this situation, I'll have my men escort you to your vehicles."

Lena's body went ramrod straight, and she glared at Ivan. "How long have you been allied with Nikolai, Ivan?"

"Lena, this situation affects all our people," Nikolai began, his voice almost unnaturally calm. Valentina knew his anger was slowly simmering under the surface, but he was masking it well. "We've come together before in times of need, and this is no different. Someone is stealing food, hydrating packs, medical supplies, and weapons. We've all been affected by these thefts, but it's our people who will suffer if we don't put a stop to them."

Lena inclined her head. "You're correct. Sergei Sokolov will be punished for his crimes."

Peter leaned against the wall. "Indeed. An armed escort has already been dispatched to the towers to retrieve him. The order was signed off by a majority about an hour ago."

Valentina felt the blood rush out of her face, and it took everything she had to remain standing. She hadn't heard anything about this order, but this was worse than they'd thought. They had to abort. Sergei couldn't be caught here. They'd have to find another way to discover the truth.

"Who approved this?" Nikolai demanded.

Someone knocked on the door, and Valentina's heart clenched. She didn't need the door to be open to know one of the guards was letting them know Sergei had arrived.

CHAPTER ELEVEN

ONE OF THE guards led Sergei into the room and said, "Sergei Sokolov to see you. His weapons have been removed."

Roman, Lena's second-in-command, walked toward him. Valentina started to intervene, but Grigory grabbed her. In a low whisper, he warned, "He needs to be searched again, Valya. Let it play out."

Roman roughly slammed Sergei up against the wall and briskly checked him again for weapons. Her fingers twitched, trying to resist the urge to draw a blade. The moment Viktor or Roman unsheathed theirs, she'd stop fighting her inclination.

Sergei turned back around and held her gaze for a long moment. In those few seconds, an entire lifetime sped by and unspoken promises passed between them. No matter what happened, she'd die before allowing anyone to harm him.

"He's not carrying any weapons," Roman announced, but he didn't move away from Sergei. The menace coming from him and Viktor was unsettling. She didn't like the fact they were between her and the man she loved. Despite Grigory's earlier warning, she moved forward to stand closer to Viktor but still within easy reach of Sergei. If nothing else, she was in a better position to provide him with a weapon.

"Well, I highly doubt this is a coincidence," Lena said, glaring at Ivan again. "You did not mention Sergei would be joining us as well."

"I asked him to join us," Nikolai announced.

Ivan nodded. "And I agreed. I want to put an end to this, and I expected all of you to want the same."

"Our reports have made it clear the weapons were being smuggled in by Pavel, Sergei's second-in-command," Peter reminded them. "Even if he wasn't directly responsible, this act of defiance was done under his supervision."

"You're correct," Sergei admitted. "I was remiss in not catching Pavel's deception earlier, but I had no involvement in these thefts. It was by my hand that Pavel was killed for betraying our people and endangering our alliance."

"You lie," Lena declared, her eyes narrowing on him. "For all we know, you could have killed him to cover up the truth."

"Sergei killed Pavel and Sofia because they abducted a woman from the towers," Valentina announced, refusing to let them continue to defame him. If Sergei wouldn't stand up for himself, she'd do it for him. "I was there and witnessed her captivity. Sofia and Pavel were torturing her. Sofia claimed Ariana's abduction was done with the approval of some of our leaders."

Ivan arched a brow. "I wasn't aware she made this claim. Did Sofia provide you with any names?"

"No," she admitted. "I knew Sofia was lying about this being a collective decision. I had been with Nikolai at the summit conference the week before and knew no decision had been made with regard to our alliance. Nikolai agreed to come to OmniLab to help assess the situation, but I came ahead of him to prepare for his arrival. However, I do not believe Sofia was being entirely dishonest."

Peter frowned. "What do you mean?"

Sergei met her gaze again, and Valentina felt his heated fire energy surround Peter and Lena. She straightened, mentally reaching out to Sergei to lend him her strength and hoping this wasn't beyond his abilities. If anything went wrong, there were no guarantees any of them would walk out of this room.

"Sofia was lying about the collective decision, but I saw Pavel's expression. He believed her words. Something or someone had led him to believe that at least one of our leaders had sanctioned Ariana's abduction."

Lena stiffened. "You're accusing one of *us*?"

Valentina blinked at her. "I am merely reporting the events and my impressions. Pavel believed it. I did not say the same."

"We are not making any accusations, Lena," Nikolai began, moving closer to her. "The four of us claim to have suffered losses from these thefts. The intention of this meeting was simply to share information with each other. Some of our stolen weapons were discovered in the possession of OmniLab residents. If we cannot put a stop to these weapons being smuggled into the towers, OmniLab has decreed our alliance will be forfeit."

Ivan frowned. "When did this happen?"

"Earlier this morning after a riot broke out in one of their towers," Sergei said, drawing their attention back to him. "Some of their residents were hurt and killed. Some of ours were also injured. We have less than twelve hours to locate our weapons and put an end to the smuggling operation or their council will vote to end our alliance."

"I can confirm Sergei's story," Grigory admitted. "We traced some of our missing supplies to the towers, but we were able to recover some of our items with Sergei's help. I do not believe he is responsible for these thefts."

Peter frowned and glanced over at Sergei. "You can't know that, Grigory. If he was simply trying to divert suspicion from himself, pretending to aid you would be a smart decision."

"Given the information I've gathered from some of my contacts in the area, I do not believe Sergei is responsible either," Valentina said quietly. They had no real proof yet, but she needed to provoke them into revealing something.

Viktor frowned. "I'm surprised to hear you say that, Valentina. I know you've been sympathetic to Sergei in the past, but the evidence against him is damning. I've shared some of my findings with you, but you've discovered something else?"

She nodded. "Yes, just recently. When we met at the towers, I mentioned to you that Nikolai had arranged to meet with OmniLab leadership in a remote location. During that meeting, we were ambushed and Sergei was shot. The weapons used were the same type that had been stolen from one of our shipments. Sergei would not have arranged to have himself nearly killed."

Lena scoffed. "He appears rather healthy for someone who nearly died."

"The healers in the towers are very skilled," Sergei admitted, and Valentina could feel him strengthening the bands of his truth barrier around Lena and Peter. So far, they hadn't said anything to implicate themselves in the thefts, but she didn't know how long Sergei could hold such a complicated energy weaving over multiple people.

Peter frowned at Nikolai. "You're *sure* these weapons belonged to one of your shipments?"

Nikolai nodded. "Yes. We realized the items were missing the following day. One of my aides reported them missing to Valentina. Later that day, Regina tried to kill me while I slept."

If Valentina hadn't been watching for any signs of guilt,

she would have missed Roman's almost barely discernible flinch. He knew something, or he knew Regina. Valentina glanced over at Sergei, and he inclined his head. He'd noticed it too.

They'd suspected Regina belonged to a unit like theirs, but now she wondered if Roman made up that unit. He could have been orchestrating the attack, but it didn't make sense. To her knowledge, Roman and Sergei had never had an issue with each other.

Opening up their bond even more, Valentina allowed more of her energy to flow toward Sergei as he spread the truth barrier to also encompass Roman. She could feel Sergei's strain in holding the energy over three people. They needed to hurry.

Valentina turned toward Roman. "Roman, I haven't had an opportunity to work with you much in the past. But your skill in strategy and tactics in well-known. Do you have any ideas who may be responsible?"

Roman's expression remained neutral. "I find it interesting that Nikolai's weapons were the ones used to target Sergei. It's rumored there's been some tension between the two of them over the past several years." He shrugged. "It would not be the first time love has caused someone to do something uncharacteristic. Sadly, it usually doesn't end well for anyone involved."

Valentina paused, considering Roman for a long moment. He had phrased his words a little too carefully. Either he was trying to tell her something or issue a warning. She just didn't know which.

Her interaction with Roman had been limited in the past. He was neither overly friendly nor hostile, preferring to keep to himself or socializing only within Lena's camp. Valentina respected him for his dedication to Lena, but that was all she really knew about him. Lena's dislike for Nikolai was well-known, and it was possible her second-in-command also shared her feelings.

Based on Nikolai's irritated expression, he wasn't thrilled with Roman or his insinuation. He narrowed his eyes. "I resent the implication. I did *not* arrange to have Sergei attacked. A laser sight was trained on Valentina, and Sergei pushed her out of the way. If anything, I'm grateful for his intervention and sacrifice in saving her life that day."

Roman inclined his head. "Indeed. You were all fortunate."

Valentina frowned. Roman knew more than he was saying, but he was a little too tight-lipped. Through her bond with Sergei, she could feel him struggling to maintain the truth barrier. They only had maybe a handful of minutes before it fell.

It was time to try a more drastic approach. Peter and Viktor might not be happy with her for revealing this information, but they were running out of time.

Turning toward Peter, she said, "I would normally not divulge information you or Viktor shared with me in confidence, but time is of the essence. If you will give me some latitude here, I believe Viktor's knowledge may help resolve this situation."

Peter studied her thoughtfully for a long moment. "Very well. If you're referring to what he shared with you at the construction tower, I'll permit it."

She nodded. "Viktor, you indicated you believed Sergei was always the target of the ambush. Why did you think that?"

Viktor shrugged. "I overheard a conversation that led me to believe it."

Valentina waited for him to elaborate. When he didn't say anything further, Peter sighed and waved his hand. "Go ahead and tell her. I want to know where she's going with this."

Viktor frowned. "I was tracing the missing shipments and a tip led me to Sofia's camp. I believe some of the weapons were stored there before being smuggled into the towers. Unfortunately, Sergei had tortured and killed Sofia and Pavel a few days earlier. When I made it clear I didn't harbor any friendly feelings toward Sergei, some of the people within the camp spoke freely in front of me. One of them mentioned they knew Sergei would be executed soon. When I heard about the shooting, it was logical to make the leap."

Valentina's eyes widened. "*Sofia* was storing them? I knew she and Pavel were lovers, but this makes much more sense. We confirmed Pavel was the one smuggling them into the towers, but we didn't know how he was acquiring them."

"Sofia wasn't storing all of them," Viktor said, shaking his head. "I searched the camp thoroughly, and I believe only a small number of weapons were held there temporarily. They are either already in the towers or being held at another location. I do not know where she acquired them."

Lena frowned. "All I'm hearing are rumors and speculation. I don't hear very many facts." She paused, and her frown deepened.

Valentina tilted her head, studying the woman's agitated body language. Lena's mouth opened and closed as though she were struggling to speak. The only explanation was she was attempting to voice a lie. Valentina glanced over at Sergei, who was beginning to perspire from the continued strain. She sent him an even stronger wave of her energy, wishing she could magnify the amount through contact. But that would be too suspicious, and they needed a few more minutes.

Roman's expression grew alarmed. "Lena, are you all right?"

"Something's wrong," she managed. "I feel strange."

Roman strode toward her. "Allow me to escort you out of here."

Valentina tensed. They couldn't allow her to leave yet. Catching Ivan's eye, he nodded and walked over to the older woman.

"Lena," Ivan interrupted, taking her arm, "you should sit for a moment. Allow me to get you a drink."

"I should leave," Lena insisted.

"Nonsense," Ivan said, leading her to a chair. "If you're not feeling well, you should wait until you're recovered. We have medics here who can attend to you. I would be remiss in allowing you to travel all the way back to your camp without medical personnel."

While Ivan poured Lena a drink, Valentina glanced at Sergei. He wiped his brow from the exertion and nodded at her to continue. She frowned. Lena's rank made it impossible for either her or Nikolai to question Lena outright about her involvement with the thefts, but it might be possible to elicit information in another way.

Turning back to Roman, Valentina said, "You mentioned love makes people act in an uncharacteristic manner. Who were you referring to?"

Roman frowned and glanced at Sergei before focusing on her again. "I believe the statement holds true for most people. That includes you, Valentina."

She paused, a suspicion beginning to grow in her mind. "Viktor was wrong, wasn't he? Was I the target of the ambush? Not Sergei?"

Roman didn't respond. Nikolai's eyes narrowed as he demanded, "If you know something, you're duty-bound to tell us."

"I'm under no obligation to answer to you, Nikolai," Roman snapped. "My loyalty is to Lena."

Valentina glanced over at Lena, but the woman was struggling to talk. Her eyes were wide, and she pushed herself out of the chair. "What have you done to me? Why am I having trouble speaking?"

"The truth has a way of emerging," Nikolai said, taking a step toward Lena. "Try to deny your involvement in the weapon thefts. Your lies will not be heard."

Lena's eyes narrowed, and she straightened. "You want to discuss lies? Then let's talk about your involvement in covering up my son's murder."

Valentina frowned, and Nikolai appeared confused too. He shook his head. "I don't know what you're talking about, Lena."

Lena clenched her fists, and anger made the older woman's features even harsher in the artificial light. "Three years ago, my son was leading one of the teams during the Pathfinder Facility takeover. When Sergei set the fire in the service wing, Leonid was among those who became trapped. You allowed him to burn to death and then helped his murderer cover up his crime."

Valentina glanced at Sergei. The pain and guilt on his face was heart-wrenching. She swallowed, wanting to go to him but unable to offer him any comfort without endangering all of them. Reaching out to him through their emotional connection, she gently brushed against Sergei with her energy to let him know he wasn't alone. His eyes met hers, and the rush of love and gratitude that flowed through their bond nearly caused her to break her resolve in keeping her distance.

"I apologize, Lena," Nikolai said gently. "I wasn't aware Leonid was your son. We lost many brave people during that takeover, and nothing I say or do will make up for your loss. Whatever you believe may have happened, I assure you, we did everything possible to try to help them."

"You lie," Lena spat, taking a step toward him. "I interviewed and debriefed many of the former residents of that facility. Too many of their stories deviated from your reports. Our other leaders weren't willing to look too closely because you and Sergei managed to get results, but your decisions that day should never have been rewarded. Neither of you deserve your positions or any sort of future. I'll see both of you lose everything and everyone you hold dear before I allow this travesty to continue."

Sergei straightened, a barely restrained fury in his eyes. "It wasn't enough to frame me for the thefts and inciting a rebellion, was it? You also targeted Valentina to get back at both of us." When Lena didn't answer, he said, "I remember your son, and he was a good and honorable man. He never would have condoned your actions. Valentina was nearly taken from us that day as well. She was not involved with anything that happened to your son. If you need to blame someone, you can blame me. But Valentina is innocent."

Valentina glared at Sergei, mentally willing him to shut up. If he kept talking, he'd likely incriminate himself further out of a misguided attempt to protect her.

Nikolai held up his hand to stop Sergei from speaking. "Those of us who were there and survived unharmed share the blame in what happened, Lena. We didn't protect our people well enough. I'm truly sorry for your loss, but Sergei is right. Valentina had nothing to do with what happened to your son."

Valentina gritted her teeth. People who were determined to protect her surrounded her, but Lena wasn't going to listen to reason. This wasn't about her. Lena had lost her son. Such devastation had crippled her, and nothing they could say would heal that damage. The only one who might have a chance to get through to her was Ivan, but even that was unlikely.

"You're wrong, Nikolai," Lena argued, her eyes going cold.

"You and Sergei share the blame. Sergei was responsible for the fire, and you were responsible for covering up the truth. Did you really think there would be no consequences to your actions?"

"By killing Valentina?" Sergei demanded, his fists clenched in silent fury.

Lena inclined her head. "You didn't seem to care about losing your position or being held responsible for the thefts. But then I heard what you'd done to Pavel after Valentina had been hurt. What better way to get back at you both than to take the person you love too?"

"Valentina, get down!" Nikolai shouted.

Not questioning his order, she dropped to the ground just as Roman withdrew a knife and moved toward her. She rolled away, but Sergei tackled Roman, grappling with him for the weapon.

She started to go to Sergei's aid just as Lena jumped forward, brandishing a gun. Only this time, Lena's intended target was Nikolai. From her prone position on the ground, Valentina withdrew her sidearm and fired at Lena just as the other woman discharged her gun.

Lena's shot went wide, missing Nikolai. But less than a second later, burning pain sliced through Valentina's chest. She ignored it, firing at Lena twice more as the woman started to raise her weapon. Nikolai fired his gun at the same time, and Lena stumbled backward into the wall, a red smear blooming on her chest.

Lena started to raise her weapon again, aiming at Valentina, but the ground and walls began to shake. Stone masonry began crumbling, causing rocks and other building debris to fall around them. Nikolai dove toward her, covering her with his body. Shouts erupted around them, and almost as quickly as it had begun, the shaking stopped.

Valentina ran her hands over Nikolai's chest, looking for

any signs of injuries. He leaned back, searching her up and down. "Are you all right, Valya? Are you hurt?"

She coughed, the dust making it difficult to breathe. Shaking her head, she said, "No. You?"

"I'm fine," he said, getting to his feet and helping her up.

Roman had crawled over to Lena and was trying to unearth her body from the rocks that had fallen on top of her. Valentina spun around, searching for Sergei, and stark terror ran through her at the sight of him on the ground. Debris had fallen around him, but it was the red stain soaking through his jacket that made her heart nearly stop.

Rushing toward him, she dropped to her knees beside him. She withdrew a knife from her arm sheath, slicing through his jacket to assess the damage. A bullet hole. Lena hadn't hit her. She'd felt Sergei being shot through their bond.

Sergei reached up to brush his fingers against her cheek. "You're not hurt?"

"Shh, Seryozha," she urged, wanting him to conserve his strength. Until she knew how bad it was, he needed to remain quiet and still. It might not be a fatal shot if they could get him help in time. Her healing skills were still shaky, but she'd do whatever was necessary to keep him alive.

She could sense Yuri through their bond, so at least he was alive and relatively unharmed. Looking over her shoulder, she saw Viktor, Peter, and Nikolai struggling to restrain Roman. The man was out of control at the realization Lena was dead.

"Nikolai!" she yelled over to him. "I need Ariana. Sergei's been shot."

Grigory motioned for him to go before stepping in to take his place. Nikolai immediately released Roman and rushed over to her. "I'll get her and Alec. Do what you can for him."

"Valechka," Sergei began, but she pressed her fingertips against his lips.

"Shh. I need you to sit up for me. I have to check for an exit hole."

She helped him into a sitting position and lifted his shirt to see if the bullet had passed through. Dammit. There was nothing.

Sergei winced as he laid back down. "Kayla must have caused the earthquake."

"She's not my concern," Valentina said, pressing her hand firmly over the bullet wound. At least this time his lungs hadn't been affected. Gut wounds were always so painful though.

"You're not going to take off your shirt this time, Valechka?"

She blinked at him. "Are you trying to get me naked while you're bleeding on the floor?"

"We could call it a dying man's last request," he said, grimacing in pain.

She frowned. "You're not in danger of dying. I won't allow it."

"I can pretend," he managed, running his fingers along the edge of her shirt and tugging it weakly.

Despite herself, she couldn't help but smile at his efforts to tease her. He was hurting so much, but even now, he was trying to distract her so she wouldn't worry. Through their bond, she could feel his agony as sharply as her own.

Leaning down, Valentina kissed him lightly and murmured, "You're such a troublemaker, Seryozha. Just hold on for a few minutes until Ariana and Alec get here. I'll need their help to remove the bullet. I don't want to cause more damage by healing you while it's still inside. Don't die, and I'll let you take off my shirt later."

He grunted but didn't argue. Movement out of the corner of her eye caught her attention, and she glanced over to see the guards who had been standing outside putting Roman into restraints while Peter and Viktor supervised.

Grigory walked over to her and frowned. "How bad is it? Can you heal him with that dragon statue?"

She shook her head. "No, it's too risky. I don't know how the statue works. If Ariana is delayed, I'll try to heal the worst of his injuries even with the bullet still inside." She glanced over at Peter and Viktor, uneasy about the thought of letting her guard down. "But I'll need to concentrate."

"Do whatever you need to do. I'll keep watch over both of you," Grigory said, placing his hand on her shoulder and squeezing it gently. "Ivan's gone to check on the damage from the earthquake. Nikolai should be back any minute with your friends."

Valentina nodded and turned back to Sergei. Even if she didn't try to heal him right now, she might be able to get a sense of how badly he'd been injured. Taking a deep breath, she focused on imagining him whole and perfect once again. Spreading her fingers outward over his abdomen, she could almost feel the bullet and the sense of wrongness coming from it. His energy and body wanted to reject the foreign invasion, but he lacked the ability on his own.

"Will you distract me to keep me awake, Valechka?"

Valentina opened her eyes and ran her hand over Sergei's forehead. His skin was cooler than normal, but he shouldn't be in danger of losing consciousness yet unless the bullet had done more damage than she'd thought. She didn't have enough experience to gauge the accuracy of her healing abilities in this type of situation. Ariana had taken her to the medical ward a few times, but her experiences were still too few to be dependable. Especially when it came to the man she loved being hurt.

Her heart thudded in her chest, and she nodded. "Yes. If

you stay awake, I'll tell you either one secret or grant one favor."

"I want a favor."

Valentina sent a silent plea to Nikolai to hurry and nodded. "Anything, Seryozha. What do you wish of me?"

Sergei put his hand over hers and whispered, "Will you marry me, Valentina Golubeva?"

Valentina froze. She blinked at him several times, trying to form a coherent thought. "Now? You're asking me this now?"

He nodded, and Grigory made a strangled noise that sounded an awful lot like a laugh. Her eyes narrowed on Sergei, and she pressed a little harder on his abdomen.

"You're not in any danger of losing consciousness, are you?"

Sergei groaned. "I might be now."

She eased up a bit and blew out a breath. "I cannot believe you."

"You agreed to owe me a favor, Valechka," Sergei said with a pained grin. "Will you be forsworn?"

Valentina shook her head in exasperation. "You're such a troublemaker."

"Mmhmm," he agreed.

Leaning forward, she brushed a featherlight kiss against his lips. "Yes, Sergei Sokolov, I will marry you. My heart and soul are yours. They've always been yours."

"Finally," he said and closed his eyes. "I thought it would take longer to wear you down. Yuri won't be pleased."

She frowned. "What?"

Sergei shifted. "He wanted more than a year of training to help me convince you. Now he'll have to suffer through it."

A laugh bubbled out of her. "What am I going to do with you?"

"Hopefully get this bullet out soon," he whispered. "It fucking burns like anything."

Valentina closed her eyes, sending a wave of healing energy over him. She felt his abdomen relax slightly under her hand. When she opened her eyes, his expression was less pained. Instead, his eyes were filled with wonderment and love as he gazed up at her.

His voice was almost reverent as he said, "I don't think I ever witnessed true beauty until I met you, Valechka."

"Seryozha," she murmured, trailing her fingertips along his jaw. He was so fierce and strong, but hearing tender words from him always sent her heart soaring. No one else had ever evoked this depth of emotion. Every day that passed, she fell deeper in love with him. He was her biggest weakness, but she wouldn't change that for anything. Sometimes, a bit of vulnerability was just as important as someone's strength.

"You always say such sweet things when I cannot show you how you make me feel."

"I love you, little dove," he whispered, squeezing her hand gently. "And I will say them to you for the rest of our lives now that you've agreed to be mine."

Approaching footsteps sounded from outside, and she lifted her head to see Nikolai and Yuri enter, along with Ariana and Alec. Ariana went over to her immediately and knelt on the floor beside her. "You weren't able to heal him?"

Valentina shook her head. "I only took away the worst of his pain. It was too risky to try to heal him completely. The bullet is still in him. Can you remove it?"

"Alec, I need you to help me," Ariana said, pressing her hand over Sergei's abdomen. Valentina started to scoot over, but Sergei reached for her and shook his head. Taking his hand, she held it against her cheek and gently caressed him with her energy. She wasn't inclined to move away either.

Alec put his hand on Ariana's shoulder. "Go ahead, love. If

you can locate the bullet, we can try to move it into a position so I can use my energy to extract it."

Valentina frowned, watching as Ariana and Alec concentrated. Unfortunately, very little was happening. Maybe it was because she was so closely entwined with Sergei now, but it required very little effort to sense the bullet. It wasn't moving, despite the combined efforts of Ariana and Alec. Ivan had medics in his camp, but it was unlikely they'd have a skilled surgery center set up here. She didn't want to cause Sergei more pain, but there had to be a way to remove the bullet without harming him further.

"Dragon fire," a voice whispered.

Valentina started, her gaze immediately searching the room. She couldn't tell who had spoken.

Yuri's head jerked up, and he scowled. "What was that?"

Alec frowned. "You heard it too?"

"So did I," Valentina admitted. Nikolai nodded, and Ariana did too.

Grigory glanced between them. "Heard what?"

"I'm not sure," Valentina said, glancing around. Peter and Viktor had disappeared. They were most likely outside or with Ivan. The guards were back and trying to excavate Lena's body from underneath the fallen rubble. But they weren't paying much attention to them and didn't show any indication of having heard anything.

Kayla came rushing into the room with Brant and Carl right behind her. She gripped the edge of the doorway, and in a nearly breathless voice said, "Oh shit. We've got to hurry. Fix him quick. We've got to go."

Alec turned toward her. "What is it? What's wrong?"

"The earthquake. It didn't just affect us here. Carl just got a call from some of our people at the underground river. Some of them are trapped in the cavern, and the water's still rising. The rocks started falling, and we've lost communication with our people. We need to stabilize the earth so they can get them out."

Ariana's gaze flew to Valentina. "You have the dragon statue with you?"

She pulled it out of her pocket. It was still the brilliant gold color, but there were swirls of pearlized red and green underneath. "Yes, but I don't want to risk harming Sergei."

"If we can use it as a focus to help combine our powers, we can melt the bullet," Ariana explained. "If you control it, he'll remain unharmed. Sergei's your mate. You won't allow anything to happen to him."

Valentina hesitated, uneasy at the thought of using an object they didn't understand on the man she loved.

Sergei squeezed her hand. "Do it."

Nikolai placed his hand on her shoulder and added, "Ariana is correct. You won't allow Sergei to be harmed, but we need to hurry. These people need us."

When Yuri nodded at her too, Valentina swallowed and placed the dragon statue on Sergei's abdomen. Saying a silent prayer for his health, she opened herself up to the surrounding energy and power within her. Ariana and Kayla reached out to touch the statuette, and the moment they came into contact with it, the strange awareness filled each of them again.

"Direct the power, Valentina," Ariana instructed.

She nodded, gathering the magnitude of each of their powers and channeling it through the dragon figurine and into Sergei. It was almost as though the statuette was acting as a filter of some kind, infusing their energy with some other elemental quality she didn't fully comprehend. Colors and images—foreign and alien—flashed through her mind. A vibration pounded against her temples, and she didn't know if it was the sound of her blood rushing through her veins or some other unearthly noise.

The combined force of their energy was almost more than she could handle. If the dragon figurine wasn't acting as a receptacle for their powers, Valentina wasn't sure if her psyche would remain intact under the weight of their combined strength. Not only was she linked with Ariana and Kayla, but there was another awareness within her. It was foreign and independent, and she had the distinct impression it was somehow tied to the statuette. She reached out toward it, but it slipped out of her grasp, directing her once again toward the bond that had grounded and sustained her for so many years.

Love for Sergei, Nikolai, and Yuri filled her heart, and she infused her energy with the strength of her emotions, channeling it toward the figurine and into Sergei. In that moment, she realized these three men were more than her bondmates or family—they shared pieces of each other's souls. They needed her as much as she needed them.

It wasn't just the bond's connection, but something that extended into the most primitive parts of themselves they didn't fully understand. It was elemental and primal, raw and pure power, and beyond her ability to comprehend. It was like catching sunlight in the palm of one's hand, with the power to either gently warm or burn them if they got too close. The longer she channeled their combined strength, the brighter and hotter their power flared until it was nearly blinding.

Whether it was instinctual or some sort of divine intervention, Valentina wasn't sure. But a sense of knowing filled her, and she opened her eyes to look down into Sergei's face. Even without checking, she knew the bullet was gone. Whatever damage had been caused by Lena's gun had been repaired. Sergei was once again whole and perfect, and completely hers, just as she belonged to him.

He sat up, causing the statue to tumble into his lap. Kayla

and Ariana sat back, shaking their heads as though slightly dazed. The dragon hadn't changed in appearance this time, although the swirls of pearlized reds and greens were much more obvious. It was even more beautiful than she'd initially realized.

Sergei cupped her face, searching her expression, and murmured, "But not as beautiful as you."

She blinked at him. "You heard my thoughts?"

He nodded, brushing his thumb across her cheek. "I feel you within me, little dove. You've always been in my heart, but this is so much more. Your love is so pure and more precious than anything I've ever experienced. You make me want to be worthy of such a gift."

"You've always been worthy, Seryozha," she whispered, leaning even closer as his heated fire energy swirled around her, drawing her toward him. She placed her hand over his heart, her love for him nearly overwhelming with its intensity. More than anything, she wanted to show him how much she valued and treasured him. "But you should not say such things until we're alone, Seryozha."

He gave her a knowing smile and pressed a light kiss against her lips. "I will have even more things to say to you then—a lifetime of things for your ears alone."

Her heart soared in acknowledgement of his words. Sergei had always known exactly what to say to her and how to chase away the shadows and darkness from her life. The world wouldn't be nearly as bright without him in it. Tracing her fingers over the area where the bullet had entered, she couldn't hide her relief at knowing he was out of danger.

"There's not even a mark, and I don't sense the bullet anymore. Are you in any pain?"

He placed his hand over hers. "No, Valechka. You've healed all my wounds, not just the ones caused here tonight.

As long as you're by my side, there is no pain. You are everything I have ever wanted."

Her stomach fluttered at his words, and she looked up into his eyes. She could easily get lost in their gray depths and the heat of his gaze. She swallowed, wishing they had a chance to be alone, but duty called. They couldn't leave their people in danger, and she knew Sergei felt the same.

Nikolai's voice was gentle as he held out his hand to help her up. "We must go, Valya."

Valentina nodded and stood. Yuri extended his hand to help Sergei up.

Sergei winked at her and said, "By the way, Yuri, I won't need to take over your training duties after all."

Yuri's gaze flew toward her. "Dammit, Valya. You agreed to marry him already? You couldn't hold out until he accepted my terms?"

She smiled sweetly. "Now why would I have done that? After all, you were the one who put the idea of marriage and babies into his head. Oh, and let's not forget giving him the advantage when I tried sneaking out to meet with Dmitri. Maybe next time you'll choose your allies more carefully."

Yuri scowled and crossed his arms over his chest.

"It's about time," Nikolai murmured and brushed a kiss against her temple. "Come, Valya. Let's go save our people and then you two can celebrate. You both deserve every happiness."

"I think we should go back to the days of having a *vykup*," Yuri muttered, following behind them as they left the building. "If Sergei wants to marry her, we should be able to extract a bride price."

"Forget it, Yuri," she said with a laugh. "You're going to have to deal with training recruits on your own."

"That's a shame," Yuri said with a sigh.

Sergei put his hand behind her back and led her up the

hill toward their speeders. "It's more of a shame that I would have agreed to two years of training."

Yuri cursed loudly. "How mad would you be if he got shot again, Valya?"

Valentina leaned against Sergei and grinned. "You're not shooting him, Yuri."

"Definitely a shame," Yuri grumbled.

CHAPTER TWELVE

THE SITUATION WAS WORSE than Valentina expected. On the drive to the excavation site, Sergei had been reaching out to their people while Kayla communicated with the ruin rats and Omnis stationed there. They were putting together bits and pieces of the story, and so far, it wasn't looking good.

From all appearances, the earthquake had originated within the vicinity of the underground cavern. The effects they'd experienced in Ivan's camp had been negligible compared to the excavation site. More than a few people had been injured and some were trapped in the cavern, cut off from all exits. With the rapids possibly still rising, the situation was becoming dire.

Valentina pulled up behind Sergei and climbed off her speeder. Kayla and Carl had arrived just minutes before them and were already rushing toward the large group congregating a short distance away.

Taking off her helmet, Valentina placed it on the seat of her speeder as the rest of their group started arriving. Grigory had stayed with Ivan back in their camp while they assessed the rest of the damage from the earthquake. Peter and Viktor had also left to check on their people. She didn't know what was going to happen to Lena's second-in-command, but it was likely he'd be subjected to a formal inquiry. In the interim, Ivan would retain custody of Roman until a decision could be made.

Nikolai climbed off his speeder and pulled off his helmet. Valentina took a step toward him and asked, "Did you speak with the people in our camp?"

He nodded. "They're all accounted for and unharmed. The earthquake didn't affect them." He turned to Sergei. "Who's in charge here?"

"Kayla and Carl, for the most part. We pulled off most of our people to work on the tower construction. I left a crew in place, but they've primarily been acting as support personnel for the excavation team."

Valentina studied the large group congregating amongst the ruined buildings and near the entrance to a large chasm. Some people were being treated for injuries, and a few were sitting down with bandages or bone molds covering portions of their bodies. The group was bigger than she expected. If she had to guess, she'd say two hundred people were living and working in the immediate vicinity, but not all of them were Coalition. "How many of our people are still here?"

"Only about fifty, maybe a little more," Sergei said, glancing in the direction she was looking. "Some are under my direct command, but we also have some who are loyal to Lena and Peter. A lesser number belong to Ivan's camp, and I believe Nikolai has even fewer. The rest are ruin rats and Omnis."

She frowned. That might be something of a problem, depending on what orders Lena had given to her people. They wouldn't find out about her death right away. Until word trickled down to their respective camps, Nikolai and Sergei could still be targets.

"Kolya, there may be some tactical issues to consider if you accompany us."

"We'll stay vigilant, Valya, but I must check on our people," Nikolai said, placing his hand on her back.

She nodded. With Lena dead, and Ivan and Peter occupied, Nikolai could act as a stand-in to make any decisions necessary to preserve life.

Ariana and Alec approached them, along with Brant and Lars right behind them. Ariana bit her lip and said, "I can feel everyone's fear and worry from here. Do we know where the people are trapped?"

"Not far from here," Sergei said, motioning for them to follow.

Valentina walked behind him, taking the opportunity to study the crumbling buildings. It was difficult to tell since she'd never been here, but based on the amount of rubble, the damage was more than a little extensive. They'd need to completely reinforce some of these buildings again if they intended to use them.

They passed by a collapsed building, and she frowned, catching sight of crates of supplies within. If their people were trapped underground, it didn't bode well for any of them. Ariana was a skilled earth channeler, but Valentina had a difficult time believing she could stabilize the earth enough to help them.

A dark-haired woman broke away from the crowd and walked over to Sergei. "I'm glad you're here. We managed to get the communication tower back up, but we're still having problems reaching our people down below."

Sergei nodded. "How many are trapped, Yuisa?"

"Four in the elevator, but another eight were down in the cavern running scans. A few of them were testing the water levels, so they were closest to the river. We don't know if any of them are alive or not."

"Assume they're alive unless we have confirmation otherwise," Nikolai ordered, his tone sharp.

Yuisa turned, her eyes widening at the sight of Valentina and Nikolai. "Oh— Of course, Chairman. I apologize. No disrespect was intended."

Valentina caught Yuri's eye, and he moved forward to stand on the other side of Nikolai. Until they figured out who the players were, they needed to be cautious. The fact no one was expecting them was to their benefit, but she didn't know how loyal these people were to Lena or Peter. Whenever Nikolai did venture out, he usually had more people protecting him.

"You worry too much, Valya," Nikolai said quietly enough that no one else could hear, except for Yuri.

"And you don't worry enough," she murmured, catching sight of Brant beside Alec. Brant didn't look particularly happy about Alec and Ariana being there either.

Kayla jogged over to them. "They're running stability scans on the area. We've lost supports in at least six areas, communication has crapped out, and a dozen people are missing."

Valentina frowned. "Do you know where they were last working?"

"We have an idea," Kayla said, motioning for them to follow her. She led them into a command tent where a few people were working. A man with light-brown hair was sitting at a console and looked up when they entered.

"Scoot over, V," Kayla said, nudging the man to the side. She took his place and pulled up a three-dimensional diagram of the underground cavern. Pointing to two locations on the screen, she said, "Okay. At the last check-in, we had one team here and another deeper below the surface. The others are in the elevator, which is about," she pointed to another area, "there."

Sergei leaned forward, studying the diagram. "We need to secure the elevator first. If those cables snap, the people won't survive. Can you rig a device to pull up the elevator?"

Kayla nodded. "Yes, provided nothing is obstructing it. We can try lowering someone to attach a couple of cables to the elevator supports. Those devices are designed to only lift the weight of one person, but we can try to hook several of them together."

Valentina frowned. "What if the area around the elevator isn't clear? The damage up here is bad enough. If these people are below ground, fallen rocks could be a problem."

Kayla blew out a breath. "That's my worry too. We need a straight shot out of the chasm to pull the elevator up. Otherwise, we'll have to manually pull them out one by one, and it'll be more difficult to get to the rest of our people. Not all of them have experience ruin diving with a cable and harness. The elevator is our best option."

Alec cocked his head, studying the display. "How much does the elevator weigh?"

"A lot," Kayla admitted with a frown. "We might need a dozen cable devices and motors to pull it up. Unfortunately, some of our equipment has been damaged. I'm not sure we have enough that are still functional."

Sergei motioned to Yuisa. "Gather a few of our people to check on our equipment. Find as many of these devices and motors as you can, verify they're in working order, and bring them to the edge of the chasm."

Yuisa nodded and ducked out of the tent.

Kayla was quiet for a moment, studying the screen. She straightened and wiggled her fingers at Alec. "Hey! Can you do your thing on the elevator and pull it up with your energy?"

Alec hesitated. "With Lars's help, possibly. It would be better if we had more air channelers, but we may be able to do it. I'm just not sure we'll have enough power to lift something that far. If it were a short distance, yes."

Valentina glanced around the room at the few remaining people she didn't know. The man Kayla had greeted was still there, standing close to a woman with fiery-red hair. Based on their body language, they were obviously a couple. Another man was working at a different console. It appeared to be a communication system, but he didn't seem to be having much luck with it.

Sergei approached her and placed his hand on her back. "You have a thought, Valechka?"

"Perhaps we should speak in private," she said quietly, not willing to discuss her idea in front of these strangers.

Sergei smiled and gestured to three people still in the command tent. "You can speak freely in front of them. Josten is one of the Shadows I worked with during our initial occupation of the towers. I've known him for over a year. Jinx and Veridian are close friends with Kayla. They'll all understand our unique circumstances."

"They're good people," Kayla said, leaning back in her chair. "I grew up with V, and Jinx has become as close as a sister. Josten saved my ass when I tried to bring down the towers with an earthquake. They all know about this energy stuff, and they're cool with it."

Brant smiled and shook his head. "You're the only one I know who ends up being good friends with people who once tried to kill you."

Josten frowned. "I only took her hostage. I never tried to kill her."

Kayla nodded. "True. Most of my closest friends have either abducted me or wanted me dead a time or two. I don't take it personally anymore."

Lars cleared his throat. "It must be your winning personality."

Kayla grinned at him. "Must be."

Valentina frowned. With her using the dragon to heal Sergei at Ivan's camp, and the people who had witnessed their display in the towers after she'd been shot, their secret was well and truly out. She glanced over at Nikolai, who smiled in understanding.

He took a step closer. "If our goal is to save our people, including those who may be trapped, we cannot remain silent. Go ahead, Valya. Speak freely. Time is of the essence."

Valentina nodded and pulled out the small dragon figurine. "Alec, would you be able to combine your powers using this? If you aren't sure you have the power to perform such a feat, do you think this would help you?"

Alec arched his brow, clearly intrigued as he studied the small statuette in her hand. "It might be possible. It worked well for you when you healed Sergei."

Kayla shook her head. "No. Valentina can direct it, but you can't. It will tolerate you because of Ariana, but it belongs with Valentina. It *really* likes her." Kayla frowned and leaned forward to view it. "Um, I don't think it was swirling like that before we got here."

Ariana approached her and studied the figurine. "It's resonating even stronger with you, Valentina. I think Kayla's right. It wants you to be the one to use it. I'm somehow picking up traces of emotion from it."

Nikolai frowned. "How can stone project emotion?"

Valentina lifted the small dragon, fascinated by the vivid swirls of red and green beneath the gold. It was almost hypnotizing, and the longer she stared at it, the more it seemed to warm in her hand. "I think... If you take me to this elevator, I believe I may able to use the stone."

Sergei frowned. "If this is dangerous to you, I do not want you to attempt it. We can try the cabling devices first."

"I don't think it's dangerous to me," she admitted. "I'm

not sure I can explain, but I think I know how to use it. I'll need all of you there to help."

Sergei didn't appear convinced, but he nodded. "I'll show you where the lift is located. Hopefully, we can access that area without too much trouble."

———

SERGEI HANDED another cabling device to Kayla. He'd offered to help set it up, but Kayla had shooed him away claiming the experts should be the ones to handle the ruin diving equipment. She was right, so he'd let her, Carl, and the rest of her group work on it.

He turned and walked back toward a stack of crates. They'd gathered a large group of people and were coordinating their efforts to locate more cables and motors. It was an exercise in frustration to find that many of their supplies had been damaged from the earthquake. Some could still be salvaged, but it would take too long to repair them, so they were searching for working items that could be used in their rescue efforts.

Valentina was standing a short distance away and speaking quietly with Nikolai and Yuri. The dragon was still in her hand, and she was showing it to Nikolai. Whatever she was saying was too low to be overheard. Through their bond, he could sense her apprehension. He knew she was trying to figure out the best way to use the statue to save their people. She'd never connected directly with Alec or Lars before, and none of them knew how it would work.

He'd be lying if he said he wasn't worried about her using that thing. Judging by the rigidity in Nikolai's shoulders and how Yuri's hand hadn't strayed from his gun, he guessed they both had reservations too.

"I hope I didn't offend Chairman Nikolai earlier," Yuisa

said, glancing over at them as she checked the contents of another crate. "I wasn't expecting to see him here. Do you think he'll be the one to take over the new tower when it's finished?"

Sergei turned back to the dark-haired woman. Yuisa had been transferred to his command only about eight months ago, but she'd proven to be capable and hardworking. "It is too soon to say. Why? Do you wish to follow his command?"

Yuisa nodded. "I've enjoyed working under you, Sergei. But you always told us you weren't going to be permanent. Some of us have been debating which of our leaders would take over. We all have different preferences. I've heard a lot of good things from the people under Nikolai's command."

Sergei pried open another crate. He wasn't altogether surprised by Yuisa's words. Nikolai had a reputation among their people as being fair and compassionate. But so much depended on whether Nikolai could retain his position now that their secret was out. If enough people were willing to follow him, it might be enough to sway any arguments. Lena's death would already upset the balance of power. They might not be as quick to remove Nikolai from his position, even if his abilities came out into the open.

"What have people been saying?"

Yuisa hesitated. "Nothing specific. Just people talking and speculating."

Sergei was quiet for a long moment, continuing to sort through the crate. Yuisa's reticence was understandable. Valentina usually got people to open up by acting as a sympathetic ear and finding common themes to build from. It worked well enough for her, so maybe it was time to try the same tactic.

In a low voice, he said, "It's my hope Nikolai will agree to take over command. I've known him for a long time, and he cares deeply about our people."

Yuisa's eyes widened, pausing with a frequency detector in her hand. "I—I've heard that." She swallowed, glancing down at the crate in front of her. "My cousin, Sveta, works in one of his camps. I don't believe she knows Nikolai, but she's met Valentina a few times. Sveta always speaks highly of her. Valentina spent a long time playing with her daughter and telling her stories. She even arranged to have some sweets delivered to Liliya as a gift."

Sergei glanced over at Valentina again and smiled. Her fierceness was undeniable, but she also possessed such a tender and beautiful heart. Children had always been a soft spot for her. "Did she?"

Yuisa nodded, putting the equipment to the side. "Liliya is always asking after her and wanting to know when her friend is coming back to visit. If Nikolai keeps such people close to him, I can't help but believe he must be a good man. I'd prefer if he were the one to take over command."

"Nikolai would be my choice too," Sergei agreed, watching as Valentina absently brushed away a lock of chestnut hair that had escaped from her ponytail again. She gave Nikolai a small smile, her blue eyes lighting up at something he said.

God, she was beautiful. And far too distracting. Turning back to the crate in front of him, he said, "I have reservations about some of the other leaders and whether they'll be a good fit for running the new tower."

Yuisa frowned and put another piece of broken equipment aside. "Me too. I hope Lena's not the one who will take control. Ivan isn't so bad, but I'd still prefer Nikolai. It's promising that he's here, though, and working with the Omnis."

Sergei cocked his head. "Have you met Lena?"

"Not exactly," she admitted. "Lena came here about a week ago, but she didn't stay long. She wanted to see the layout of the area and how we operated. I did meet Roman though. He wanted copies of the shipping manifests and delivery schedules. He said they were considering taking over shipping distribution to and from the construction site until Pavel could be replaced."

Sergei's jaw clenched, a suspicion forming in his mind. If Lena had been involved personally, no one would have questioned her orders. "Did they store their supplies here?"

She nodded. "Some. Roman told us not to touch them and they'd have their own people handle distribution. I got the impression they didn't trust our competency."

"Are they still here?"

Something in his tone must have caught her attention because she looked over at him and frowned. "Yes. Did we do something wrong by allowing it?"

Forcing himself to gentle his voice, he said, "Not at all. I'd like you to show me these supplies though."

"Sure," she agreed and pointed up the hill to an abandoned building. "I'll take you. I'm not sure what kind of condition they're in from the earthquake. We weren't sure if we should check on those or wait until one of Lena's representatives contacted us. They might have some cabling devices in there."

"Just a moment," Sergei said and walked over to Nikolai, Valentina, and Yuri. "Yuisa just informed me Lena's been storing supplies here. You may want to come with us. It might be what we've been looking for. If not, we'll have more of a selection of equipment we can use to rescue our people. Most of the equipment we've found so far isn't usable."

Valentina's eyes narrowed, and she put the dragon figurine back into her pocket. "Where?"

"Just up the hill," Sergei replied, leading them back over to Yuisa. The dark-haired woman's eyes widened at the sight of all of them joining her.

Nikolai stepped forward. "Show us where the supplies are being kept."

"Of course," she agreed and hastened up the hill.

———

VALENTINA KNELT beside another crate and cursed loudly at the lettering on the side. "This is another one of ours."

Sergei moved forward and pried it open with one of the tools Yuisa had brought to them. Valentina looked down and blew out a breath. "It looks like about half of our missing weapons are here. We'll have to compare the numbers with what they confiscated in the towers, but at least they've been located."

"There's more food, hydrating packs, and medical supplies here too," Yuri said from the other side of the building. "No cabling devices though. Most of these items were meant for our civilian camps."

Nikolai frowned. "We'll need to reach out to Ivan and Peter to get accurate numbers from them and start redistributing supplies to our people. At least our weapons won't end up in the hands of the Omni residents. We'll let Alec know right away so he can relay the message to his council."

The dark-haired woman who had accompanied them frowned. "I'm sorry. I had no idea these items belonged to you."

Valentina straightened and approached her. Softening her expression, she said, "Your name is Yuisa, correct?"

When she nodded, Valentina smiled. "You've done us a great service today, Yuisa. We've been looking for these supplies for the past several weeks. You had no reason to think anything was wrong. You were simply obeying the instructions of one of our leaders, just as any one of us would have done. No one can fault you for that. But now, thanks to you, we'll make sure our people have the proper supplies they need."

Yuisa's face filled with gratitude. "Thank you for your kind words, Valentina."

Sergei approached them. "If someone else takes over control of the new tower, I believe Yuisa may be looking for a new post."

Valentina studied Sergei for a moment, understanding immediately what he wanted. Focusing again on Yuisa, she tilted her head to regard the younger woman. "I see. None of us can predict the future, but Nikolai is always looking for loyal people. In fact, we recently had an opening in our command center for an inventory specialist. Since you have experience handling such things, perhaps you might be suited for the position."

Yuisa gaped at her, but hope shone brightly in her eyes. "I'd love to be considered for such an opportunity."

"Good," Valentina said with a smile. "We'll make sure your efforts here are suitably rewarded. In the meantime, would you go through and inventory all these supplies? You can send me the report personally. If anyone from Lena's camp reaches out to you, direct them to me."

"Absolutely," Yuisa agreed, pulling out her tablet. "I'll get started right away."

Valentina murmured her thanks, and Sergei led her out of the building and back toward the chasm. She glanced over her shoulder to find Nikolai and Yuri were right behind them. Hopefully, some of their other workers had managed to locate the rest of the cabling devices they needed. "Yuisa told you she wanted to join Nikolai's service?"

"Mmhmm," Sergei agreed, putting his hand on her lower back. "But I would say you were the motivating factor."

She frowned, looking up at him. "What do you mean?"

"Her cousin lives in one of Nikolai's camps and has a

young daughter named Liliya who's taken a shine to you." Sergei darted a glance at her and teased, "Something about sneaking her sweets, playing with her, and telling her stories?"

"Oh," Valentina murmured with a small smile. "Yes. She's an adorable little girl. Her mother had fallen ill, so I offered to watch Liliya so she could get some rest. The child is a delight."

Sergei stopped and pulled her against him. Without another word, he lowered his head and kissed her. All coherent thought disappeared, and her fingers unwittingly curled into his jacket. She softened against him as he deepened the kiss, wrapping his arms around her.

Yuri cleared his throat. "Is this how it's going to be from now on? Whoever finds the next batch of missing weapons gets a victory kiss from Valya?"

Nikolai chuckled. "I wouldn't count on it, Yuri. But he's right about one thing. You're beginning to attract an audience."

She pulled back, and Sergei grinned at her. He cupped her face and pressed another light kiss against her lips. "Good. Now they'll know you're mine."

"Or they'll know you're mine," she teased.

"I have no objections," he said, putting his arm around her. Valentina leaned into him as they headed back to the chasm.

Kayla glanced up at them when they approached. "Good. You're back. We're almost finished. Carl's just checking the last device."

"We found the missing weapons," Sergei announced.

Relief flooded through Alec's expression. "At least that's one problem that's been resolved. I'll send a message to Ariana's father. They'll agree to suspend the vote given this new information and what's happened here at the river. But I have a feeling our alliance will no longer be in jeopardy."

Nikolai nodded and walked over to where the cabling devices were set up. "How is this going to work?"

Alec looked down into the chasm. "We were just talking about that. Even with the dragon figurine, we're going to need to drop down to get close to the elevator to maximize our chances for success."

Kayla stood and brushed the dirt off her hands. "We've got harnesses for up to ten people. Once we get to about the same level as the elevator, we can attach some cables to it. If the energy thing doesn't work, we'll try a more conventional approach. Either way, we need some additional supports attached to the elevator in case things go wrong."

Valentina frowned. "What are the chances of any aftershocks?"

"We're not sure," Alec admitted. "I don't know how, but the earthquake doesn't appear to be natural. We just got confirmation from some of our scientists in the towers. Until we know what caused it, we're putting a halt on all excavation in the area. I'm not sure if something we did affected the stability of the chasm."

"I told you it wasn't me," Kayla grumbled and tightened another cable connection.

Brant snorted. "But it *was* you who almost knocked over the towers."

Lars grinned. "And when you got upset about Carl being hurt in Sergei's camp."

"Yeah, yeah. I see how it is. Cause an earthquake once or twice and suddenly everyone's blaming you." Kayla huffed and picked up a harness. "So... who's going down?"

Valentina reached into her pocket, brushing her fingers against the dragon figurine. It was a little unnerving how she understood what it wanted. Maybe it was a sign from the heavens or some other mystical force at work, but she was inclined to follow its directions for now.

Gesturing to her bondmates, Valentina said, "The four of us need to go down. Ariana, Alec, and Kayla need to go too. Everyone else is optional, but the seven of us need to go."

Alec frowned. "I'd rather Ariana stay on the surface. Brant can remain with her."

Ariana shook her head. "No. If we need to use the dragon, I need to be involved. Lars should also go in case this doesn't work. Between you, Lars, and Yuri, you may have enough wind power to lift the elevator."

Brant took a step forward and added, "I'm going too. If we're not sure what's causing the earthquakes, I may be able to help if it's energy-related. At the very least, I should be able to detect it and possibly find out where it's originating."

Kayla glanced over at Carl. "Okay. Carl's going to come too. He knows these ruins better than anyone. That's our ten. Everyone else is going to have to wait here. Let's get loaded into the harnesses and start the descent. Veridian and Jinx will monitor the equipment from here."

Valentina nodded. "Let's do it."

CHAPTER THIRTEEN

Valentina landed on the rocky outcropping and spoke into her headset, "Cable Four. Stop the descent."

Sergei gripped her cable and pulled her away from the edge. Valentina kept the harness on but disabled her microphone to avoid any conflicts with communication on the surface. While Sergei reached forward to help Nikolai with his landing, she studied the small outcropping and cavern where they were standing. The elevator was just a short distance below them, and judging by its current position, they weren't going to be able to pull it out with the cables like Kayla had suggested.

The earthquake had dislodged some rocks, and the elevator was on its side, lodged between some of them. Kayla was lying on her stomach at the edge of the rocky outcropping calling back and forth to the people within. It sounded like the four individuals trapped inside were alive, but they all had some minor injuries.

Nikolai moved to stand beside her. She glanced up to see Yuri descending next. Alec and Ariana would be right behind him, followed by Lars and Brant.

"I don't know, Kayla," Carl said quietly. "That's a lot of open space between here and there."

"It is, but I know I can make that climb," Kayla said, studying the distance between the ledge they were standing on and the elevator.

Carl frowned. "We can launch an anchor bolt into the cavern wall to help you cross, but it's still risky."

Kayla gave him a small smile and leaned against him. "Ruin rats don't die that easily. Besides, you'll be the one guiding my cable. You won't let anything happen to me."

Carl sighed and wrapped his arms around her. "Go ahead and set it up. But if there's any instability or I even suspect you're in danger, I'm hauling you back here. I don't give a damn what arguments you make."

Kayla beamed a smile at him and pressed a quick kiss against his lips. Without another word, she bent down and started setting up the spare cabling device they'd brought with them.

Sergei leaned in close to her and whispered, "Please don't tell me you're considering joining her. I'm not sure my heart could take it."

Valentina smiled and unhooked her harness from the cabling device. "I've never claimed climbing as one of my strengths. I will leave such things in the hands of those with more experience."

"Good," he said, giving her a quick kiss before turning away to help Ariana onto the ledge.

Valentina scooted over to give them more room and handed her cable to Carl. The ledge where they were standing was large enough they could all fit comfortably upon it. They were fairly far underground, within a large chasm that had opened centuries ago. Some of the buildings that had once stood on the surface had slid into its depths. Many of them had been totally destroyed, but others were relatively untouched except by age and neglect. She leaned over the edge to peer down below, trying to determine how far the chasm extended. It was too dark to see much.

Nikolai wrapped his arm around her waist and pulled her away from the edge. "Careful, Valya."

Kayla finished collecting everyone's cables and started to climb across the width of the chasm to the elevator. Everyone watched her progress with a sense of anticipation.

Valentina leaned in close to Nikolai and whispered, "Do you think it's a mistake to try using the statue?"

Nikolai frowned. "I don't know. It worries me that we're depending on something we don't understand. But why don't you tell me your concerns and we can figure it out."

"I wasn't expecting it to be quite so hazardous down here," she admitted quietly, not wanting the people trapped in the elevator to hear her concerns. "The effects when we used the figurine for the first time were pretty dramatic. I'm worried about not being able to control it. It's not just the people in the elevator at risk if things go wrong."

"We don't have to do it," he reminded her gently. "They can try to lift the elevator with their air abilities. But the first time we used the figurine, you were seriously injured and weren't the one directing the power. When you used it earlier with Sergei, he was the only one affected. There were no other environmental effects. The earthquake happened before you used it."

Valentina nodded. "You're right. It hasn't been an issue when I was the one directing it. I think the figurine wants me to use it. I know that sounds silly, but it almost feels alive to me."

"We can have it analyzed as soon as we get back," he promised and brushed a kiss against her temple. "But right now, if you're having doubts, we can explore other options. The choice is yours."

Valentina withdrew the dragon from her pocket. It was strange, but there was a sense of rightness about being here with it. "I'll do it. I'm worried about these people, and I would never forgive myself for not trying to help them. With the elevator being on its side, we can't get the door open to pull them out. It doesn't look like we'll be able to rescue them unless we cut through the metal bars. That much vibration could be dangerous down here."

"We'll stop using the figurine if we notice any ill effects," he promised, squeezing her midsection lightly. "When I warned you about the danger to our people before, you stopped the power immediately. You can do it again."

Valentina lifted her head, watching as Kayla started making her way back across the chasm. She'd managed to affix the cables securing the elevator in place. Now it would just come down to trying to move aside the rocks and lifting it back to the surface. Once that was completed, they could send the elevator down to the lower levels to rescue the rest of their people.

Sergei moved to stand on the other side of her and rubbed his thumb against the back of her hand. She looked up at him, and he murmured, "It will be fine, Valechka. You won't allow anything bad to happen to them."

She frowned. "Are you still reading my thoughts?"

He grinned. "Mmhmm. I'm rather enjoying it too. It will be even more interesting to see how you respond when I take you to bed. Perhaps we can even try some sensory deprivation to see how well you can direct me."

Valentina blinked at him. That definitely had some interesting and intriguing possibilities.

Yuri moved along the edge toward them. "Now that Sergei's distracted you from whatever you're worried about, it looks like we're ready to try this."

She narrowed her eyes, but Sergei chuckled and kissed her

nose. "It would have worked longer if Yuri hadn't pointed it out. I shall have to distract you more thoroughly later. It looks like Kayla has returned."

Valentina turned to see Carl helping Kayla back onto the ledge. Kayla issued some instructions to the team on the surface, and the cables she'd connected to the elevator grew taut.

"Stop," Kayla ordered. "Okay, hold them there. Hook up a few more power supplies to it. We'll let you know when the elevator's in position so you can try to raise it."

Everyone turned toward Valentina, waiting expectantly. Valentina swallowed and pulled off her gloves, shoving them into her pocket. She'd need direct contact with the figurine to make this work. "Go ahead, Ariana. You too, Kayla."

Ariana nodded and moved forward, placing her hand on the dragon. Kayla pulled off her gloves and did the same. The strange sort of awareness filled Valentina once again, and she felt their powers flow into her. Focusing on the statue, she gathered their collective powers and infused it with her own brand of elemental energy before directing it into the stone dragon.

The hair on Valentina's neck lifted, and she stared in wonder at the statuette, which was now glowing with that unearthly golden light. All her senses were amplified as power poured into her. She could feel the rock ledge beneath her feet, the sharp tang of ozone in the air, the molten fire deep within the earth's surface, and most especially the dense moisture of the surrounding air. Even further beyond that, she could sense a rush of elemental power in what she assumed was the river. It called to her, beckoning her to hasten, and she hesitated.

A sense of impatience filled her. It startled her for a moment because it wasn't her emotion, but it belonged to someone else. Valentina wasn't sure how she was picking it up, but she was confident it wasn't coming from any of her bondmates. Maybe she was tapping into Ariana's ability to read emotions and it was originating from the people within the elevator. But either way, it brought her attention back to their purpose.

Valentina took a steadying breath and exhaled slowly, focusing her thoughts on the elevator. Reaching out with the energy of all the elements, she directed the figurine to begin loosening the rocks around the elevator. They began crumbling away, falling into the depths below. The elevator lurched, and Nikolai squeezed her shoulder.

"Hold it steady, Valya," he ordered. "We can't allow the elevator to swing back and hit the wall on this side of the chasm."

She nodded, immediately recognizing the wisdom of his words. Concentrating again, she used the air energy threads to weave a protective band around the elevator. It was tight enough to hold the elevator in place but still allow the people trapped within it to breathe. With another part of herself, she reached out, pulling more of the rocks away with earth energy. There was a metallic groan as the elevator shifted and swung slightly out into the open area.

A wave of relief surged through Valentina, but she still didn't release the energy. If anything went wrong, she needed to tap into it quickly. "Kayla, tell them to start pulling it up."

Without removing her hand from the dragon, Kayla spoke into her headset. A moment later, the elevator began lifting into the air. Valentina watched it, holding it steady with their combined power. When it was almost to the top, she gradually loosened her grasp on it and knew the cables were holding it.

"Okay," Kayla said a few minutes later with a relieved sigh. "It's on the surface. They're prying open the doors to unload everyone. Once they're out, they'll send the elevator back down to rescue the next group. We don't have communication with them yet, but we're now picking up their vital signs. They're showing signs of stress, but they're all still alive."

Carl spoke into his headset and said, "It sounds like they've located more cabling devices too. They can bring us up soon. Veridian and Jinx are setting up the equipment."

"Good." Valentina slowly released the energy she'd been focusing through the dragon figurine. With everyone safe, some of the urgency was beginning to lessen.

"It was here," Nikolai murmured.

Yuri's brow furrowed. "What was?"

"My premonition. I didn't recognize the location immediately, but everything fits. When I felt Valya's fear and sense of urgency just a few minutes ago, I knew this was it. This was the spot from my vision."

"That was days ago. You don't usually see events so far into the future," Sergei said with a frown. "Have your abilities increased?"

Valentina glanced over at Ariana and Kayla, recalling the dream she'd had after they'd used the figurine the first time. Both women had been present, but she didn't remember much else. The dragon statuette flared brightly, and she winced, immediately averting her eyes.

The ledge they were standing on began to tremble and shake. It collapsed a moment later, and Valentina plunged downward into the darkness below.

CHAPTER FOURTEEN

VALENTINA SCREAMED, sliding along the rocky outcropping. Rocks bit into her hands as she tried to grab anything to stop her rapid descent. The ground continued to shake, pebbles and rocks falling along with her until she landed on a hard surface.

Everyone rolled to an abrupt stop. Ariana winced, breathing heavily, and said, "I'm keeping the ground steady, but I don't know how long I can hold it. I need to form a stable ledge so we don't keep sliding."

The dragon figurine had disappeared when they fell. Valentina couldn't even help her by using it to enhance her power. She looked over to find Sergei and Nikolai beside her. Sergei appeared relatively unharmed, but Nikolai's arm was covered with blood. The anchor bolt cable they'd use when Kayla crossed the chasm was wrapped around Nikolai's arm, cutting into it. Yuri was bleeding profusely from a gash on his head. Everyone else was alive and conscious, but they were all sporting some injuries.

Valentina felt Ariana tapping into her power. A moment later, the ground trembled and rose beneath them, lifting to form a rocky ledge. Valentina rolled over and crawled to Nikolai while motioning for Sergei to check on Yuri. If she didn't take care of Nikolai now, he might lose his arm.

Reaching into the pack at her waist, she withdrew a small multipurpose tool and started to cut the cable wrapped around his arm. The wound was deep, slicing through muscles and tendons but stopping before it had cut through the bone. Nikolai winced, and she placed her hand over his arm and directed her healing energy into him. His arm began to knit back together, and Nikolai placed his hand on hers.

"Thank you, Valya," he murmured, his expression growing more relaxed as the pain dissipated. "The rest is minor. Check on Yuri."

She nodded and crawled toward Yuri, catching sight of Ariana checking on everyone too. With the two of them being the only healers, they had their work cut out for them.

Sergei moved aside so she could sit next to Yuri. A deep gash stretched across his forehead and had just barely missed his eye. He'd been lucky, but she needed to stop the bleeding. She lifted her hand and pressed it against his forehead, ignoring the pain in her palms from her own injuries. She couldn't heal herself, but she could help the people she loved.

Yuri grimaced and opened his mouth to object, but she gave him a stern look. "Keep your mouth shut, Yuri. Don't fight me on this."

His mouth twisted into a smirk. "If you want to keep me pretty, go ahead, Valya."

Valentina smiled and focused on his injury, using her energy to repair his wounds. The wound immediately began to weave together, and she intuitively knew it hadn't been serious. Head injuries always bled so much.

Bending down, she pressed a light kiss against Yuri's cheek. "All better, and you're still pretty."

Yuri sat up, and she turned around to assess everyone else.

Alec had helped Ariana to her feet, and Kayla and Carl were looking over the edge. Brant and Lars were also unharmed and trying to figure out where they were in relation to the drop-down point. Valentina pulled off her harness and tossed the useless piece of equipment on the ground.

Kayla tapped on her earpiece and swore. "We're cut off temporarily. The earthquake must have knocked out our communication equipment again. It looks like we're on our own until they get it back up and running."

Carl was still looking over the edge. "I think we're farther down than the level where you found the underground river, Kayla."

Kayla nodded. "Yeah. We haven't done as much exploration down here."

Valentina blew out a breath. At least they weren't in any immediate danger, but that wasn't a guarantee if another earthquake hit. It also wasn't very reassuring that Carl and Kayla didn't know this area well.

Sergei reached over and carefully lifted Valentina's hand, frowning at the blood covering it. Their rapid descent had cut open her palms and taken off a few layers of skin. One of the cuts was a little deeper than she'd initially thought, but it wasn't as bad as it looked. But that didn't seem to matter to Sergei.

Valentina smiled at his concern. "It's not so bad, Seryozha. I've had worse bumps and scrapes. The most important thing is that we're all alive and relatively unharmed."

"I don't like seeing you injured," he said, lifting her other hand and cradling it gently while he assessed the damage. "You're still bleeding."

Ariana turned toward her. "Allow me to heal you, Valentina."

She shook her head. "It's minor. The bleeding's almost stopped, and it's helping to wash out some of the grit. Let's get to safety first, and then you can. I'd rather you keep your energy reserve in case something happens again. The dragon figurine is gone, so we can't merge our abilities. I dropped it when we fell."

"I see it glowing," Kayla said, peering over the edge. "It's not too far. We should be able to climb down to retrieve the dragon pretty easily. It looks like it's on a more stable level anyway."

Valentina walked over to the edge. Kayla was right. She could make out the gold glow sitting in a pile of rubble. It was a good drop, but they might be able to make it without too much trouble.

"I can form a ramp," Ariana suggested. "Or we can try to use our air abilities to lower ourselves down."

Nikolai frowned. "I can help you with the ramp. It's been a long time since I attempted such a thing, but I should be able to do it."

Ariana nodded and offered Nikolai her hand. "We can form a connection and combine some of our energy to create it. Kayla, if you'll link with me too, your power will come in handy. We won't be able to use as much compared to what the dragon statue can handle, but every little bit will help."

Valentina watched as they clasped hands, and the ground trembled. It was different from the earthquake, lesser some-how, and a moment later, another rock formation lifted in front of them. It elongated itself, stretching outward and sloping downward, forming a rocky path to the ground below them.

Alec put his hand on Ariana's shoulder. "Take what you need, love. You're trying to do too much and depleting your reserves."

Ariana put her hand over his. "Thank you. That helps. Nikolai's much stronger than I realized. He and Kayla did most of the heavy lifting that time, but you're right. I'll need to rest soon."

Valentina reached outward, surrounding Nikolai with her power. He walked over to her and kissed her forehead. "Thank you, Valya, but I'm afraid Ariana directed most of it. We're fortunate to have such a skilled energy user as a teacher."

Ariana beamed a smile at Nikolai. "You've been an excellent student." She darted a quick look over at Kayla and teased, "One of these days, maybe Kayla will let me pin her down so I can finish teaching her."

Kayla snorted and moved forward, walking down the rocky path. "If I had known how much Sergei and everyone was going to show me up with this training stuff, I would have handled our first few meetings a little differently."

Sergei chuckled. "If you had approached your training with more discipline, it's doubtful we would have been able to kidnap you in the first place."

"Damn, that's a good point," Kayla admitted. "You didn't get me just once either. That's twice I could have kicked your asses."

Carl followed Kayla, moving carefully down the path. "You know, Kayla, these abilities have a lot more potential than I realized. If Ariana's willing to show you how to create something like this path, think about how much scavenging you could accomplish in the ruins."

Kayla made a small noise of agreement. "I think you're right. If these earthquakes keep happening, installing ramps into and out of our work areas would prevent a lot of accidents and downtime."

"Aha," Ariana said, her eyes twinkling with amusement. "I may get you into a training session after all."

"It's about time," Alec muttered.

Kayla huffed. "I'm starting to think you're all conspiring against me."

Valentina smiled and followed them down the path with Sergei right behind her. A low rumble reached her ears, and she lifted her head. "What is that?"

"The river," Kayla said, still navigating the path. "We're closer than I thought. Either that or this is another branch of the river."

"Hopefully, it's not the same branch that flooded the cavern," Brant said from behind her.

Kayla glanced at him over her shoulder. "What's the matter, Brant? Can't swim?"

"With my luck, you'll push me in," he grumbled.

Kayla laughed and hopped off the path, prowling around the area to investigate. Carl followed close behind her, speaking too softly for Valentina to hear what he was saying.

Valentina stepped off the path and glanced around. This area appeared to be part of a cave with a solid, rocky ground beneath their feet. At least they didn't have to worry about another ledge collapsing. An earthquake or the flooding river was most likely their biggest concern now.

Walking over to the glowing figurine where it lay in the rubble, she bent down to pick it up and brushed off the dirt. "It doesn't appear to be damaged."

She felt Sergei approach from behind, and he wrapped his arms around her waist. She automatically relaxed against him as his heated energy swirled around her. Leaning over her shoulder to look down at the dragon, he said, "It's lighting up this whole area. I believe it's even brighter now than it was when you used it on that ledge."

Valentina nodded, turning over the figurine in her hands. She didn't see a scratch on it. It made her wonder what it had been carved from that it could withstand such a fall. Even the delicate wings were still intact.

"I sense something," Ariana said, gazing around the cave.

Alec frowned and approached her. "I feel it through our bond. Could what you're picking up be more echoes from the past? I believe we're close to the area where you sensed it before."

Ariana shook her head. "No, it's different. When you last brought me here, I felt something, but I was trying to block it out. Now that we're bonded, I don't have to shield quite so much."

Lars walked over to them, his gaze sweeping the cavern. "There's a strange quality to the air. Maybe the smell? I can't put my finger on it, but something's not quite right. What exactly do you sense, Ariana?"

"I'm not sure I can put it into words. Emotions have different textures, and this is unlike anything I've ever experienced. It's almost impatient, but there's also curiosity. Those emotions are too simple to describe the complexity of whatever I'm picking up though."

Sergei tightened his arms around Valentina. "Do you feel anything, Valechka?"

She hesitated. "Not exactly. When we were on the ledge and right before it collapsed, I felt impatient. It wasn't me though. I thought I was picking up on Ariana's empath ability because we were connected through the figurine. I assumed it was coming from the people in the elevator."

"That's possible," Ariana admitted. "You could have been using a variation of my energy when I channeled it toward you."

Alec closed his eyes and inhaled deeply. "I think Lars is right about the air being different. I'm not sure how, but it doesn't have the same quality on the surface. I don't think it's dangerous, but there's something off about it."

Valentina gazed around the cavern, noting the dips and

jags in the earthen walls. "Something about this cavern is familiar. I dreamed it."

Nikolai cocked his head. "You mentioned having a dream the other day. I know you've been practicing your abilities lately. I'm wondering if you're tapping into my prophetic visions."

Alec frowned. "That sounds likely. Was there anything you remember?"

Valentina shook her head. "Nothing specific. Ariana and Kayla were with me in the dream. It was more just feelings and impressions. But I think we're supposed to be here."

"I hear something," Yuri said, staring off where the cavern extended into darkness.

Valentina tilted her head. "The river? I hear the low rumblings from it."

"No, something else. I can't quite make it out. It may be nothing."

"Guys!" Kayla called out, jogging back over to them with Carl. "You've gotta come see this. I think the earthquake opened another entrance to the river. The water's higher, but it's not flooded. If our people were in danger from the rising water, it's probably lessened in their location."

Carl nodded and gestured to an area behind them. "This spot is ideal for us to tap into the river. Given the location, we should be able to drop our equipment directly down without affecting the stability of the ruins. No supports are necessary. We won't have to worry about anything collapsing. It's a long way down, but that's much better than the alternative."

"Then we can harness the river as a viable water resource," Alec said eagerly, moving toward them. "Show me."

Sergei put his hand on her back and led Valentina toward the area Kayla and Carl had discovered. The dragon figurine flared brightly, and she halted.

Ariana stopped in her tracks and whirled around. "I sense eagerness again. It's coming from the dragon."

Valentina swallowed and held up the statuette. "I think it wants us to go this direction."

Sergei's eyes narrowed. "It's communicating with you?"

"I don't know. I'm getting impressions when I hold it, but nothing concrete."

Nikolai frowned. "Perhaps you should leave it here, Valya. I don't like that it's connected to you like this, especially since we don't know what *it* is."

Kayla cocked her head. "Um, I'm getting mixed signals from it now. But it really doesn't like the idea of Valentina leaving it behind."

Valentina lowered the dragon. "What do you mean? What mixed signals?"

"It's lost, but it's also found," Kayla began and then shrugged. "I don't know how to explain it, but you need to bring it with us."

Valentina cradled the figurine in her hands. "Given the precariousness of our current situation, I'm inclined to keep it with us. We've seen what it's capable of accomplishing and its potential for destruction. I think caution is warranted though, especially if we need to use it again. But I'm not willing to leave it behind and risk anyone else finding it."

Nikolai frowned. "I can't fault your logic, but be careful, Valya. I would rather lose it than risk anything happening to you."

Sergei reached out, his hand hovering over the figurine. He paused and lifted his gaze to meet hers. "May I touch it?"

She nodded and held it out to him. His fingers brushed against the wing, and it flared even brighter before dimming again.

"Okay, now *that's* weird," Kayla muttered. "It likes you too.

Still not as much as Valentina, but it definitely has an affection for you."

"I think it's because you're so closely bonded," Ariana said, studying them and the statue. "It's resonating with both of you. When you touched it just now, it recognized you somehow. But I'm not sure you can use it. I believe Valentina may still need to direct it."

Sergei frowned, clearly not pleased with that idea. Valentina smiled up at him and placed her hand on his arm. The rawness of her palms burned, and she pulled her hand away. Sergei captured her hand, his touch gentle, and he turned toward Ariana. "Can you heal her? She's in more pain than she wants to admit."

Before Ariana could respond, the dragon figurine flared even brighter, filling the cavern with its golden light. Valentina gasped at the sensation of heat that flowed into her hands. It was similar to Sergei's energy but slightly different.

"It healed you," Sergei murmured in amazement, lifting her hand to study it. He stroked his fingers over her unblemished palm. "I do not know what magic that dragon holds, but I have no objections to keeping it in your possession if it will protect you from harm."

The figurine pulsed in her hand. She had the distinct impression it was pleased by Sergei's comment.

Curling her fingers around it, Valentina said, "Let's go see the river. I'm curious about it, and the dragon wants me to take it there too."

CHAPTER FIFTEEN

A CRACK HAD FORMED in the wall of the cavern, leading to an even larger chamber beyond it. It was wide enough that several people could fit through side by side comfortably, but it was angled in such a way that it had been almost hidden from view until Valentina was nearly upon it. She couldn't help but wonder if Kayla's ability to find lost objects had led her to find it, just like she'd found the river initially.

They entered the dark cavern, and she lifted the statue, using the radiant glow to help cut through the oppressive shadows. The smell of sulphur was strong here, and the roar from the river was even louder. But it was the sight of the river itself that made her halt in stunned shock.

Sergei interlaced his fingers with hers and pressed a kiss against her knuckles. "The first time I saw the river, I thought of you. I've been wanting to bring you here."

"It's beautiful," she whispered, awestruck by the wildness of the flowing water.

It was the purest form of her element, and it called to the innermost places within her. This entire cavern possessed an almost otherworldly air, manifesting all the elements in a primal display. It was captivating, exhilarating, and more humbling than she expected. The sheer power in the rapids as they crashed against the rocks made her once against realize how fleeting their lives were in comparison. They would all be gone one day, but this river would remain as it had for an untold number of centuries.

Valentina looked up at Sergei, letting him see the raw emotion the river had awakened. His gaze softened, and he reached up to brush his thumb against her cheek. "As beautiful as the river may be, it cannot compare to you. You took my breath away the first moment I saw you, and my heart followed right after that. The look in your eyes right now, Valechka, that sense of wonder and awe... That is how I feel every time I look at you."

"Seryozha," she whispered, blinking back tears. She placed her hand on his chest, directly over his heart. Hers was full to bursting from the emotions his words evoked. "Why do you keep saying such sweet things to me?"

"Because you'll remember them and tear off his clothes the moment he gets you alone," Yuri said, moving forward into the cavern. "I think he practices in front of the mirror. I've caught him making eyes at himself a few times."

She narrowed her eyes at Sergei, who grinned and wrapped his arm around her. He leaned down to nuzzle her neck and murmured, "That is part of it. But I would not say these things if I did not mean them."

Valentina couldn't help but smile. "You are such a troublemaker."

"Only with you, Valechka," he murmured, embracing her again with his heated fire energy.

Trailing her fingernail down his chest, she accompanied the gesture with her water power and nipped at his bottom lip. "Yuri's right. I'm cutting off your clothes as soon as we get back to the towers. Now, behave and I'll reward you later."

Sergei gave Yuri a triumphant look, and she shook her head in exasperation. They were impossible.

Nikolai walked a little closer to the river and asked, "Were the rapids this high in the other location?"

Kayla nodded. "When I originally found it, yes. It might be a little higher here, but not much. Our people said the other cavern has risen about eight or nine feet higher than it used to be. The rapids don't appear quite so treacherous either."

Lars sniffed the air. "What's causing the sulphur smell? Is it the water?"

The dragon warmed slightly in her hand, drawing her attention back to it. Valentina detected an unmistakable sense of eagerness emanating from it. "I think it wants Ariana, Kayla, and me to link with it again. But I don't know why."

"I'm not sure that's a good idea down here," Sergei advised with a frown. "We don't know if it might flood the area or trap us with another earthquake."

Ariana shook her head and walked over to her. "It won't. We're safer here than out in the other cavern. I don't understand how I can feel emotions from it, but I can sense its sincerity. It won't cause any harm to us, but it wants us to do this. I think it may be a test of sorts."

"Ari, I'm not sure you should do this," Alec began, but Ariana put her hand on his arm.

"Please trust me with this, Alec. I would never do anything that would put you in harm's way, but I know this is safe. I believe Fate has brought all of us here together for a reason. It hasn't steered us wrong yet, and I'm inclined to trust in it."

Alec's expression softened as he gazed at her. "Be careful, love. Sometimes, Fate gives us trials before offering its rewards. I don't want anything to happen to you."

Ariana smiled at him and reached over, placing her hand on the dragon figurine. Alec muttered a curse under his breath as the strange glow spread outward from the statue to envelop Valentina and Ariana.

"Oh, fucking hell," Kayla muttered. "It wants me to join in too."

Carl frowned. "Sweetheart, are you sure that's a good idea?"

Kayla shrugged. "Probably not, but I don't want to miss out on all the fun. I hope you're ready to save my ass again if things go to shit."

The moment Kayla touched the figurine, the glow surrounded all of them. The golden light filled the rocky cavern, chasing away the worst of the shadows.

A huge rock formation took over the entire far wall of the cavern and disappeared under the rushing rapids. The color of the stone was the same original deep-green the dragon statuette had once been, but Valentina could make out traces of pearlized colors in hues of gold and red. The stone was beautiful, with its patterned dips and edges, and unlike anything she'd ever seen.

"Wow," Kayla murmured. "I wonder how much OmniLab would pay for a piece of *that* stonework."

The rock formation moved, and Valentina nearly dropped the figurine as a huge reptilian head emerged from the river. Water splashed onto the ground near their feet as the green-scaled head lowered itself to rest on the rocky shore in front of them. The river receded a bit but still flowed around what she guessed was the dragon's underbelly, feet, and tail.

Sergei grabbed Valentina around her waist and hauled her backward, away from the creature. He angled himself in front of her in a protective stance, but Valentina was too busy staring. The body was almost the size of Lars's entire living quarters. Probably larger.

"Fuck me," Brant whispered. "That's not a rock. It's a dragon."

Two large eyes opened and blinked golden irises at them. The color was an almost exact replica of the light emitting from the dragon figurine.

"Your friend is very observant," a voice sounded in Valentina's mind.

Nikolai and Yuri also moved to stand in front of her like protective sentries. Carl moved in front of Kayla as Alec did the same for Ariana.

Lars made a pained noise. "If the dragon decides to roast us, we're all in trouble. There's nowhere to escape."

The dragon huffed at them, the sound almost like a wheeze. The sulphur odor became even stronger as a wisp of smoke emerged from two cavernous nostrils.

"You may stand down, mates of the Fates. I intend my friends no harm. I did not bring them all this way to simply watch them expire."

"I hear him," Yuri said quietly. "It's the same voice I heard before, but I can understand it now."

"The dragon is *talking* to you?" Carl whispered, eyeing the dragon warily.

"I don't hear it," Lars said with a frown.

"Me neither," Brant admitted. "I don't know if that's good or not."

Valentina looked over at Sergei, Nikolai, and Alec. They appeared to hear the dragon too. Ariana and Kayla were staring in rapt fascination at the dragon, and Valentina knew they could hear the voice as well.

The dragon's golden iris focused on Yuri. *"You hear the voices of all winged creatures. That was my gift to you. Through you, I may speak to Atropos."*

Valentina's eyes widened. When they'd first admitted to possessing powers, Lars had tested their abilities back in the towers. He'd told Yuri he had the ability to hear winged creatures. She knew Yuri had gotten warnings in the past while they'd been out on assignment. It was one of the reasons he'd always excelled as a tracker and scout. But apparently, that translated to him being able to hear dragons too.

Sergei frowned. "I don't know that name. Who is Atropos?"

The dragon blinked again, its gaze now focusing on Valentina. *"Atropos. Morta. Cutter of threads. Ender of Life. I cannot remember all your names. They are inconsequential. But you are one and the same."*

"He's talking about Valya, but I'm not sure we should correct him," Yuri whispered. "You don't really argue with a dragon."

Valentina moved forward to stand beside Sergei, fascinated by the strange creature. On some level, she instinctively knew the dragon didn't mean them any harm. Granted, it may view harm differently from them, but she didn't think its intentions were malevolent. She felt a strange sort of kinship with this creature, something she didn't altogether understand.

"I'm called Valentina."

"Come closer, daughter," the dragon urged. *"Hair of fire. Eyes of the sea. I recognize you."*

"Valechka," Sergei warned, putting his hand on her arm. "I do not think this is wise."

Valentina covered his hand with hers. "Trust me with this, Sergei. If it wanted us dead, it would not be speaking to us now."

Sergei hesitated and released her, and she took a step toward the creature. All the stories her grandmother had told her came rushing back. She'd thought they were just fanciful lore passed down through generations, but now she wondered about the reality. She glanced down at the water where the dragon was still partially submerged, but it was too dark to see clearly.

"What are you looking for, daughter?"

Valentina frowned. "I was trying to see if you had three heads or only the one."

The dragon blinked at her. *"Why would I have need of three heads when you are The Three?"*

Valentina paused, glancing at Ariana and Kayla out of the corner of her eye. Between them, they numbered three. Was that what the dragon was saying? She swallowed, remembering how Ariana had said there were always elements of truth in every story.

"I've heard stories about dragons. You look similar to one called *Zmei Gorynich*, but it was said he had three heads."

The dragon seemed almost pleased. *"I was called that name once long ago, but it is not a true name. You know these stories?"*

"Some," she admitted, fascinated by the pair of reptilian eyes gazing at her. They were almost as big as she was tall. "My grandmother told them to me when I was a girl. They took place centuries ago though. How can you be the same dragon from the stories?"

"We cannot die," the dragon replied, a trace of something akin to sadness or loneliness in his voice. *"We exist and slumber when we must. But eternity grows tedious."*

"Everything eventually dies," Kayla said, taking a step forward.

"Ah, Clotho, the spinner of threads," the dragon acknowledged. *"You are the youngest of three. Life energy begins with you."*

Ariana also moved forward. Alec made a pained noise and moved closer to her, but he didn't intervene. Ariana clasped her hands in front of her and said, "Atropos and Clotho. I recognize those names from when I studied ancient mythology. You're referring to the three Fates who shape destiny, aren't you?"

"Yes, Lachesis, Measurer of Threads," the dragon acknowledged. *"You choose whether to allow the thread to continue with your healing gifts or to hand them off to your sister to be cut."*

Yuri frowned. "Who are the Fates?"

Ariana glanced over at him. "They were three women who shaped destiny. It was said they controlled the thread of life of every person, and even the gods were bound by their authority. The youngest spun the threads of life, the middle one measured the threads, and the eldest cut them."

"Indeed. The Fates reappear in times of great need and come together to accomplish their goals. It has been centuries since they last walked the earth."

Alec frowned. "Is the dragon saying you three represent those same Fates?"

Ariana nodded. "Yes. Kayla is the youngest, bringing about creation with her life or spirit energy. I measure their lives, and Valentina ends them."

Yuri cleared his throat and muttered, "Always nice to know a dragon recognizes your ability to handle a weapon, Valya."

Valentina tilted her head to study the dragon. She wasn't as familiar with the names or mythology Ariana mentioned, but she knew about this dragon. Or at least, she knew the folklore about the dragons. If she, Ariana, and Kayla represented the three heads, that left another part of the story unanswered. "How many tails do you have, *Zmei Gorynich?*"

"How many tails do you have, Valentina?" the dragon responded, a trace of mirth in his tone.

"None," she said with a frown, suspecting that was the wrong answer.

"Are you sure? I count three bonded to your spirit. Your sister has bonded to another. The youngest holds her own. There are seven in total, as Fate has always decreed. Time is cyclical, like the emblems you adorn."

Valentina's eyes widened as she caught sight of the ouroboros symbol on Brant's uniform. It was a stylized emblem of a dragon looped around to form an "O" and grasping its tail in its mouth. The Coalition's emblem was also formed from a circle with a line embedded through it to mark their path. Perhaps their two respective cultures had more in common than she'd realized.

Turning back to the dragon, she considered the numbers again. "In the stories I heard as a child, *Gorynich* was said to have seven tails. In other stories, the hero possessed a whip made from seven silks bound together. You're saying those weren't tails or silks? They were bond connections? We were always Fated to form these bonds with each other?"

The dragon continued to blink at her. *"A weapon is always stronger when bound together. You are stronger together, Valentina."*

Kayla frowned and held up her hands. "Whoa. Wait a minute. I don't know about all this talk of whips and tails or about this Fate stuff. How can it be Fate if I was briefly bonded to Alec? If I hadn't removed it with Brant's help, we'd still be bonded."

The dragon huffed, a wisp of smoke rising from its nostrils. *"You were never meant for a bond, Clotho."*

"Kayla," she said, gesturing to herself. "Just Kayla."

The dragon's eyes twinkled. Valentina had the impression it was amused by the conversation, which was a little disconcerting. Although, entertaining a dragon was much better than dealing with an angry one.

"So many names. Very well, Kayla. You were never meant for a bond."

"Then we were right. Alec was always meant for me," Ariana murmured, gazing up at the man standing beside her.

"Yes," the dragon agreed. *"Do you have a name preference, little healer?"*

"Ariana," she replied. "What shall we call you?"

"Well met, Ariana. I have had many names over my lifetime. But you may call me Gorynich since that is the name your older sister prefers."

Ariana smiled. "It's a pleasure to meet you, Gorynich. How did you come to be here?"

"Your youngest sister tried to wake me years ago," the dragon replied, focusing again on Kayla. *"Someone tried to cut her thread before it was time. I awakened enough to ensure she survived before I went back to sleep."*

"You helped save me in the ruin collapse," Kayla whispered, her eyes wide in astonishment. "I remember now. I heard you in my thoughts back then just like I'm hearing you now. You led Leo and Veridian's mother to me so they could take me to safety. I didn't want to leave you, but you said it was too soon. You warned me to keep my abilities secret. That's why the thought of going to the towers scared me for so long." Her brow furrowed. "You're what's been pulling me toward the ruins all these years. You've been missing and lost. I wanted to find you."

The dragon huffed, two plumes of smoke trailing out of its nostrils. *"I have not been missing or lost. I have always known exactly where I am. You connect and weave the threads of life together. That is your function and your purpose. Lost, indeed. Who has been filling your head with this nonsense?"*

Kayla glanced over at Alec, who appeared equally confused. Kayla shook her head. "I don't understand. I've always been able to find objects that have been missing. You're saying that's not what I was doing? I've been connecting threads of life instead?"

"Threads of Fate," Gorynich corrected. *"You connect the Threads of Fate with their intended recipient. Some things are not meant yet, so you will not be able to connect them, but each object you discovered has a purpose. You may not understand it, but your comprehension was never a requirement."*

"Then I *was* supposed to find the dragon figurine," Kayla said, glancing at the glowing statuette in Valentina's hand.

"*Indeed. You were not meant to find it until you were ready to reunite with your sisters.*"

Valentina shook her head. All of this was too overwhelming to believe. "Why did you want me to have the figurine?"

The dragon focused its golden eyes on her again. "*My ties have always been closest to your bloodline, Valentina. You look much like Zabava. Even your thoughts remind me of her.*"

"Zabava was the princess from the legend," she whispered, recalling the story her grandmother had told her. "Some stories said you abducted her, but that wasn't true, was it?"

"*I am not in the habit of kidnapping or harming innocents, as some of your stories claim. Zabava was a friend, and I gifted her with abilities.*"

Sergei wrapped his arms around Valentina's waist, drawing her against him. "If you do not wish any of us harm, why did you lead us here?"

"*The time for sleep has passed, fire wielder. It has been centuries since the Fates walked this earth. They only converge when there is great need. I can smell the taint of this world from my resting place, and if there is a chance to bring your world back to life, I must assist them.*"

Valentina tilted her head, studying the dragon. Each scale was enormous, at least a couple feet in length. It was impossible to tell how thick they were, but the dragon was well protected. It watched her in return, but Valentina couldn't bring herself to be afraid of it. She had no doubt it could kill all of them with little more than a thought, but she simply didn't believe it would ever harm them intentionally.

"You can help bring life back to the world?"

The dragon shifted its head a fraction, but it was enough

to cause a nearby boulder to dislodge from the wall. Sergei tightened his arms around her, and she placed her hand on his arm to reassure him they were safe. Part of her wondered how the dragon had managed to get down here in the first place, but if it was a creature of magic, she was sure it had its ways.

"In part. Your people once called me a hydra. The water is my dominion. It is only through my efforts that this river has remained pure. It is my gift to you, but there are many other sources of water which need to be revitalized if your people are to survive."

Kayla frowned. "We've been trying to harness the river for months. Our equipment kept getting destroyed in the rapids. Were you doing that?"

A whiff of smoke unfurled from the dragon's nostrils. *"A gift is freely given, not taken or demanded. I gift this river to the three of you now. Your equipment will no longer be destroyed. You may do what you wish with it."*

Valentina felt Sergei relax. If the dragon were being honest, this would take a great deal of pressure off their people. But it didn't negate some of the other obstacles they'd been trying to overcome. "With all due respect, *Zmei Gorynich*, the rapids have risen dramatically. This has endangered our people here. Some of them are still trapped in the cave above us. Were you the cause?"

"Your people are safe. The ones on the surface are lowering the noisy metal contraption to rescue them. I will not interfere. Now, tell me, what do your stories say about dragons?"

Valentina blinked at the dragon, wondering how he knew all this. But she had no reason to doubt the dragon's word. Trusting the trapped people were safe, she said, "I'm not sure what you wish to know. We originally didn't have a word for dragons. You were called *zmei* in our folklore, but that just means snake. I mean no disrespect, but your kind were originally a representation of evil. We later borrowed the word *drakon* from the west. Over the centuries, you became less of a threat and more of a curiosity and fascination."

"Then times have indeed begun to change and the cycle has begun again," the dragon mused. *"What else do you know?"*

She frowned, thinking back to her childhood. "The stories of you and *Tugarin Zmei* were the most popular ones told to children. *Chudo-Yudo* was another. Your arrival was heralded by dark clouds, thunder and lightning in the sky. It was said you enjoyed the water but also the mountains."

"And have you seen these things? Dark clouds? Thunder and lightning?"

Valentina started to say no but stopped, and her eyes widened. "I have not seen them for myself, but when the dragon figurine was used to heal me, such events were reported. There were storms and even an earthquake."

"Indeed. You three combined your energy, fusing the direction of Fate together to accomplish your goals. It never heralded the arrival of dragons. It was the result of intense power."

The tip of the dragon's tail emerged from the water and lay beside its head on the rocky shore. Valentina stared in amazement at the pointed, arrowlike tip. It could do some serious damage if given the inclination. But even with its potential for destruction, there was still a remarkable beauty and elegance in it.

Valentina lifted her gaze to meet the dragon's golden eyes again. "In the short time we've been here, the water has receded and become less fierce. It happened the first time when you lifted your head, and again just now when you removed your tail. You haven't always been submerged, have you?"

Regret, sharp and pungent, flowed into her mind. Underneath, she also had the impression the dragon was a little embarrassed.

"*No. But I became hungry while I awaited your arrival. You three are as stubborn as the last Fates. Even I need to eat.*"

Valentina floundered, not wanting to offend a hungry dragon. She'd seen Yuri cranky when he hadn't had a meal. She didn't want to think about irritating a hungry creature of this size. "My apologies. I was not aware you were hungry."

Nikolai tensed. "I'm not sure how we can manage to keep you fed. In the old stories, dragons were said to eat people. Were the stories wrong about that too?"

"*Bah,*" the dragon complained, but his eyes twinkled. "*Humans are much too crunchy with not enough meat. Energy sustains me. Water energy, preferably.*"

Valentina's mouth twitched. "That's why you've been slumbering in the river. How long have you been here?"

"*Time loses meaning over the centuries. One day I grew weary, so I decided to rest.*"

Valentina held up the dragon statue. "This brought us to you. Do you know what it is?"

"*Ah,*" the dragon focused on the small object. "*It appears to be a scale. Not very usable in its current form, but an adequate enough representation.*"

Kayla gaped at the dragon. "Someone carved up one of your scales?"

"*So it would appear,*" Gorynich agreed. "*An explorer visited this cavern centuries ago. I offered him a scale. He agreed to carve it in my image and leave it for you in accordance with my instructions. We spent a great deal of time together while he carved. Learning about the changes in your world was a welcome distraction, but once he left, I went back to sleep to wait. The lives of men are far too fleeting compared to my own.*"

Ariana frowned. "Forgive me if my question is too presumptuous, Gorynich, but you said you could help revitalize our world. I'm interested in learning more, but your...

resting place is somewhat problematic. Will you try to fly yourself out?"

Kayla's eyes widened. "Holy shit. You'll cause another earthquake if you do that."

"I don't think that's a concern," Sergei admitted. "If the stories are true, Gorynich can leave anytime."

Nikolai chuckled. "I suspect you're right. In fact, I wouldn't be surprised if you've left many times over the centuries."

Ariana bit her lip. "Are the stories true, Gorynich? Are you a shapeshifter?"

Alec's eyes widened. "We always believed we were descendants of the dragons and had lost our shapeshifting abilities. Is that true? Are we like you?"

The dragon blinked at Alec. *"Do you wish to be a dragon?"*

Alec frowned. "As wonderous as your true form may be, I'm not sure it's very practical."

"I never said this was my true form."

Valentina's curiosity was almost overwhelming, but intuition warned her that it might not be wise in prying too deeply into the dragon's origins. He'd been forthcoming enough with information, but he'd worded some things in such a way that led her to believe he'd chosen his words with care. In the short time they'd been speaking with him, his language had changed, gradually becoming less formal and stilted. He was adapting, learning just as much from them as they were from him.

The dragon focused on her again, and its voice echoed within her head. The cadence was different, though, and she knew it was only speaking to her, Ariana, and Kayla.

"You are perceptive, Valentina. Some questions from the Fates I may answer, but some I shall not answer at all. As Fates, you may guide, but the final choice will always be left to the individual. That includes questions."

Kayla's eyes widened. "You can use targeted mind-to-mind contact, but can you also speak to everyone? Carl, Brant, and Lars can't hear you."

"Um, Kayla," Brant began, looking decidedly uncomfortable, "not real sure I like you volunteering me for anything right now. It hasn't ended well for me in the past."

Carl made a small noise of agreement.

"Speak for yourself," Lars said. "I'd love to be able to talk to a dragon."

The dragon stared at Lars for a long time. Energy, more vibrant and encompassing than anything Valentina had ever witnessed, filled the room. The dragon's scales shimmered from their captivating green color and became the same golden color as the figurine. Valentina averted her eyes as the light became almost blinding.

A moment later, it was gone.

Valentina blinked, trying to adjust her sight again to the dimness in the cavern. The dragon was gone. In its place stood a young woman with golden hair that fell nearly to her waist. Her eyes were the same green color the figurine in her hand had once been. Other than a simple white dress, the woman was wearing no other adornments or even shoes.

"Holy shit! You're a girl," Kayla managed.

The woman smiled and glanced over at Valentina. By all appearances, she was a woman of no more than twenty-five, but there was a weight to her gaze which belied that illusion.

"I believe Valentina told you that even girl dragons can breathe fire."

CHAPTER SIXTEEN

LARS'S MOUTH DROPPED OPEN. "A girl dragon who speaks."

"I'm not sure we can still call you Gorynich," Nikolai said with a frown. "Not only will that raise some questions, but it doesn't fit this other persona."

The dragon turned toward Valentina once again and clasped her hands together, emulating the same body language Ariana had displayed only a few minutes ago. "You have the gift of changing personas with ease. Will you name this new form so I might walk among you?"

"Inna," she whispered immediately. "It was the name of my great-grandmother."

The dragon blinked at her. "You would gift me with a family name?"

Valentina nodded. "You called me daughter. You referred to Ariana and Kayla as my sisters. If you were friends with Zabava and she is of my family line, then I can do no less."

"You honor me," Inna said quietly with a trace of emotion in her voice, and she bowed her head.

"You're the one who's honored us," Valentina admitted. "You saved my life that day when the dragon carving healed me. You saved the life of the man I love when he was shot a few hours ago. You've been guiding and protecting us all for years and we didn't know it. I consider Sergei, Nikolai, and Yuri to be my family because I trust them with my life. You've already shown us we can trust you with ours."

Inna lifted her head and smiled, the expression making her appear a bit more human. There was still an alien quality about her, especially in the rigidity of her movements, but she was quickly adapting. "Will you teach me about this new world of yours, Valentina? Much has changed over the centuries, and I will need a guide."

Valentina returned her smile. "I have a feeling you won't need a guide for long, but yes. I would be happy to teach you."

Lars frowned. "Our communication is still cut off. We're going to have some challenges getting back to the surface unless our new friend can help."

Inna turned toward Sergei. "You have not reconnected the communication system?"

Sergei frowned. "My ability with electronics requires proximity. If the antenna was knocked out on the surface, I can't reconnect it from here."

Inna walked over to him. "Show me your communication device."

Sergei offered her his earpiece. "That's one part of it. But the other part, the antenna, is on the surface."

Inna lifted the device and said, "Remarkable. All these little circuits. Your people continue to amaze me." She handed him the device. "Take it. I will show you how to connect with the other equipment. Location is irrelevant."

Sergei accepted it, and Inna placed her hand over his. Valentina's eyes widened at the flow of energy that swirled around them and through the device. Almost immediately, their equipment crackled to life.

Kayla yelped and pulled out the earpiece. "Holy freaking feedback. It worked. A little loud, but it worked."

Inna turned to look at her. "I had forgotten how sensitive human hearing can be." She lifted her head to regard Sergei. "Can you duplicate the energy pattern in the future?"

He nodded, staring at the device in amazement. "Yes. I would have never considered such an approach. Thank you."

Inna inclined her head. "If you wish to return to the surface, you must make a choice. You have many options available to you in escaping from this cavern. How will you do so?"

Yuri arched an eyebrow. "Is this a test?"

"If you'd like, wind channeler," Inna agreed. "If you were alone here and unaided, how would you leave?"

"I'm assuming you expect us to use our talents somehow."

Inna didn't reply and simply stared at Yuri. Valentina lowered her head and bit back a smile. She suspected Inna wasn't going to make it easy on him, which could prove to be rather interesting.

Nikolai glanced over at Yuri. "If I were alone, I would create a ramp like we did to get down here."

Inna nodded. "Very good. And you, Valentina? How would you escape?"

Valentina paused for a moment. "If I only had to rely upon my talents and not tap into any others, I could use the water from the river to float to the surface."

Yuri scowled. "Well, the obvious answer is I'd shoot up to the surface on a blast of air, but that's a little beyond my skill level."

Inna held out her hand to Yuri. "I will show you."

After the briefest of hesitations, Yuri placed his hand in hers. Valentina watched the same strange swirl of energy envelope Yuri, and his eyes widened. "I can generate that much power?"

Inna blinked at him. "You are the bondholder of one of the Fates. Your limitations are of your own making. You are not a true *drakon*, but rather kin to one. However, you have been gifted with the abilities of a *drakon*."

Valentina frowned. "Kin? OmniLab calls us *Drac'Kin*. That's where it originated from? We're kin of the dragons, and we share your same abilities?"

Inna nodded. "Within the restrictions of your current form, yes."

"Whoa, wait a minute," Kayla said, holding up her hands. "Are we restricted if we're not in our current form?"

"Which form would you like?"

Ariana gaped at her. "We could be dragons, couldn't we?"

"If that is your wish," Inna agreed. "You three may take the appearance of such, but it will not be a true form."

"Holy shit," Kayla muttered. "I could really be a dragon."

Valentina considered Inna for a long moment. "What are you not telling us?"

"Nothing is free, daughter," Inna said gently. "Transmutation is a great ability but also carries a heavy cost. You will be nearly invincible compared to your more fragile human form, but you will not be able to share the ability with your mates. The energy cost is also very dear."

"That's why you've been sleeping so long," Valentina guessed. "You were regaining your strength."

"In part, but it is also a form of protection while we wait for another cycle to begin. Each form carries its own set of benefits and drawbacks. In times past, we've freely walked among you."

Valentina tilted her head. "That's how you met Zabava, isn't it?"

Inna nodded and lowered her gaze. "We were friends, in the same way other human girls form friendships. I shared my secrets with her and taught her our ways. When people witnessed Zabava using her new abilities, they began hunting her. I took on the dragon form and flew away with her, protecting her from those who wished us harm."

Valentina frowned. "That's where the stories came from about dragons kidnapping princesses and stealing them away. They would have assumed you were evil, not protecting her."

Inna nodded, and Valentina could see the pain in her eyes. "I cannot blame them for their suspicions. I knew enough of humankind to recognize their inability to accept her new gifts, but Zabava saw her abilities as a way to help her people. When they turned on her in fear, I intervened. I took her to safety and did my best to protect her, but I could not reunite her with her family."

Ariana blinked back tears. "That must have been so hard for you. It sounds like you cared for Zabava very much."

"I did," Inna said quietly and lowered her head again. "She taught me a great deal."

Valentina swallowed, both touched and dismayed by what had happened. She couldn't erase the past, but she might be able to ease Inna's sadness.

Taking a step toward her, Valentina said, "The stories my grandmother told me were different than the ones heard by other children. They'd been passed down from her mother, and her mother's mother beyond that, going back generations. In these stories, the dragons were friends with the heroes, never the enemies. Zabava must have told her children about you, because my grandmother made me promise I would tell my own children one day about the heroic dragons."

Inna was quiet for a long time. "Thank you for your kind words, Valentina. The opinions of other mortals never troubled me much, but Zabava was different. I sense within you the same spark she possessed. I'm glad you finally arrived. I've wanted to meet you for a long time."

Alec frowned. "You mentioned the explorer visiting you, but no one else. Have you been alone all these centuries? The only dragon surrounded by humans?"

Inna turned toward Alec. "I never said I was the only one."

Kayla's eyes widened. "How many dragons are there?"

"Four in total. But the others, like myself, retired from the world and have been sleeping for the past several centuries."

Valentina tilted her head. "They're your bondmates, just like Sergei, Nikolai, and Yuri are mine."

Inna smiled at her. "You are very perceptive, Valentina. Yes. We share a bond, but not quite the same as yours. Ours exists in a different dimension, but the connection remains. We each share a different elemental alignment, strengthening one another. If you want our help in revitalizing your world, we will need to awaken each of them."

Valentina's head was spinning. It was hard enough to imagine one dragon, but the idea of four of them existing in the world unnoticed for centuries was surreal.

Inna turned toward Brant, studying him thoughtfully. "You are questioning your purpose in all this?"

Brant hesitated. "It's more curiosity than anything. You've spoken about alignments, but there's been no mention of Shadows. I'm not sure how we fit into this."

"Shadows? That is what you call yourself?"

Alec frowned. "Brant's my half-brother. He has the ability to negate abilities, but he does not possess his own."

Inna paused for a long moment. "Do you wish to be more like your brother?"

Brant's head jerked in surprise and then he frowned. "I honestly don't know. I never really considered it before. I've used energy when Kayla shared hers with me, but I've also found merit in not having my own. I can suppress other people when they're out of control or going too far. I'm not limited by any particular alignment. The only ones I lose effectiveness with are Kayla, Ariana, and Valentina."

"It sounds as though you've already discovered your purpose," Inna said gently. "Without your aid, the bond between Kayla and Alec wouldn't have broken. Without you leading other Shadows, Kayla would have turned the towers to dust in an earthquake. You also helped unite your brother with his rightful bondmate and taught Valentina the healing skill she needed to save Sergei's life when he was stabbed. Do not minimize your importance. There is balance in all things, and you are critical to maintaining it."

Brant stared at Inna, a look of wonder on his face. "I'd never looked at it from that point of view."

Inna walked over to Lars and opened her hand to reveal a green pendant. "Your mother and Alec's mother shared a bond that surpassed the normal boundaries of sisterhood. They shared a womb and a connection until the day they died. They both protected Kayla from harm so she could fulfill her purpose. Your mother's last thought was of you and your sister. She loved you well. I promised her I would return this to you one day. The thought gave her some peace in the end."

Lars accepted the pendant, running his thumb over the green stone and staring at it sadly. "I never thought to see this again."

After a long moment, Lars lifted his head and looked over at his cousin. "I want you to take this, Alec. You gave me your mother's pendant without ever knowing for sure if we would find this one. Inna's right. Our mothers were closer than normal sisters, and you've always been like a brother to me— even when I didn't want to believe it." He looked down at the pendant again. "I think she'd be pleased to know your future wife was wearing it and that it would be passed down to your children."

Alec nodded, but Valentina could see the impact Lars's words had on him. There was no doubt in her mind Alec cared deeply for him. Alec accepted the pendant and said, "I'm glad you've come back to us, cousin."

When Lars nodded, Alec placed the necklace around Ariana's neck. She blinked back tears and walked over to embrace Lars. "Thank you."

Lars hugged her tightly. "We're family now, Ari."

Ariana nodded and kissed his cheek. She turned back to Inna and said, "I know Edwin was responsible for the earthquake years ago, but we've been plagued by earthquakes several times over the past few days. Do you know what's causing this?"

Inna nodded. "It was me."

Kayla gaped at her. "You caused it? But why?"

A suspicion formed in Valentina's mind. "The first one happened when we initially used the dragon figurine."

Inna nodded. "The merging of your powers awakened me rather abruptly."

"The next time was right after Sergei was shot," Valentina murmured. "I felt the bullet penetrate him through our bond, and the ground started shaking almost immediately. Lena targeted me next, but the earthquake prevented her from firing again. You saved me, didn't you?"

Inna inclined her head but remained silent.

Sergei wrapped his arms around Valentina. "Thank you, Inna. That's at least three times you've helped Valentina, with the third being right outside this cavern. If there's ever anything I can do to repay you, I'm at your disposal."

"You've protected her well for a long time, fire wielder," Inna said with a small smile. "If you need training to remain by her side, I will offer it. Valentina will require your help when it comes time to awaken my siblings."

Nikolai frowned. "Siblings? Not bondmates?"

"You cannot hold me to your same human standards, earth shaker. I am as intertwined with my bondmates as you are with yours. Your names and titles matter little to me. We are connected. Their strength is mine, and my life is theirs."

Nikolai bowed briefly. "You have my apologies if I've offended you. I believe I understand. I love Valentina dearly, but it's not the same type of love Sergei feels for her. It cannot be measured. It's simply different."

Inna nodded. "Qualifiers are a human design. They limit and confine relationships but rarely encompass true emotion. You do not need to adhere to those standards. You each possess alternative ways to express yourselves."

Kayla lifted her head to look up at Carl. "I've never felt limited in communicating with you, only by my ability to express words."

Carl smiled and tucked her hair behind her ear. "You've always excelled at showing me your feelings without words, sweetheart. I don't have any complaints."

Kayla wrapped her arms around Carl's waist and leaned against him. Valentina couldn't help but smile. They were well suited, strengthening one another, and defending against the other's weaknesses. She lifted her head to regard Sergei. He'd always done the same for her, encouraging her to keep true to herself. It took a special sort of person to accept one's flaws and still be willing to stand by their side.

Sergei's gaze softened. "Valechka, when you look at me like that, I would move heaven and earth for you if asked."

She cupped his face and pressed a light kiss against his lips. "I would do the same for you, Seryozha."

Alec put his arm around Ariana. "I'd like to invite you back to the towers, Inna. Whatever you need from us, we'll happily do our best to accommodate your wishes."

Inna inclined her head. "I wish to stay near Valentina and

her bondmates, if you do not mind. I would also ask that you do not share my identity with the others within the towers."

Alec frowned. "Of course. Valentina has been staying in Lars's quarters, but I'm sure he'd be willing to offer you one of his rooms."

"Absolutely," Lars agreed. "I have plenty of space. The room next to Valentina is available. If there's anything else that would make you more comfortable, please let me know."

"Access to a source of water will be necessary."

Ariana smiled at Inna. "We can definitely accommodate that. There's a pool you can use as often as you wish."

"Then I accept," Inna said with a small smile. "I would also ask that you allow me to teach what you will need to know. Your abilities are vast, but you're all deficient in your knowledge."

Hope shone brightly in Ariana's eyes, and she nodded. "I would appreciate such guidance. I've spent years going through our archives trying to understand my talents better, but our knowledge is limited."

Valentina frowned. "I would be grateful as well, Inna, but I would like to know your expectations in exchange for this knowledge."

"Only your assistance in helping awaken my siblings," Inna admitted. "I know that may sound trivial, but it will not be an easy feat. I need to ensure all of you are as strong as possible before the endeavor. To that end, I will share information no other human knows, and once our task is complete, you may do what you wish with this knowledge. However, our time is limited, and if we are to repair your world, we need to act soon."

Ariana frowned and looked up at Alec, who appeared equally worried. "Why is our time limited? Are we in danger?"

Inna gave her a small smile. "No, Ariana. Not from this. But travel will be difficult once your little ones are born."

Ariana's eyes widened, and Alec moved even closer to her. "Ariana's pregnant?"

Inna shook her head, and her eyes took on a faraway look. "Not yet. But soon enough. Twins. A boy and a girl. We must be well on our way before then. Shortly afterward, Valentina's child will be born."

All the blood rushed from Valentina's head, and Yuri began a coughing and choking fit that left him wheezing. Nikolai slapped him on the back as he doubled over trying to breathe.

Sergei placed his hand protectively over her stomach and turned to Inna. "A child? We'll have a child together?"

Inna nodded. "Yes. A girl. She will be bonded with Ariana's son."

Ariana's eyes shone with emotion. "Then we'll be sisters in truth."

Valentina swallowed, her mouth suddenly dry. "You're sure about this, Inna?"

"Yes. You will have a girl within months of Ariana's children being born. Kayla's child will follow later and shall be bonded with Ariana's daughter."

"What the fuck?" Kayla demanded, her eyes wild with panic. "Oh, hell no. No kids. What the hell are you thinking? Take off this woo-woo curse."

Inna studied Kayla for a long moment. "This is not something for me to decide. If you as the Fates have decreed it, so it shall be. You control your own destiny, Kayla. Nothing will happen until you are ready and prepared, but I suspect you will change your mind in the years to come."

Kayla frowned and relaxed, but her eyes were still suspicious. "Years?"

Inna nodded.

Carl turned Kayla around in his arms. "Neither one of us knows how we're going to feel about kids in a few years, sweetheart. I'm not ready for a child right now either. We're still learning about each other, and I'm happy just treasuring every day with you. Maybe this is something we're willing to explore one day. But there's nothing to run from. No one is pressuring you to do anything. You have options, sweetheart."

Kayla stood on her toes and pressed a kiss against Carl's lips before turning back to Inna. "Is this set in stone? Or is Carl right?"

Inna smiled. "Kayla, you know better than anyone that you always have options. Fate may guide you, but it's ultimately your choice."

Kayla nodded and leaned against Carl again. "Okay. I can handle that."

Valentina swallowed and lifted her head to look up into Sergei's eyes. "We've never talked about children."

Sergei grinned and wrapped his arms around her. "No. I was planning to wait until after we were married to convince you about children. I figured you couldn't get away by then. I expected it to take another year or so to convince you after we were married. Nikolai thought it might take a bit more time. Yuri thought I'd have to get sneaky."

She blinked at him. "You all discussed this?" Whirling around, she caught sight of Nikolai's guilty expression and Yuri's smirk. Valentina blew out a breath. "I cannot believe you."

Sergei chuckled and turned her back toward him. "If I played by the rules, Valechka, I never would have gotten you to agree to marry me so soon."

Valentina reached up to cup his face and pressed a light kiss against his lips. "Sometimes, I'm glad you're such a troublemaker, Seryozha. And I always planned to marry you too."

ABOUT THE AUTHOR

Jamie A. Waters is an award-winning science fiction and fantasy romance author. Her first novel, Beneath the Fallen City (previously titled as The Two Towers), was a winner of the Readers' Favorite Award in Science-Fiction Romance and the CIPA EVVY Award in Science-Fiction.

Jamie currently resides in Florida with her two neurotic dogs who enjoy stealing socks and chasing lizards. When she's not pursuing her passion of writing, she's usually trying to learn new and interesting random things (like how to pick locks or use the self-cleaning feature of the oven without setting off the fire alarm). In her downtime, she enjoys reading, playing computer games, painting, or acting as a referee between the dragons and fairies currently at war inside her closet.

You can learn more by visiting: www.jamieawaters.com

CPSIA information can be obtained
at www.ICGtesting.com
Printed in the USA
LVHW112343200819
628405LV00001B/54/P

9 781949 524000